Reaching into his shoulder holster, Bryant pulled out his suppressed Ruger Mark II pistol. Clicking off the safety with his thumb, he let the muzzle of the pistol lead the way over the coaming of the deck. As the eyes in the black balaclava-covered head of the SEAL cleared the edge of the deck, he froze in place. Squatting down in the shelter of a small boat resting in a cradle at the port side of the ship was an Iraqi sentry.

In his position at the boat, the Iraqi on the deck only had to move his hands away from his face and open his eyes to see Bryant not six feet away. Without moving, Bryant held his position. His dark eyes centered on the Iraqi while staying focused on the front sight of the Ruger. Bryant watched the man he was about to kill.

The Iraqi on guard pulled his hands away from his face as he leaned his head back. Rubbing his eyes, the man finally opened them and looked around the deck.

Books by S. M. Gunn

SEALS SUB STRIKE: OPERATION BLACK SNOW
SEALS SUB STRIKE: OPERATION OCEAN WATCH
SEALS SUB RESCUE: OPERATION ENDURANCE

SEALS

SUB STRIKE
OPERATION BLACK SNOW

S.M. GUNN

AVON BOOKS
An Imprint of HarperCollinsPublishers

AVON BOOKS
An Imprint of HarperCollins*Publishers*
10 East 53rd Street
New York, New York 10022-5299

Copyright © 2004 by Bill Fawcett & Associates
ISBN 0-06-009549-0
www.avonbooks.com

First Avon Books paperback printing: November 2004

Avon Trademark Reg. U.S. Pat. Off. and in Other Countries, Marca Registrada, Hecho en U.S.A.
HarperCollins® is a registered trademark of HarperCollins Publishers Inc.

Printed in the U.S.A.

10 9 8 7 6 5 4 3 2 1

SEALS

SUB STRIKE
OPERATION BLACK SNOW

CHAPTER 1

★★★★

1990
Iraq

When there was a difficulty in getting what he wanted, Saddam Hussein did not hesitate to throw money at the problem in order to solve it. He had learned from his dealings with the West and the rest of the world that there were few difficulties that couldn't be solved with a copious flow of cash. The bigger the difficulty, or the more desired the final product, the more Hussein was willing to spend. This flow of wealth was not bottomless, and the eight-year war with Iran had almost bankrupted Iraq in spite of her huge oil reserves.

It didn't matter that the people of Iraq were suffering in the aftermath of their long struggle with their neighbor to the east. The vast oil wealth of Iraq was available to Saddam alone—to spend as he saw fit. Anyone caught cheating Iraq, and by proxy Hussein himself, might find it very difficult to live long enough to enjoy their profits. That threat did very little to stem the flow of people, and even countries, offering Saddam what he wanted.

With his thug's mentality, what Saddam wanted most of all was weapons—the more powerful, the better. A nuclear weapon was the Iraqi dictator's ultimate desire. But during the war with Iran, chemical weapons had turned the tide for the Iraqi forces facing the Iranian hordes. In spite of his personal fear of disease, Saddam had been assured that biological weapons could cause even more damage than nerve gas. And that the psychological effect of a disease being delivered as a weapon would be even greater than the actual body count might warrant. His own fears made it very easy for Saddam to believe others would feel exactly as he did.

The invasion and annexation of Kuwait had gone smoothly and quickly just a few short months before. The fact that the largest creditor of his war debts was being ground under his rule should have delighted Hussein. His joy was eliminated by his very bad misjudgment of the world's reaction to his invasion. Led by the United States, a coalition of forces was gathered under United Nations approval with the intent of driving Iraq out of Kuwait. The U.S. was building up strength in the Persian Gulf and Saudi Arabia since early August, only days after the Iraqi invasion had been completed.

Backed by UN resolutions authorizing and increasing use of direct action against Iraq, the U.S.

and coalition forces had become a major threat to
Saddam's plans for a unified Middle East—free of
what he considered the Israeli problem. This unifi-
cation would be conducted under his "benevo-
lent" leadership, which Hussein considered only
right.

To continue his plans, Saddam wanted weapons
capable of destroying people on a massive scale.
The Iraqi nuclear program was receiving massive
support, but was still months away from delivering the sudden destruction Saddam wanted.
Months were not available to Iraq or Saddam.
Time was short, so money and material were being poured into ongoing chemical and biological
weapons programs. The first program to give the
dictator what he wanted would be viewed under a
vary favorable light from Baghdad. Saddam wanted
results, and he wanted them right now.

1054 ZULU
33° 12' North, 42° 28' East
Bunker 38
Al Muhammadiyat Test Range
Iraq

The large man in green fatigues wore dark sunglasses under the black beret that covered his gray-
ing hair. He looked out across the empty section
of desert in front of him. There was nothing to be
seen anywhere beyond the high chain-link fence
surrounding the huge ammunition storage site
that was his responsibility. The dozens of sand-
covered, carefully camouflaged concrete bunkers

were spread out in an orderly fashion behind him. He was standing in front of the open door and blast shield of one of these bunkers, looking out at absolutely nothing but sand, rock, and the occasional scorpion or venomous snake.

Colonel Hafiz Kassar al-Tikriti had proven himself more than a capable and trustworthy man. During the invasion of Kuwait only a few months before, he had demonstrated bravery and ability while operating as the Staff Intelligence Officer with the 2nd Armored Brigade of the Iraqi Republican Guards' Medina Division. His technical knowledge helped his personnel pinpoint very desirable scientific equipment in Kuwait City and quickly arrange for its transport to Iraq. So why did his reward seem so much like punishment?

The recent addition of two gold stars underneath the eagles on his shoulder boards was a welcome weight, though the responsibilities that went with his recent promotion to full colonel in charge of the weapons facility were heavier than he liked. His rise in the ranks of the Republican Guards had not come about just because he was from President Hussein's home town of Tikrit. He well knew the value of following a precise timetable, and just when such attention to detail is most important. This was one of those times.

Another thing the colonel had learned during his military career was how to play to an audience. And there was only one person in the immediate vicinity that he was responsible to. The present location might be the armpit of Iraq, a spot so remote not even camels cared to pass through it. But it was his assignment, one he would carry out to the best of his abilities.

Colonel Kassar watched the second hand of his Rolex sweep around the face of the watch. The information under the security cover on his aluminum clipboard had been very expensive to obtain. He would not waste one moment of the time that information gave him, or react too quickly and make all their efforts useless.

Checked for accuracy only the day before, Kassar trusted his watch now as the second hand swept past the twelve o'clock position. The other hands of the watch indicated 7:55 in the morning. Seeing this, he placed a nickel-plated whistle between his lips and blew a shrill blast.

The shattering noise of the whistle was repeated across the compound as whistles were blown by lower-ranking officers and the sergeants below them. The desert became a beehive of activity as men and vehicles left the shade of their protected positions and raced out across the sands. The colonel turned and entered the front door of Bunker 38 at the Muhammadiyat weapons storage facility and test range. The reason for all the secrecy and careful timing of the morning, as well as the technicians responsible for it, were inside the bunker.

Abu Waheed and Jaleel al-Dossadi were standing back as Colonel Kassar stepped into the cool darkness, away from the brilliantly sunlit open doorway.

"It is one minute exactly," said Kassar, "past the time that the American Keyhole spy satellite has passed over the horizon. The information our

Soviet friends have so graciously supplied us with states that the next Keyhole satellite, the KH-11/7, will not come over the horizon and invade our air-space until 10:14:40. You have two hours and eighteen minutes to conduct your test and have everything removed from the test site. Radar is reading clear for the moment, and most of the American spy plane overflights come in intermit-tently in the afternoon. I suggest you get moving."

There was little more the two technicians could say. Abu Waheed climbed into the cab of the GAZ-66 truck he was standing in front of. In the back was a tarp-covered payload. The driver be-hind the wheel started the engine, and ran the ve-hicle out the front door as soon as Waheed had shut the door. Jaleel al-Dossadi joined several other men in a much smaller, tan-colored UAZ-469. The jeeplike vehicle quickly followed the truck.

The technicians and their cargo were on their way. Now Kassar faced the small group of people still in the bunker with him. The three body-guards could be dispensed with for the moment. Ignoring them was about as safe as not paying at-tention to cobras you saw near your feet. But not giving the utmost respect to the man the body-guards flanked, Abdul Talfaq, made playing with cobras seem like a desirable entertainment.

Talfaq was a big man in his early thirties, stocky, powerfully built. His black hair was slicked back and oiled, as was his black mustache. The nephew of Saddam Hussein on his mother's side, he was head of Iraqi Secret Service Organization, the SSO—in charge of protecting Saddam himself, as well as overseeing all operations of the Iraqi intelligence organizations—which made Talfaq the second most powerful man in Iraq. In addition, Talfaq was responsible for what Hussein considered his most important projects—the development of weapons of mass destruction—and was in charge of the Ministry of Industry and Military Industrialization, one of the most powerful ministries in the Iraqi government.

MIMI ran all military procurement in Iraq, the standard items as well as the nuclear, chemical, and biological weapons programs. The bulky item on the back of the GAZ truck that had just left the bunker was a warhead for the new al-Hussein rocket. Instead of high explosives, the warhead was filled with the final test simulant for a biological weapon.

"I had been led to believe that the last of these tests had been conducted back in August," Talfaq said. "We do not have the time to waste resources on manufacturing and loading simulants."

A handsome woman spoke up from nearby, where she was standing next to an older man.

"Those tests were of the R-400 aerial bombs," Dr. Badra Hushmand said. "They were loaded with a wet-slurry agent. The efficiency of that weapon has been proven by earlier testing. The consistency of this new agent is very different and has to be tested at least once."

"The freeze-dried and milled *Bacillus subtilis* that this warhead was filled with had to be made anyway," said Dr. Saeed Hushmand, the older man with Bandra. "The production machinery had to be set up and calibrated. It was much more efficient to use a simulated agent to do that. In this state, *Bacillus subtilis* acts the same as anthrax would."

"Out of the more than sixty-one kilograms of material in that warhead," the woman said, "only ten percent is the simulant. The rest of the material is inert."

"Make no mistake," Talfaq said in a dangerously soft voice, "this test had better prove your device and agent. A new director and associate director could be located for the Iraqi Biological Weapons Research Center. Replacements would be found much more easily than the remains of anyone who failed to deliver results at this late stage."

Abu Waheed was more than happy to see the weapons storage bunker disappear in the distance behind him. Saeed Hushmand was the director of the top secret research center. As such, he was the single scientist most responsible for the biological weapons program. To direct such an undertaking, Hushmand had to be a scientist of no small skill and dedication. And the man constantly showed a single-minded devotion to the idea of turning diseases into weapons of war, weapons of mass destruction.

Saeed's sister, Badra Hushmand, was also a scientist. She had received her advanced degree in microbiology from her studies in Germany. Her skills had helped place her as the associate director of the research center.

A scientist in name only, and despised by those who worked for her, Badra had a lust for power and prestige that was plainly seen by anyone she considered her inferior. In the throat-cutting world of Iraqi politics, she blended in well with the rest of the carnivores in Saddam's higher circles. Badra Hushmand had more than her share of blood on her hands, and just about everyone but her brother knew it.

Badra was quick to take the credit for anything that went right in the bioweapons program. She was only faster when it came time to shift the blame for a failure on someone else. This was not something that endeared the woman to those who worked under her, including Abu Waheed.

With Abdul Talfaq in the bunker, along with his Republican Guard thugs, the atmosphere in the closed area had become much too politically charged for Waheed's comfort. Talfaq wanted to hand to Saddam Hussein the means to control all of the Middle East and the bulk of the world's oil production.

The destruction of Israel with a biological or chemical weapon would bring the Arab world around to realizing the leadership of the man who finally eliminated the Israeli Problem from the Middle East. If he happened to defeat and reduce the United States—the world's last superpower, at least for the time being—to groveling at his feet for oil, so much the better.

Besides escaping from the politics of the situation, the technical aspects of the upcoming test were difficult enough, Waheed wanted to get his friend Jaleel away from the bunker and the nest of vipers inside of it. Jaleel al-Dossadi was a brilliant technician. His years of work in the military had given him an encyclopedic knowledge of ordnance and the tools of war. But the man whined that coming from Saddam's home village of Tikrit made him invulnerable to the petty intrigues of others.

Abu could see that the biological weapons program was very important to the government of Iraq, and that meant it was also important to Saddam. With importance came power, and where there was power to be had, there was intrigue. He could still remember as a small boy being with his uncle Abdulla in the desert, the old man pontificating at length on the intrigues of what he despairingly called civilization. And the simple desert nomad had been proven right from just about everything that Abu had ever experienced in his government's service.

The missile warhead adaptation and filling project had not been going well. The freeze-drying equipment Iraq had obtained from a pharmaceutical equipment company in Belgium had been plagued with technical problems. The lyophilization process was supposed to remove all the moisture from a solution of biological agent mixed with a sugar stabilizer. By freezing and removing the moisture under a hard vacuum, the bacterial solution—in this case an anthrax slurry—was reduced to a hard cake of material.

Milling the bacterial cake to a fine powder, only five microns or less in size, effectively weaponized the anthrax—turned it into a powder fine enough to bypass the human body's normal protective systems. The fact that the powder could be stored, handled, and loaded into various delivery systems made it an effective biological weapon. This was what Saddam Hussein and the people around him wanted—and Abu Waheed was put in the position of trying to deliver it, and taking the blame if there was a failure.

And there had been lots of failures. The laboratory-scale lyophilizer equipment had been difficult to adapt to the production scale demanded by the Hushmands and those above them. Once the freeze-drying process had finally been brought under control, other problems had developed in the milling process.

For one, the Soviet Union had refused to supply Iraq with their own air-milling system. They had produced a technique for weaponizing anthrax that had been conducted on a major industrial level, completely in secret, inside the Soviet Union. But with the difficulties the Soviets were having with their own economy, they didn't want to be caught giving the Iraqis what effectively constituted a poor man's atomic bomb in lethal terms.

So Waheed and his fellow technicians and scientists had been forced to work out the systems on their own—while still delivering the weapons they could make. Thousands of liters of liquid anthrax slurry had been loaded into bomb casings the Iraqis had bought earlier on the world's arms market. Expal BR-250-WP aircraft bomb casings were originally intended to be loaded up with white phosphorus. The hollow body of the bomb with the central explosive burster well was easily adapted to being loaded with a liquid biological agent instead.

Nearly one hundred bomb casings had so far been filled with Botulinum toxin, the deadliest known natural toxin on earth. More than half that number of bomb casings had also been filled with liquid anthrax slurry. So the Iraqi BW R-400 bomb had been produced—but not without its own difficulties.

The bioagent production and filling line at the Aqaba facility had been destroyed by an accidental spill contaminating the site. Not only had the anthrax agent spilled, something had caused a chain of explosions that completely wrecked the loading facility. The blasts had probably been the high explosive bursters to the bombs, but knowing the reason did not help rebuild the production line. The loss of irreplaceable equipment had been a terrible setback, but not even that was not as bad as the loss of a number of scientists, skilled technicians, and trained workers.

The accident at Aqaba had taken place in October, and the incident blamed on Kuwaiti resistance fighters backed by the American CIA. In spite of the official explanation, Saddam Hussein, or Abdul Talfaq, had the director of the facility and his security chief killed. It didn't really matter who ordered the executions, they served the same purpose—to convince everyone involved of Saddam's sincerity in wanting biological weapons, at any cost.

CHAPTER 2

★ ★ ★ ★

Virginia Beach is a popular tourist spot for much of the year. Even during the Christmas season some diehard visitors are walking about. Located south of Norfolk, facing the waters of the Atlantic, the city appeals both to vacationers and locals looking to take advantage of its food and entertainment opportunities. Fewer spots are popular during the winter months, but there are still some that stay open year round and do a good business.

One of the local feeding spots was relatively new, and relatively successful. Already making a name for itself, the Iceberg Bar and Grill was located on one of the main thoroughfares in Virginia Beach, an excellent location, and it offered a good value for your money. Drinks were reasonable, the food was great, and the place had appeal for everyone.

The owner of the Iceberg was a tall, slender, ex-Navy man who was friendly, sociable, skilled in the kitchen and with the customers—and was probably the most deadly man many of those customers would ever meet in their lives.

Ken Fleming had an easy smile, his teeth about as bright as his bald head. His limp was the reason he had left the Service, the result of a parachuting mishap when he had been an active duty Navy SEAL. After his Navy career had ended, he established the local watering hole that was the Iceberg. It was the same hard work and devotion to a cause that Fleming had used to become a SEAL that helped him make the Iceberg a growing concern. The fact that his old Teammates, as well as others from the Teams up the road at the Little Creek Amphibious Base, were regular customers didn't hurt his bottom line either.

Fleming was busy preparing to cater a change of command ceremony at SEAL Team Four late the next morning. The bulk of the kitchen staff were bustling about, preparing food for the catering service as well as feeding customers out front. Waitresses constantly moved back and forth, slipping by one another smoothly as they delivered orders to and from the kitchen. Amid all this activity, a door in the back of the restaurant was ignored by all of the staff except Fleming. Hanging from the knob of the door was an old rubber swim fin known as a "Duck Foot." It was a sign that the occupants of the room beyond that door were not to be disturbed.

Inside the room were the bulk of Fleming's old Teammates from Fourth Platoon, SEAL Team Two. Only now the men had been gathered together into a new unit, one necessitated by the danger of weapons of mass destruction in the hands of terrorists and rogue nations around the world. The destructive power of nuclear weapons was a threat the military and public had been familiar with for a long time. Chemical and biological weapons could be just as destructive as a nuclear weapon in terms of body count, and could do it far more inexpensively and relatively simply.

The job of the Navy's Special Materials Detachment, the SMD, was to go where no one else wanted to go, and take control of weapons that no one even wanted to think about. They would seize chemical poisons so deadly that the amount on the head of a pin would be enough to kill you several times over. Or face a disease that had ravaged mankind for centuries, only to be turned into a weapon of war by someone insane enough to do so. The SEALs would take these weapons away from terrorists, military groups, or even nations, if they were called upon to do so.

The men of the Navy's SMD took their job very seriously. But not so seriously that they didn't refer to the unit as "the Smud" among themselves.

The men of the Special Materials Detachment had recently returned from having spent nearly five months in the Middle East. Arriving in Saudi Arabia in August, the SEALs immediately continued on to a mission in the Red Sea. Off the coast of Sudan, they successfully boarded and captured a cargo ship that had been transporting a cargo of modified Scud missiles along with some technicians trained to operate them.

The missiles the SEALs found were the modified Scud B designs produced in Iraq as the al-Hussein. But what they hadn't located were the warheads to the missiles. Their skills and training had equipped the SEALs to deal with a biological or chemical weapon. Nukes were still under the purview of the Explosive Ordnance Department, but there was nothing that said the SEALs of the SMD wouldn't be called up to secure and set security on even a nuclear weapon. However, they found none of these on the cargo ship off Sudan. The missiles they discovered hadn't been fueled and weren't fitted with any warheads at all.

The information that the al-Hussein missile had a removable warhead was valuable in and of itself. It increased the probability that there were chemical and biological warheads for the weapon under development.

So the search went on to locate the weapons with which Saddam Hussein was threatening his area of the world. The violent dictator had used chemical weapons when he gassed the Kurdish people of northern Iraq. To try to turn the tide of the Iraq-Iran war, Hussein had ordered the use of both mustard and nerve gases. Thousands had died painful deaths, suffering the burning blisters of mustard gas or the suffocating, body-wrenching spasms of nerve agents.

Biological weapons were strongly desired by Hussein. Detailed CIA reports had been made available to the SEALs as part of their training in the subject. But these hell weapons, banned by treaty throughout the world, had yet to be confirmed or located.

The SEALs had proved that Saddam Hussein had sent missiles and their support equipment to Sudan with the hopes of increasing the tensions in that part of the world. If a biological warhead had burst over the heads of the population of Egypt, Sudan would have had an easier time taking control of Egyptian lands they considered properly Sudanese. And with such an attack, part of the international pressure coming down on Iraq and Hussein for his invasion and takeover of Kuwait might have been lessened.

In spite of their best efforts, and though completely successful in their execution, the SMD had not found any of the weapons they had been sent after. Even a successful operation loses some of its flavor if the target comes up mostly empty. And during the balance of the time they had spent in the Kuwait theater of operations, the SMD hadn't been called out on a hot operation. The existence of the Special Materials Detachment was still so classified that the SEALs within it had not been able to relax and spend any time with the rest of the SEAL detachment on duty in Saudi Arabia and the Persian Gulf.

The men remained deployed over the Thanksgiving holiday, and then over Christmas, which wasn't a particularly unusual situation in the SEAL Teams, or even in the Navy as a whole. For the SMD SEALs, their contact with home had been extremely limited due to security considerations—also not an unusual occurrence in the Teams. And that situation had weighed heavily on the men—especially those with families. There was a reason that marriages in the SEAL Teams often ended in divorce. It took a strong bond for a woman to accept what being married to a SEAL could entail.

The commanding officer of the SMD, Lieutenant Greg Rockham, knew the feelings of his men very well, and he shared them. The lightly built man with sandy hair and a square jaw had a family of his own. Not even the commanding officer of the SMD could bypass security considerations to contact his wife Sharon or his three-year-old son Matt. And meanwhile, the men were starting to get on each others' nerves.

Originally, the SEALs had been scheduled to return to the States back in November. But intelligence reports from agents and sources inside Iraq had told of a number of unusual weapons tests, and the descriptions gathered and analyzed by the intelligence organizations had coalesced into a new emphasis on biological weapons in Iraq. The program was getting a big push from the powers in charge in Baghdad, which meant Saddam Hussein himself wanted biologicals as well as chemicals at his command. So the SEALs of the SMD had been put on alert for a possible mission as soon as a target had been identified and confirmed, and their deployment in Saudi Arabia extended. No target, either suspected or confirmed, had been positively identified. Without a target, there hadn't been a mission.

Finally, after weeks of waiting for a go-ahead signal that had never come, the SMD was sent back to their families in and around Little Creek, just a few miles from Norfolk, Virginia. The threat of a possible domestic WMD attack by a terrorist group armed with a chemical or biological weapon had grown serious. The political and military situation was dire enough that the Joint Special Operations Command wanted its premier Navy WMD unit available for a quick deployment to the United States in case of an attack.

Now, the men were back at what had become their traditional watering hole. It was after duty hours but still early in the evening. Business was brisk enough in the front rooms of the Iceberg, but the men of the SMD were in the back, isolated from the crowds. Their Do Not Disturb signal— the rubber swim fin on the door—made sure that no one would bother them, which anyone who might have come through the door appreciated. In spite of their having been together in close proximity for months, the men still gravitated together after duty hours.

Normally when the men were off-duty it was a time for relaxation and building unit cohesion. More than one SEAL officer had learned that it was good for the men to not only work hard together, but to play hard together. That simple rule could draw a group of men closer than even family ties.

Lieutenant Greg Rockham wanted to be with his men right now, and he wanted to be home with his wife and his son as well. The family had spent some time together after Greg returned from his Middle East deployment, but Sharon could tell then that something had gone wrong on the mission. She had been a SEAL wife long enough, however, not to ask her husband about the details of something that was most likely highly classified.

In fact, nothing had gone wrong on the deployment; it just hadn't gone as right as it should have. The men of the SMD had conducted a hard operation and pulled it off flawlessly. Yet, the intelligence had been wrong, and the big prize—a weapon of mass destruction—wasn't found. Recovering something like that would have gone a long way to turning world opinion against the Hussein regime in Iraq. And it might have given the U.S. a boost in coming up with the proper defenses against such a weapon, such as vaccines or other medical developments.

They had come back with a gold mine of information for the scientists and engineers. The two al-Hussein missiles the SEALs found were poked, probed, photographed, and measured—before being blown apart with high explosives. With the information the SEALs had gathered, ordnance engineers felt that they had an even better chance to tweak the Patriot high altitude aircraft defense systems in Saudi Arabia into something that could even shoot down an incoming Scud missile.

Rockham realized that telling the men that they had found valuable intelligence wasn't received with enthusiasm. They weren't angry at what they hadn't been able to accomplish so much as disappointed. He knew that could lead to frustration among highly trained and motivated men such as those under his command. And such frustration could lead to other things even more damaging.

Most of the eighteen men assigned to the Special Materials Detachment were now at the Iceberg. Lieutenant (junior grade) Shaun Daugherty was back at Little Creek in the cramped quarters of the SMD, doing some of the paperwork that never seemed to end no matter how elite the unit one belonged to. He had insisted that Rockham go on to the Iceberg along with the men.

The men at SEAL Team Two had been conducting the watch for the SMD while the men were deployed. Now it was time for the small unit to take up their own slack again. Mike Ferber had the watch back on the SMD quarterdeck. He was the leading petty officer in the unit, second only to Senior Chief Frank Monday in enlisted rank. But the unit was so small that everyone had to pull their turn at the duty, and Ferber had come up on the rotation.

Pete Wilkes wasn't around that evening, at least not yet. It was one of his girls' birthdays, and he'd missed enough of them over the years he had spent in the Teams. Then again, it always seemed to be the birthday of one of his girls. He had four kids, all of them female. Sometimes, the guys joked that Wilkes had joined the Teams just for the male companionship—he was so outnumbered by the females in the Wilkes household.

One other member of the unit wasn't in attendance at the Iceberg that night because of women. Larry Stadt—Kraut to his Teammates, for his chiseled Nordic good looks, blond hair, and blue eyes—said he'd seen quite enough of his Teammates over the last several months and was going to be out with softer, prettier company for the evening.

Smiling as he lifted his glass of beer, Rockham knew that Stadt would find his lady, at least one of them, and spend his time with her. And before the evening was over, the chances were good that he would show up at the back room at the Iceberg to drop in on his Teammates. Even Wilkes would probably show up after the girls were put to bed. The men in the Teams were a lot like a big family, and even more so in the small, tightly knit SMD. And just like a big family, an occasional argument broke out among the kids.

The biggest kid in the unit was Roger Kurkowski, who had yet to grow up completely. A very competent man in the field, Kurkowski was someone you wanted at your side, or watching your back, in a life or death situation. In other situations, he could be a pain in the ass. And right now one of those pain situations seemed imminent.

The men were all enjoying a beer or two after their long, relatively dry spell in Saudi. The Moslem country didn't allow spirits, so the drinks had been few and far between over the past months. A cold beer tasted pretty good, even if it was starting to get chilly outside, with the late fall weather. There were a lot fewer tourists and a lot more locals at the Iceberg.

Mike Bryant, John Sukov, Wayne Alexander, Dan Able, and Ryan Marks were sitting around a table conducting the same poker game they had been playing for months. Markers were all that Frank Monday allowed in the way of bets, and Rockham wasn't about to counter any dealings with the men on the part of his senior chief petty officer. Monday knew that if money changed hands, tempers could flare and a good chance to relax could be destroyed for the men. So only markers were used, and the total tallies for the poker game were getting into some serious numbers. The scores were kept, but the markers were forgiven at the end of a day's play. But that didn't cut back on the enjoyment of the play for everyone involved, or for those observing.

Sitting across from Ryan Marks, John Grant was drinking his usual one beer. The big Native American liked to drink with his Teammates, but he also had the discipline to recognize that he didn't handle his liquor well. So he always limited his intake voluntarily, something Rockham respected in the man. And something that Kurkowski felt he could take advantage of.

Roger Kurkowski was a clown who liked to play a practical joke whenever he could. Every time he had a chance, Kurkowski had been spiking Grant's beer. When his head was turned or

Grant was otherwise distracted, Kurkowski would slip a little more whiskey into John's beer. Then the bottle would go back into Kurkowski's pocket. It wasn't going to take long for Grant to notice the taste, or Kurkowski's actions.

The gag was a mild one, as far as Kurkowski's idea of a funny joke went. Two other members of the unit, Sid Mainhart and Ed Lopez, were watching Kurkowski and quietly discussing among themselves as to just when Grant would notice the gag. Mainhart was Kurkowski's swim buddy and shooting partner—which was as close as you could get to another man in the Teams; closer than brothers. Training together for so long and at such intensity as was done in the Teams quickly taught you how the other man thought in any situation. But Mainhart had also learned that Kurkowski rarely thought when he was trying to pull a gag.

Finally, Kurkowski's time ran out. Grant, watching the reflection in the almost empty beer glass held by Ryan Marks at the next table, saw the movement of Kurkowski slipping the bottle forward. Snapping around, unbelievably fast for such a large, muscular man, Grant grabbed the bottle of whiskey between his thumb and fingers before Kurkowski was able to pour a drop.

The quiet noise of conversation in the room stopped as everyone took in the scene. Kurkowski's penchant for jokes was well known to the crew, and so was the fact that none of them had ever seen John Grant lose his temper. Tonight just might be a learning experience for everyone involved.

But John didn't do anything—he just held the bottle immobile. This was not a small thing. Kurkowski was one of the unit's breachers. His job was to knock open a door during a takedown. Built like a barrel with thick, black hair, Kurkowski was a strong man, even by SEAL standards. And he had just learned how much stronger than he the quiet Native American was.

"No, thanks," John said in his deep, sonorous voice.

Realizing he had been caught out, Kurkowski just smiled and waited for Grant to let go of the bottle. When the big Indian did release it, Kurkowski pulled it back and dumped the last of the contents into his own beer.

Greg Rockham looked over at Frank Monday with the same feeling of relief that he was sure the SEAL senior chief felt. He knew that things were taut among the men when Kurkowski started pulling dumb stunts and didn't even laugh at them himself. Something was going to have to be done about the situation, and soon.

The men couldn't be given leave since the unit had to remain on call and on alert. But the months of forced inactivity, interspersed with periods of excitement and then disappointment as another mission came up and went down without action, had raised the stress to an unacceptable level. They were still playing their poker game, but the general conversation and kidding around had faded.

Greg remembered some advice from earlier in his SEAL career. Master Chief Rudy Boesch had been on the quarterdeck at SEAL Team Two since the Teams were founded, and with the UDTs before that. Every morning, Rudy had been out leading the men of SEAL Team Two in PT and their morning runs or swims. Even in his fifties, Rudy was near the front of the pack during the runs and there were always a lot more men behind him than leading him.

Rudy believed there wasn't any problem that couldn't be dealt with by a good run or workout. Exercise didn't make a problem go away, but it gave you something good to do while you let your mind work on it. So that's what Rockham decided he would do—take the SMD out on a "run."

CHAPTER 3

★ ★ ★ ★

It was a simple mid-morning meeting in a very secure location. It wasn't that the meeting required extraordinary security, but that Navy captain Nick Moisen's office in the Pentagon was well-protected against accidental intruders—or even intentional intruders, by Pentagon standards.

The outer door of the office suite opened up onto Corridor 4 on the third-floor, D-ring of the Pentagon. The door was closed behind a five-pin cipher lock. Just getting onto the corridor had required showing a Marine guard—an armed gunnery sergeant sitting at a desk—proper identification, which he carefully checked against a list of appointments.

Once you were buzzed into the outer office of the suite, a very serious Navy chief yeoman announced your arrival to the inner office. Just look-

ing at the chief's eyes told you that he had a
weapon nearby and knew very well how to use it.

The final door to the inner office had the weight
and feel of just what it was—painted steel, secured with a Sargent combination-dial lock. The
location wasn't so much an office as a bank vault,
one that protected its secrets very well.

Aside from the impressive security in the doors
and corridor, Captain Moisen's office looked very
much like any other mid-level government func-
tionary's place of work. It included a plain-
looking brown wood double-pedestal desk, a
smaller desk with a computer terminal on it, and
several solid-looking five-drawer filing cabinets,
each with a combination lock dial and a flip sign
below the dial. All the signs read LOCKED.

Creature comforts were minimal but sufficient.
A brown upholstered couch was on a wall of the
office, below a briefing board covered with a
black drop-curtain. An old leather armchair, also
brown, faced the desk. The chair, couch, and desk
all looked like they had been part of the original
furnishings of the Pentagon when it was first
opened during World War II. Behind the desk,
Moisen sat in a modern, padded black leather executive chair.

Of medium height and slightly overweight, with
a round face and receding hairline of light brown
hair, Captain Moisen himself wasn't nearly as impressive as his office location would have indicated. He looked like any one of thousands of
mid-level executives or bureaucrats. In a crowd, he

wouldn't have been given a second glance—which was exactly what a captain in Naval Intelligence wanted. His easy smile masked a sharp and shrewd mind—something his instructors at the Naval Academy had quickly noticed. In fact, over the years, Moisen had developed a persona that allowed him to almost disappear in an empty room. To underestimate him because of that skill would have been a serious mistake.

Lieutenant Greg Rockham was not the kind of man to make mistakes. In the SEAL Teams, mistakes, at best, made you a bad operator. At worst, they cost men their lives. Rockham had known Captain Moisen for the better part of a year now. The Special Materials Detachment had been a pet project of Moisen's—one he'd worked hard to create. Now that Rockham saw a possible problem coming up with the special unit, he wanted Moisen's help in providing an answer. But the meeting wasn't going as well as he might have hoped.

"So you're saying that the unit can't do its job with the manpower it has now?" Moisen asked.

"No, not at all sir," Rockham said quickly. "In fact, the men can do their job, and do it well. The results of our field work demonstrate that. The problem is, we have too few qualified people to address the level of commitment we need to maintain. We pulled off the takedown of the *Pilgrim's Hope* well enough. There were no casualties on our side and no civilians were hurt. But in spite of the overall success of the operation, the men were disappointed that we didn't find the weapons on board that we were sent after. It was as if we had won the big game but only part of the opposing team had shown up."

"The missiles that you did find provided some very valuable intelligence," Moisen said. "Their design proves that Hussein does have an ongoing hidden weapons program. Those missiles were intended for warheads a lot more destructive than just simple high explosives would be.

"Your men should feel very proud of the mission they conducted—that you conducted. It was hardly their fault that the warheads were not aboard that cargo ship. They may not even exist yet, if Saddam's scientists have run into any serious technical difficulties. But now, once a warhead is ready, there won't be anything to launch it with, at least not in the Sudan."

"That may be, sir," Rockham said, "but the men were still disappointed with the results. One of them said it was like kissing your sister. Nice enough, but no big thrill. Then when we had to sit on our hands in Saudi—"

"There isn't a mission available every day," Moisen interrupted.

"No sir," Rockham said. "In the Teams, we know that better than just about anyone. We've trained for years without a hot operation coming along—that's something we're used to. What the men aren't used to is just sitting on their hands and not being able to do anything but studying and PT. Because of our security classification and alert status, that was all we were able to do for the last four months in Saudi Arabia.

"The rest of the Persian Gulf had SEAL detachments conducting a number of real-world operations as well as active training. We couldn't take part in that. Then we get pulled back to the States to sit on our hands again. The men are starting to get on each other's nerves. Nothing serious yet, but we're starting to lose our edge. And that's something that can be very serious."

"So what do you suggest?" Moisen asked.

"First, that we eliminate the port and starboard watches for the time being," Rockham said. "I will see to it that the entire unit is ready to go—both squads will be on a first alert status. All of our equipment will be prepped and ready to load. We can be in a wheels-up condition within six hours of receiving an alert."

"If you feel that you can function with your men in that situation and still accomplish your mission," Moisen said, "there's no way that I'm going to argue with it. The situation in the Persian Gulf is going to heat up before very long. Within weeks would be a smart bet. I didn't know whether we would need your people ready to go here in the States to react to a terrorist threat or in the Gulf to act with the coalition forces. So we have to leave all the options open right now. But changing the alert status system for your unit doesn't seem to address the lack of personnel—to me, it seems to make it worse. What more are you suggesting?"

"Consolidating the alert status of both squads doesn't do anything more than put them together as a single unit," Rockham said. "Effectively, we are that anyway. What it does give me is the opportunity to do something that will help their attitude.

"What I want to do is take them out West on a seventy-two hour field training operation. That would mean we'd increase our reaction time to an alert on the East Coast, but we would still be inside of CONUS," Rockham explained, using the acronym for the continental United States. "At the same time, it would greatly reduce our reaction time to the West Coast if we had to join up with the Teams there."

Being closer to the West Coast was a serious consideration, since Special Warfare Group One at Coronado assembled SpecWar Task Force One, which was conducting operations in support of the coalition forces in the Persian Gulf.

"And there's some additional benefit to the unit from going out to Nellis right now," Rockham went on. "As I'm sure you know, the Air Force has developed some new insertion techniques using their newest stealth aircraft, the B-2 bomber. The training officer at Special Warfare Group Two has hooked me up with the proper people, and this looks like something we could not only do well, but would be a new tool for us.

"I haven't received all the details yet, but it looks to be right up our alley. From the very first days of the Teams back in the 1960s, we experimented with jumping from all kinds of aircraft. From what the Air Force is asking, this looks like an extension of those days. That, and it gives them another mission to help justify their half-billion-dollar B-2s to Congress."

Moisen leaned back in his chair and regarded the young SEAL officer. Rockham had always proved himself more than competent, and he read his men better than anyone else could. Moisen knew that anything he wanted had to be in the best interests of the men under his command.

"Just where do you intend to go," Moisen asked, "and what do you intend to do when you get there?"

Reaching into the briefcase sitting on the floor next to his chair, Rockham pulled out a thick interagency mail envelope—the kind secured with a string between two buttons. Standing up, he placed it in front of Moisen.

"You will find a complete briefing and oplan here, sir," Rockham said, referring to the operations plan, as he sat back down.

Unwinding the string, Moisen opened up the envelope and removed the two file folders inside. Over several moments, he scanned the contents of the folders while Rockham sat and waited. For years, Moisen had cultivated the ability to read a page almost at a glance. It was a very valuable skill for someone in the Intelligence community. He did not let many people know that he possessed such an ability.

"Give me the essentials please," Moisen finally said.

"The Air Force wants us to spend several days training and conducting jumps from the B-2 they have at Nellis. If the technique works, we'll use it as our insertion platform for the field training exercise.

"The basic problem will be a live-fire exercise in a secure training area in the Nevada desert. There is a target site that is perfect for our needs in the range area northwest of Nellis, at a place called Dog Bone Lake. The objective is at a mock-up of an Iraqi air base the Air Force already has in place at that location. The specific target for the SMD is a jet aircraft parked at one runway with a pair of spray tanks mounted under the wings.

"My contacts in the Air Force have confirmed that there is a target in place suitable for our needs and that the area has been cleared for our operations. We will conduct a night HAHO"—high altitude, high opening—"jump into the target area and march in with both squads acting as separate elements. We will eliminate the target and then conduct a seventy-two hour escape and evasion exercise."

"Why the live-fire aspects of the exercise?" Moisen asked. The enthusiasm Rockham radiated for his subject was contagious, and Moisen found himself caught up in the idea of the mission.

"Doing the operation as a live-fire with small arms and explosives will put the men in a state of maximum alert," Rockham said. "They will have to stay sharp about themselves and each other. It's the only way to prevent accidents, and even then, there will be a certain level of danger to the operation. But that's how we have to do things, sir. We fight how we train, and we train how we fight. It's the only way to get the job done.

"That's also the reason I'm conducting the infiltration as a night HAHO jump. A hop-and-pop HAHO jump is difficult enough during the day. Any number of things can go wrong when you open up your canopy immediately on exiting the plane. It will let you fly a good distance, but being on oxygen for the jump just means there's that much more than can go wrong. Doing a HAHO at night makes things harder by an order of magnitude. And it's also how we would be doing it for real.

"Making things hard for the men will force them to concentrate on the task at hand. All of the little irritations and mickey-mouse crap that's been building up for the last several months will be pretty much gone as soon as we start operating. There just won't be any room for petty irritations—I'll see to it that the men have enough real irritations to deal with," Rockham finished with a big grin.

"Why the three-day trek across the desert?" Moisen asked.

"Mr. Murphy is always ready to mess things up somehow during an operation," Rockham said. "If you give him the slightest opening, he will slip in and foul things up. So I'm just planning a simulation of his arrival. The plan will be to have the initial extraction called off so we'll have to move to another extraction site. It's a common enough occurrence on a real-world op. The only thing is, we'll have to cross some pretty hostile terrain to get to our extraction site.

"The men have been back here in Virginia long

enough. If Desert Shield heats up fast, I want them to still be acclimatized to the conditions over there. And there will be additional benefits to the training operation as well.

"I've been in touch with the people at Nellis and coordinated with them on the whole operation. They think it's more than feasible to conduct the op in the time frame I have projected. They also think it will be of use to their people as well. Their search-and-rescue people will be conducting the extraction, and there's going to be an air-drop of supplies on the second day of the operation. The whole thing is coming together very quickly, but that would also be an aspect of a high-priority real-world operation."

"If I authorize the expenditures for this exercise," Moisen said, "how are you going to maintain your alert status and keep your response time short?"

"We're going to be on a regular communications schedule with the people at Nellis," Rockham said. "In addition, I've already confirmed that our beeper system will operate in the training area we've selected. If we're needed, the Nellis people can come in and jerk us out of the field. Even being in the desert on what is effectively survival training, we won't be exposed to the elements for so long that our operational efficiency would suffer.

"As far as our alert gear goes, we'll have most of a loadout with us at Nellis. What we don't take into the field with us will remain under secure storage at Nellis. In addition, the staff at SpecWar

Group Two and SEAL Team Two are holding our alert loadout at the ready. If the balloon goes up, they are prepared to put our gear aboard whatever transport is assigned.

"We probably won't need all of these precautions, sir," Rockham continued. "But I would want them in place even if we weren't going across the country. I want this exercise to launch quickly for a reason. It will give the men something they all can fight without giving each other grief.

"This schedule won't give them much time with their families, but there's no helping that. I wish I had more time with my own wife and son. But at least the men were able to have part of the holidays at home. There's a bunch of our brothers who are deployed over in the Gulf who haven't seen their families over the holidays at all."

Moisen looked across his desk and liked what he saw. Here was a young officer with enthusiasm for his job, tempered with real concern for his men. The sacrifice of family was something that every military man had been asked to make at one time or another—that wasn't going to change. But this young officer was asking for more time to be given to his men, even at the cost of his own family time. He put the welfare of his men before his own, and the needs of his country before even that.

If Rockham needed his help to complete a difficult job, Moisen decided, then he would do whatever he could. Expending close-held funds for an unscheduled training exercise would just mean that he would have to scramble a little harder to locate the money. That search wouldn't be as hard as coming up with air transport, since just about everything that could fly was assigned to the Gulf effort and to getting materials to the coalition force build-up.

Even the aircraft could be located, if that was necessary; it just wouldn't be easy. It wasn't as if Rockham was asking for a free ride to the sunny West—though Moisen suspected that a blowout in Las Vegas, which was a stone's throw from Nellis Air Force Base, was planned as the wrap-up to Rockham's training syllabus.

CHAPTER 4

★ ★ ★ ★

2045 ZULU
SMD Headquarters
Building B417
U.S. Naval Amphibious Base
Little Creek, Virginia

"Just what in the hell has gotten into Rock?" Mike Bryant said. The young SEAL spoke while he scooted forward on his knees, rolling up the steel cables and rungs of a caving ladder laid out along the ground.

"I have no idea, but we had better get this gear stowed," Larry Stadt said. "Chief Monday said the boss wanted this climbing gear loadout checked out and in the boxes by the end of work today. So we'll get this last box on the pallet and wrap up the paperwork. We miss that meeting at 1600 and the chief will come down on both of us. I don't want to pull the duty any sooner than I have to."

"Hey, all of us have to stand the watch and answer the phone when our turn comes up," Bryant said.

A few men larger than a standard SEAL Team operational platoon, the SMD was broken down into two squads, first and second. Those squads were further broken down into two fire teams of four men each or eight shooting pairs of SEALs. In addition there were two corpsmen, giving the SMD eighteen men, which included the two officers. Though their manpower was small, the material they had available was substantial. The Navy had been lavish with their issue of weapons and materials for the unit. This kept a full loadout of gear mission-ready at any time, and gave the men another complete set of equipment to train with.

The gear had been rotated so everything was ready to go at a moment's notice. Batteries were up to date, weapons zeroed for accuracy, and ammunition used up and replaced with fresh. Each squad had its own gear loadout, and the men most familiar with a specific department's equipment took care of those boxes: Ordnance handled weapons, ammunition, and explosives; Air Ops dealt with parachuting and air drop rigging; Sub Ops was in charge of diving equipment; and Medical and Chem/Bio overviewed the specialized protective, sampling, and handling gear the SMD used for its specific mission.

As the lead climbers of their respective squads, Bryant and Stadt inspected and secured the materials used for climbing aboard ships, oil rigs, buildings, or mountains. The heavy piles of ropes, cables, coiled caving ladders, and odd hooks, poles, and caribiners had been taken out, checked, and were now being repacked in four-foot-square cardboard "triwall" boxes lined with heavy plastic bags. The two SEALs quickly finished their tasks and picked up the now heavy containers. They had been working outside their unit headquarters on an old concrete building foundation slab, which afforded them room to roll out and check such things as the thirty-foot caving ladders.

Though the Navy had been open-handed with equipment, it had been tight-fisted when it came time to find a building to house the SMD. Building B417 was about twice the size of a two-car garage. With all of the unit's gear, the available space in the building ran out fast.

Wooden pallets lay on the floor of the largest room in the building, behind a rolling overhead door, the pallets ready to be stacked with equipment containers. Once the triwall boxes were sealed, they would be secured and tied down with steel strapping. Then a forklift could lift the pallets, to be quickly loaded aboard whatever transport the unit would be using. Most of the pallets were already loaded with boxes of gear from the other departments when Stadt and Bryant added their contributions to the loads.

With their equipment properly packed and stowed away, the two SEALs had plenty of time to get to the meeting. Walking into the building, Stadt and Bryant saw most of their Teammates sitting or standing around the crowded office area. As the ranking man of the detail, Larry Stadt approached Senior Chief Monday with the paperwork for their job.

"Here's the 1149s, inventory, and manifest sheets," he said, handing over a sheaf of papers. "Everything is good to go, ready to be sealed and strapped to a pallet."

"Okay," Monday replied, "I'll check to see if Mr. Daugherty or Rockham want to do a look-over, and then we'll seal everything up. How did you two finally decide on how to pack up the climbing poles?"

"Mike came up with a good one for those," Stadt said. "Found some really heavy cardboard tubes that we could cut to size with a handsaw. The Seabees cut us some wood plugs for the ends and we bundled up the new fiberglass climbing poles inside the cardboard and screwed the caps on."

"We can get all of the tubes we want," Mike Bryant added. "On my way in this morning, I stopped at that carpeting store on Virginia Avenue, and the guys there said they toss them out all the time. They hold those new pole sections tightly and they don't rattle."

"Good job," Monday said as he set his full clipboard down on the desk he was leaning against. The tall senior chief SEAL had more experience under his belt than any two members of the rest of the unit combined. One of a decreasing number of Vietnam combat veterans still active in the Teams in the 1990s, he well knew the value of using the skills and ingenuity of his men. Monday looked like he would be a slow thinker, with his unruly black hair and round face framed by two big ears. But his slow smile and easy way masked a very sharp mind. Few things escaped his notice, and his attention to details set an example for the men who worked for him.

"Rock and Mr. Daugherty are still over at Group Two," Monday said to the men in the room, "but they called and told me they would be here in just a few minutes. So settle in."

"Any idea what this briefing's about?" Pete Wilkes asked from the back of the room.

"You'll know as soon as I do," Monday said.

"And that's right now, Senior Chief," Rockham said as he walked into the room.

Shaun Daugherty followed Rockham. Going up to a bulletin board that took up a large portion of one wall, Daugherty started to pin up a long, thin roll of paper.

"An opportunity for some good training has come up that I intend for us to take advantage of," Rockham said. "The Air Force has a new and very expensive toy that they want to share with us."

The noise and moving about in the room came to a halt as every man listed to what Rockham had to say. The look in the men's eyes ranged from careful wariness to excitement. They waited to hear what he'd say next.

"We are going out West to conduct a training operation in Nevada," Rockham told them.

"Vegas again," Kurkowski said.

A round of laughter went through the room at Kurkowski's mention of their last trip out West. The unit had celebrated its successful certification operation with a two-day blowout on the strip in Las Vegas. Even Chief Monday had a big grin on his face at the memory of that weekend as he growled out, "Okay, pipe down."

Rockham had a smile of his own as he looked at Kurkowski. "Maybe," he said, "but first we're going to have a fun-filled couple of days jumping, courtesy of the U.S. Air Force."

Kurkowski's face fell at that news. Everyone knew that he didn't particularly like jumping from a perfectly good aircraft. But Dan Able was the only SEAL in the room with a real frown on his face. He would do whatever was asked of him, but Able had never liked parachuting.

"This information is classified top secret," Rockham said, "for obvious reasons. It seems that the Air Force is trying to justify spending a train car full of money developing and fielding the new stealth bomber. So some bright mind came up with a way of using the B-2 as an insertion platform for special operations. If the system works, we'll be able to insert a team from an aircraft that isn't detectable by radar. I don't have to explain to you just how valuable a technique that will be.

"The Air Force wants us to test out their technique operationally on a controlled basis. The system has been tested extensively, and I've been told that it does work well. But now they want someone else besides their development people to try out the new ride. Since every one of us has received their top secret security clearances, we're invited to be the first ones on the ride.

"Tomorrow morning at 0800 hours we will be heading out. For the next several days we'll be training on their new system. Then we'll be conducting jumps from one of the two operational B-2s in the country. If everything works out as planned, we'll use the new technique to insert the unit on a high altitude, high opening jump on a target in the desert. We'll open at 25,000 feet and cover several miles of desert before landing."

As Rockham spoke to the men, Shaun Daugherty had been unrolling what was now identifiable as a large sheet of maps. He secured the bottom of the roll and stepped back from the map. Now everyone in the room could see that the large sheet had been assembled from nine smaller maps taped together at their edges.

"This is Dog Bone Lake in southern Nevada," Rockham said, pointing to an elongated feature extending north and south between two of the maps. "And before any of you look forward to a water jump, you should know that this place hasn't been wet for a couple of thousand years or so.

"In the upper half of this dry lake there's an airstrip set up as an Iraqi airfield. The Air Force has regularly used this area for target practice, but it has been declared clear for our exercise by Explosive Ordnance Disposal. There is an Iraqi-marked MiG-19 jet fighter on the strip at that lake fitted with a pair of chemical spray tanks. That jet is our primary objective. The mission will be for us to insert into the area of the objective by HAHO jump. Once there, we will approach and confirm the target. After examination, we will destroy the target with demolitions and withdraw for extraction.

"There will be no aggressors on this operation, but it will be a live-fire exercise. Targets have been put in place around the area, and we will treat them as enemy forces. Targets that are engaged will be put down by hits in the kill zone. Miss, and it means more range time for all of us. Any questions so far?"

There were none. It was still early in the briefing, and the men expected to receive a lot more information. Even though it would be another training exercise, each man treated the situation as if it were a real-world op. The fact that it was a live-fire exercise was not lost on any of them. The normal danger just from jumping into an area and conducting training had been greatly increased by adding the factor of live ammunition and explosives.

Right from the beginning, the mission was starting to do just what Rockham had hoped it would—bring the men close together again by giving them a mutual problem to deal with. Now he had some news that he hoped they would enjoy even more.

"As of right now," Rockham said, "we are under a new organization for training. We have been authorized to train as a single unit and operate under a single alert status. That worked well for us while we were in the Gulf, and I see no reason to go to the two-squad alert rotation. Once we get enough men into the unit to make a complete second platoon, we'll go back to rotating alert status."

The alert rotation system had one squad on first alert and the other on second alert. While on first alert status, the members of a squad had to be on base within an hour of hearing the alert over their pagers. It also meant that the squad had to be ready to deploy within six hours of the men arriving on base. In only seven hours, a squad of the SMD had to be prepared to deploy anywhere in the world.

The squad on second alert status didn't have things much better. They had to report to the base within four hours of an alert. Six hours later, they too had to be in a wheels-up status and heading out to wherever they were needed. The two squads didn't have to carry their own food, tents, and bunks with them, but needed the weapons, materials, and equipment to deploy for ninety days without special resupply.

The switching status had sounded good at first, since some of the men would at least be able to head a short distance away from Little Creek and spend time with their families. But the rotation also split the very small unit and caused more friction. Rockham wanted to do away with it when he saw how strained things had grown between the men during their long, static deployment in Saudi Arabia. Captain Moisen had given him permission to do just that.

The rotation had been a pain, and the men were glad to be rid of it, even though they knew something had to take its place. Vocal approval of the new situation sounded out from a number of the SEALs in the room.

"Okay," Rockham said, "you don't get something for nothing. We will have to maintain our deployment loadout even more tightly than we have been doing. And the bad news is, we'll have to take it with us when we go out on training missions."

A small groan went around the room at that announcement. The complaint was mild enough, but the workload wouldn't be. The new situation meant that the unit would travel with twice the amount of gear they needed to work with. And that meant more transport, handling, and security.

"We'll look like a Gypsy caravan moving out for the summer," Kurkowski said.

"So much for traveling light," Wayne Alexander said.

A chuckle went around the room at Alexander's comment. At five feet four inches, Alexander was the shortest man in the unit. But he was anything but the weakest. He was built like a fireplug and could hump the heaviest load over long distances. His rucksack was always fully packed, and half the time he carried an M60E3 machine gun as well. Alexander never traveled light.

"We're going to be traveling anything but light," Rockham said, as if picturing Alexander's usual load. "At least until we get to the training area at Nellis Air Force Base."

"Just outside of Las Vegas," Kurkowski said again.

"You said that already," John Sukov said. Big

John wasn't the largest man in the unit, but at over six feet tall and at more than 210 pounds, he could hold his own with most men, and was not above poking fun at Kurkowski or anyone else in the unit on occasion.

"Can it," Chief Monday growled, and the wise-cracks stopped immediately.

"We have to get to Las Vegas before anyone can do anything, Kurkowski," Rockham said. "And moving this outfit is going to take twice as much work as any time before. All department heads should have their paperwork in to Senior Chief Monday by now. If there are any shortages, we have to address them tonight. I want the unit packed and ready to move out by 0630 hours to-morrow morning. I know Pete Wilkes has to get back to his ladies. So the sooner everything is ready tonight, the sooner we can go home and tell our families we're going to be hitting the road again."

Pete Wilkes, a member of second squad, had the largest family of anyone in the unit. He had been married to his wife Michelle for fifteen years and they now had kids aged fourteen, eleven, nine, and seven. In the world of the SEALs, the fact that Wilkes never looked at another woman while the SMD was out on an operation or training showed he had a very solid marriage. With his oldest daughter starting to show a serious interest in boys, Wilkes was torn between wanting to deploy with his Teammates and staying on his front porch with a shotgun.

There was another round of light laughter that

went through the men as Wilkes raised his head and smiled at Rockham's joke. Only a short time earlier there wouldn't have been even a laugh at such a mild razz as Rockham had given Wilkes.

Rockham was glad to hear them joking around. It sounded a lot more like their old style of operating than the way they had over the last several weeks, even after getting back to the States from Saudi Arabia. It was confirmation that the training curriculum he had set up would take all of their energy and more.

CHAPTER 5

★ ★ ★ ★

0237 ZULU
14033 Princess Drive
Virginia Beach

It was well into the evening before Rockham had
finished up his paperwork at the Special Materials
Detachment. Finally, he was back in his car and
passing through Gate 5 of the Little Creek Naval
Amphibious Base. While driving, the SEAL officer
thought about how many times he'd headed home
after dark during his career in Naval Special Warfare. Too many times, he thought.

Shaun Daugherty had been with Rockham
back at headquarters, pushing paper across their
desks. Both men were making sure that everything
was ready for their upcoming training operation.
Even though Rockham had been planning the
event for a while now, there was always last
minute documents that had to be shuffled, signed,
and filed.

A lot of the work involved in moving the relatively small number of men in the SMD could be delegated to the more than competent petty officers and chiefs who made up the unit. The trust that Rockham and Daugherty had in their men showed in the amount of responsibility they did delegate. But in the final analysis, the local chain-of-command for the unit ended on the desks of the two officers. It was Daugherty and ultimately Rockham who held the final responsibility for the welfare of the men and the functioning of the special unit they made up.

Few of the men were around when the two officers finally wrapped up their workday. Still single himself, Shaun had asked Rockham how his wife Sharon had taken the news about their training operation out West. The unit had only been back in the United States and the Little Creek base for a few weeks after having been deployed for months in the Persian Gulf. Now they were leaving again.

A lot of men in the Teams had sacrificed their married lives for their careers, and Daugherty knew this well. If he was ever going to be a married, active duty SEAL officer—and there was someone he was very interested in—he would have to know how the other guys dealt with their families. Rockham not only was another married officer, he had a young son.

"Sharon knew who and what I was when she married me," Rockham had told him. "And she has been a Team wife and stood by my side for nearly eight years now. She can understand what I do, and why I do it, even though I can't always explain things to her about where the unit is going, or why. I know that sometimes she would prefer that I was doing something else, but she accepts and deals with the situation as she can.

"It's Matt who pays the biggest price for my career in the Teams. He's proud as hell of his daddy and has no trouble telling anyone that. But he's only a seven-year old boy. So far in the last year, I've missed both his birthday, Thanksgiving, and Christmas. That means a hell of a lot to someone his age.

"In finding Sharon, I was lucky. She can accept my career and work with the restrictions on family life that comes with the bill. Not many guys can find women like that, and I wish you luck."

Now, as he pulled up the driveway to his modest ranch home in Virginia Beach, Rockham reflected on what he had said to Daugherty. A large part of the local community around his home on Princess Drive was made up of Navy families. In fact, there were so many SEAL families in that neighborhood, it was practically a Special Warfare community of its own.

When Rockham, or any of his married people, left on a deployment, their local Teammates who were still in the area checked up on the families left behind. There were so few men in the SMD that they all left the area for a deployment with no one left behind, but SEALs from the other Teams checked up on their families.

Teammates from SEAL Team Two especially, the source for most of the manpower for the SMD, stopped by the house regularly. The lawn was cut at the Rockham home, and the little household problems—a broken ceiling fan, hornet's nest, or leaking washing machine—were taken care of by a Teammate who knew how to deal with the problem. Kids were ferried to school functions when the mother wasn't able to, sporting events were attended, and the families cheered the surrogate children on. It wasn't a substitute for a father and husband being home, but it helped.

Getting out of the car at his single-story, ranch-style home, Rockham knew that his family was well cared for no matter what his situation or assignment. Entering the house through the side door, the first thing he saw was his son, sound asleep, curled up in the recliner near one wall of the family room. As he looked down at Matt, his wife Sharon slipped her arms around her husband and hugged him from behind.

Resting her head against his shoulder, she said quietly, "He wanted to stay up for you."

"I'll put him to bed," Rockham said.

Reaching down, the powerful SEAL effortlessly picked up the small boy. As he held Matt in his arms, the boy groaned softly in protest at the disturbance. But he lay sleeping quietly in his father's strong arms as he was carried back to his room at the far end of the house.

After putting his son in bed, Rockham returned to the kitchen and sat at the table in the dining area. Sharon was plating up the dinner she had kept warm for him. She knew from long experience that the nights before her husband had to leave on a trip were usually late ones, and had prepared an evening meal that reheated well.

"Coffee, dear?" she asked from the kitchen.

"I'm about coffeed out," Rockham said. "I think a beer would go nicely with dinner tonight."

Sharon took two cold, brown glass bottles out of the refrigerator. She came into the dining nook with a plate in one hand and the two bottles in the other.

"So how did Matt do in school today?" Rockham asked as his wife set a full plate in front of him.

Putting one of the beer bottles next to his plate, she sat down before answering. "Some of the older kids at school were talking about how the U.S. was only fighting for the oil in Kuwait. They said that's what was being talked about on the news. Matt wasn't accepting any of it. He said his daddy didn't fight for oil, he fought for people. Not too bad for a first grader I think," she said with a warm smile.

"No," Rockham said, "not too bad at all. He thinks more clearly than many adults I know."

"Children are like that," Sharon said. "They can cut through a lot of the smoke screen that blocks what the adults can see. He gets that from his father, I believe."

Sharon looked at her husband with a soft smile on her face. Where other wives might have protested about their husbands always being away, she accepted it and worked her life around it. Rockham knew that she also helped other wives who had a harder time when their SEAL husbands had to deploy. Even though the SMD was very small and very classified, the wives of the married members helped support each other. As the wife of the commanding officer, the leader of the unit, Sharon accepted the traditional role of her position and tried to set an example for the other wives.

CHAPTER 6
★★★★

Thoughts of wives, families, girlfriends, or the pet dog were absent from the minds of the SEALs the next morning as they hustled to get the SMD on its way. Muster was held at 0600 hours, and a number of individuals, Rockham among them, had been hard at work since well before that time.

Larry Stadt arrived at SMD headquarters just as muster had begun. Senior Chief Monday didn't change his tone of voice or raise an eyebrow as he came in. The chief simply made a mental note of the late arrival and growled a quick, "Belay that" as Kurkowski started to make a comment.

The remark made the day before, about the SMD resembling a Gypsy caravan, seemed an apt description as a pair of trucks with the bulk of the unit's gear and supplies was packed. A SeaBee who had come to SMD headquarters with a fork-lift made quick work of lifting the pallets full of gear boxes up onto the truck beds.

A double load, needed for eighteen men, went on board the trucks. The boxes and bags contained the clothing and personal gear of the men as well as all of their special equipment, ammunition, weapons, and demolitions. All the men took extreme care to be certain that every piece of material was properly stowed for maximum safety and security. In spite of that, the Air Force loadmaster for the transport air-craft would have had a fit if he knew exactly what it was that the SEALs were bringing on board with them.

The only piece of gear missing was the usual picnic basket of chow the men looked forward to from their old Teammate Ken Fleming. A care package of good food and drink from Ken's Ice-berg Bar and Grill was a welcome break from the boredom of a long military flight. But there hadn't been time to give Fleming a heads-up, or to stop by and pick up anything even if it had been ready. Rockham was pushing hard, and had the men de-ploying as if it was a hot operation rather than a training op.

What Lieutenant Rockham wanted, Senior Chief Monday delivered. Gear was up on the vehi-cles in record time and the unit was out the gate and on its way. Once the men and their vehicles had arrived at Langley Air Force Base near Hamp-ton, less than an hour's drive from Little Creek, even with the morning traffic, they received the really bad news.

Air transport was limited, with the Desert Shield buildup reaching a critical level. The clouds of active war were gathering over the Persian Gulf, and Kuwait was going to be liberated soon. But the logistics needs of such a distant war used all of the transportation it could get. Even with their high priority, the men and equipment of the SMD had to settle for what was available to them to head out West.

Sitting on the tarmac was a C-130H from the Air Force Reserves. The big, bulky transport craft with its four Allison T56-A-T5 turboprop engines was a real workhorse of the military aircraft world. It was dependable, tough, loud, and slow. It would be at least a six-hour flight to Nevada in the big flying truck—the four blades of the turboprop engines adding their own unique roar to the sound of the flight.

All of the men had been on long, slow military flights before. There was nothing to do but accept the situation and make the best of it. The canvas webbing and tubing frame seats lining the sides of the aircraft's cargo area hadn't been designed for long-distance comfort. Not long after takeoff, John Grant took advantage of the limited comfort of being between the two rolled-up Zodiac F470 inflatable boats secured to one of the pallets. Stretched out on the hard rubber, the big Native American was soon sound asleep.

The short, powerful body of Wayne Alexander

seemed to completely accept any situation. He was asleep sitting in one of the canvas passenger seats even before John Grant had stretched out. The off-key buzzing roar of Alexander's snoring could even be heard over the noise of the C-130's turboprops.

On top of one of the cargo boxes, Roger Kurkowski, Sid Mainhart, and Ryan Marks resumed the poker game they had been running on every long SMD trip. The game had taken on the trappings of a religious ritual while the unit was in Saudi Arabia—the SEALs playing on an almost daily basis. The only difference at the moment was, with Wayne Alexander asleep, his normal seat at the game was taken by Mike Bryant.

Rockham, Daugherty, Chief Monday, and Mike Ferber were spending their time on the flight going over the training schedules for the SMD once they got to Nellis Air Force Base in Nevada. Even in Special Operations, there was never an end to the military paperwork necessary for an operation.

The balance of the unit tried to make themselves as comfortable as they could, resting, reading, or attempting to sleep. The loadmaster of the crew came by some hours into the flight with hot coffee and food for the SEALs. The coffee was good, but it did little to make up for the boxed lunches that were the staple fare for such military flights. The good eats from Ken Fleming were missed by most members of the unit.

After nearly six hours in the air, it was approaching 1530 hours for the SEALs. But the lo-

cal time was only about half past noon. Chief
Monday noted that the extra three hours would
help the men do a real day's work after sitting on
the plane for so long. The very loud fart from the
direction of Wayne Alexander was considered a
normal bodily function of the man and not a comment on the chief's work ethic.

"Hey, you can see Las Vegas," called out Larry
Stadt from where he was looking through one of
the small portholes in the sides of the C-130. All of
the SEALs were now in the canvas seats lining the
sides of the aircraft, strapped in for the upcoming
landing. A few of the men looked out the other
portholes to see the city passing by below them.

Pink tile-roofed houses rising up from the
desert floor were spread out in rectangular tracts
plopped between the tan and brown mountain
ranges. The taller buildings of the Las Vegas strip
couldn't be seen from the SEALs' vantage point.
The tile roofs and mostly white houses swept past,
the occasional sudden splash of green showing a
golf course in the irrigated desert.

2445 ZULU
36° 14' North, 115° 02' West
Nellis Air Force Base
Nevada

The C-130 flew lower and passed near the city
as it lost altitude going down to Nellis. The Air
Force base, only seven miles to the northeast of
downtown Las Vegas, nestled between the same
mountain ranges that framed the famous city.

With a crunch and loud roar, the cargo plane set its wheels down on the runway, the props changing pitch to help slow the big aircraft.

After taxiing for what felt like forever to the SEAL passengers inside, the C-130 came to a stop in front of a hangar complex. One of the small hangar buildings had a high-security, alarmed storage area for the exclusive use of the SMD. With the help of some waiting Air Force handling gear, the pallets full of gear belonging to the SEALs were moved from the C-130 and stowed away.

"Hey," said Kurkowski, as the Air Force people made quick work of unloading the aircraft, "this bit about having a high priority could be something I could get used to."

"Don't get too used to things," Chief Monday said. "We've still got to get ourselves squared away before the real work can even begin."

In spite of the chief's misgivings, it only took a few hours of shuffling about for the men and officers of the SMD to be assigned quarters and get their records in the proper hands for the duration of their stay at Nellis. Air Force Second Lieutenant Mark Pruitt had met the SEALs after their plane arrived. He was at the storage hangar and had a blue-painted Air Force bus ready to transport them. After having guided the SEALs through the maze of buildings and offices at Nellis, he left them in a large hangar at the far eastern side of the airfield.

"This will be the main classroom area for your training," Pruitt said. "The entire area has been declared off limits to regular Air Force personnel, so you shouldn't be disturbed."

Without another word, the lieutenant climbed back onto the bus and told the driver to return to the other side of the field.

"Huh," Daugherty said to Rockham. "Do you think it's something we said?"

"Probably just didn't want to know any more about what we were doing than he had to," Rockham said. "These Air Force guys can be strange as hell about security."

The hangar where the SEALs were dropped off was behind a long stretch of chain-link fence. The armed Air Police guard at the gate snapped to attention as Lieutenant Rockham approached him. But in spite of his show of respect, the guard took a careful look at the ID cards of each man before opening the gate so they could enter the hangar area.

The only visible furnishings in the huge building were several rows of student chairs with small desks attached. The chairs were lined up in front of a podium and several long tables. Behind the tables were the bulky shapes of equipment covered in large dropcloths, with a stack of folded gym-floor padded mats like those found in high school off to the side. Next to the stack of mats was some odd-looking scaffolding with boxes and piles of cloth underneath.

As the SEALs stood looking about, a door opened from the office area at the side of the hangar and three serious-looking sergeants walked in. The black man leading the trio was dressed in an Air

Force flight suit with a huge patch of chevrons on his arm. There were two peaked chevrons above a central circled star, and six rockers surrounding and below the same star. The sergeant looked like he'd been in the Air Force since being ground crew at Kitty Hawk. The other two wore black jumpsuits much like those often worn by the SEALs themselves. On the upper right chest of the jumpsuits were black patches with gold lettering.

The Air Force sergeant leading the group was short and stocky and appeared almost as wide as he was tall. His chest was so heavily muscled that his arms couldn't hang down straight by his sides. Instead, they stood out at slight angles from his shoulders.

The other two sergeants appeared to be very fit and moved with crisp, confident strides. As they approached the SEALs, the words U.S. ARMY could be read underneath a set of gold parachute wings on the black leather patches of their jumpsuits.

"Good afternoon, sir," the black sergeant said as he stopped in front of Lieutenant Rockham and saluted smartly.

"Good afternoon, Sergeant," Rockham said, returning the salute.

Before the SEAL officer could utter another word, the stocky sergeant turned away and walked up to the podium. "If you gentlemen would please take a seat," he said in a loud voice, "we'll get started. We don't have a lot of time to familiarize you with this equipment or these techniques if we want to keep to your planned training schedule."

Rockham had wanted things to move quickly to keep his men busy and their minds on their training. But this Air Force sergeant kept an even brisker pace. As the SEALs sat down, the sergeant kept talking.

"I am Chief Master Sergeant Fitzhugh," he said from the podium. "The two men with me are Master Sergeant Edgars and Staff Sergeant Posey."

Both men nodded as they were introduced.

"These NCOs are both Army Special Forces sergeants," Fitzhugh continued, "assigned here for the development of this training. They are members of Company B of the 2nd Battalion, 1st Special Warfare Training Group (Airborne). I'm certain that all of you gentlemen recognize that unit. They run the U.S. Army Military Freefall Parachute School down at the Yuma Proving Ground in Arizona. All of you have completed that advanced course, otherwise you wouldn't be here."

Each of the SEALs well-remembered that grueling five-week course. They had done more than thirty freefall parachute jumps while attending it. At least two were daylight high altitude, low opening jumps on oxygen and with full field equipment. Then there had been at least two nighttime HALO jumps, also with oxygen and full gear. Sid Mainhart, the newest SEAL in the unit, had completed the course less than a year ago. These instructors were hard-core professionals with more time in the air than the average angel.

"We have checked your medical records,"

Fitzhugh said, "including your HALO physicals. I have been assured that all of the physicals are up-to-date, or at least less than two years old. Since this unit made a HAHO insertion jump west of this air base early last year, you gentlemen are at least somewhat familiar with the ground surfaces we have in this area."

Several of the SEALs were surprised to hear that Fitzhugh knew about the unit's certification operation. The jump he was talking about had been made only the year before at the Indian Springs Air Force Auxiliary Field about forty miles northwest of where the unit was now.

An Air Force chief master sergeant was at the same rank as a Navy master chief petty officer. This was the kind of man that high-ranking officers listened to.

"That jump was made from a C-130 aircraft flying at about 26,000 feet," Fitzhugh said. "Effectively, it was identical to the aircraft that you arrived in today. Forget everything about jumping from a cargo transport. The jumps that you will be making here will be from a much different aircraft, and you will not be exiting from the rear ramp—there won't be any."

Staff Sergeant Posey had walked over to one of the smaller cloth-covered objects in the room. At a nod from Fitzhugh, he pulled the cover off and exposed what it had been hiding—a boxy, angular sheet-metal seat with a very tall back.

"Gentlemen," Fitzhugh said as he warmed up to his subject, "let me introduce you to a highly modified version of the Advanced Concept Ejection Seat, known as the ACES II for short. This is a third-generation ejection seat used in a wide variety of aircraft. From the A-10 to the F-16, right now over a half-dozen production and experimental aircraft use this ejection seat to save pilots' lives. By using the seat, there is an eighty percent chance of survival for a pilot during an emergency ejection. Aircrew who stay with their aircraft under the same circumstances have about a fifteen percent survival rate.

"This seat will eject a pilot at a peak catapult acceleration of twelve g's. That's twelve times the force of gravity. For a two hundred pound man, that means he would suddenly weigh more than a ton. Standing on the ground, zero-zero conditions in the Air Force, the catapult rockets of this seat would throw a man two hundred feet straight up into the air."

"We're going to eject from a jet?" Dan Able said from his seat, a concerned look on his face that was mirrored in the faces of a number of his Teammates.

"No, not quite," Fitzhugh said with a grin, the first one the SEALs had seen from him. "We wouldn't do that even to Navy guys. This seat has had its ejection and stabilization rockets removed for use. You won't be ejected from the insertion platform."

Both Army sergeants had moved over to a much larger piece of equipment hidden under a tarp. Pulling the cloth down, they uncovered a long complex cylinder with flat disks on both ends. Along the sides of the more than eighteen-inch-thick central cylinder were mounted rows of ACES II ejection seats, five seats to a side. The whole assembly looked to be more than twenty feet long.

Each of the seats were flat-sided boxy assemblies. The ribbed metal sides of the seats stuck out beyond where the actual seat ended and the occupants' legs would hang down. There was some padding on the back of the seat, but the center section was almost completely cut away. An assortment of buckles and webbing straps made up the bulk of the seat's equipment, but they were not the most visible components.

On what would be the front of the armrests of a normal seat were two bright yellow handles lined with black stripes. The handles were located so they would be outboard on either side of a seated person's knees. All the seats hung from a metal frame that extended out from the central cylinder and down the back of each chair. Even in the "stripped down" configuration that Chief Master Sergeant Fitzhugh had said the seats were in, the ACES II was a complicated-looking piece of equipment.

"This," Fitzhugh said, "is a modified version of the Boeing Advanced Applications Rotary Launcher, what we call the AARL. The original version of the launcher can hold up to eight bombs that weigh considerably more than a ton each—so it is more than strong enough to hold your entire unit along with all of their jump and field gear.

"This AARL will drop the seats selectively from either side of the launcher, starting from the rear and moving to the front. Each seat will fall free of the aircraft, where a drogue parachute will deploy 1.35 seconds from the time of release. The seat will release a restraining harness approximately 1.5 seconds after the drogue deploys. That puts the jumper in a freefall situation."

"You mean the seat is released from the aircraft and we're all ejected?" Mike Bryant said. He had done the most parachute jumps of any SEAL in the SMD and was normally the lead jumper on an insertion. He had never heard of anything like this technique.

"No," Fitzhugh said, "you are not ejected. In this case, gentlemen, you won't be actually jumping—you'll be dropped like a bomb."

CHAPTER 7
★ ★ ★ ★

After Chief Master Sergeant Fitzhugh's introduction to the AARL-ACES II insertion system, the SEALs of the SMD spent the balance of their first afternoon and a good part of the evening learning about the new equipment. Fitzhugh and the two Special Forces sergeants knew the system completely. They had all been involved in its development and testing.

In addition to being technically competent, all three sergeants were excellent instructors. Recognizing fellow professional military men, the SEALs welcomed the information the three NCOs were able to impart to them, absorbing the information with a minimum of their usual joking around.

Early the following morning, Senior Chief

Monday had Mike Ferber lead the unit through its
morning physical training and conditioning run.
The men hadn't been back from the Persian Gulf
that long, but Rockham and Chief Monday
wanted everyone to be acclimated to the desert as
soon as possible. In January, the Nevada desert
wasn't particularly cold during the day, but the air
was extremely dry and the nights could easily be
below freezing.

Mike Ferber had been an instructor at the Basic
Underwater Demolition/SEAL training course at
what they called the Schoolhouse in Coronado,
California, only a few years earlier. As someone
who had been a head instructor for the intense
first phase of training, when the infamous Hell
Week was held, Ferber was in standout physical
condition. Having been named Instructor of the
Year back at BUD/S, Ferber had maintained his
very high level of physical conditioning. He stood
out even among this fit group of SEALs.

The two Special Forces sergeants were staying
in another section of the Transient Quarters, separate from the area the SEALs were in. Both SF
sergeants had decided to join the SEALs for their
morning workout and run, and both quickly confirmed that the SEALs reputation for physical fitness was well earned. In spite of the brisk chill of
the early morning desert air, everyone working
out was soon coated in a film of sweat. Sets of
push-ups, jumping jacks, crunches, and other cal-
isthenics were interspersed with sets of stretches
and warm-ups.

The forty-five minutes of hard exercise were

followed by a brisk five-mile run around the main
roads of the air base. Roger Kurkowski explained
to the two Special Forces sergeants that they had
cut the PT session and run short so as not to use
up valuable training time.

Bringing up the rear of the running formation
was Wayne Alexander. Almost always coming in
last for a run, Alexander also kept up and finished
no matter how long the run. On long hikes with
heavy equipment loads, he just kept going, even
when the other SEALs were winded. The man was
a living pack mule.

Coming up to the end of the run. Alexander
overheard Kurkowski's comment to the Army sergeants. "Hey, Kurkowski," he said in his normal
loud tone of voice, "if this PT is so damned easy for
you, how come you're always trying to sneak out
of the runs?"

Alexander kept trotting to where the rest of the
unit was walking off the run, ignoring his Teammate and the two Army Special Forces sergeants
with wide smiles on their faces.

After PT the morning would be spent on additional classroom training on the new jump system. This time, the activity was going to be a lot
more physical than it had been. When the SEALs
returned to the classroom hangar, a new piece of
equipment was standing uncovered near the desks.

One of the modified ACES II seats was attached
to a strange-looking set of scaffolding. The seat
was attached to a curved rail, something like a re-
versed S with a straightened bottom part. There
was a cable attached to the top of the seat that ran

up into the scaffolding and disappeared into the mechanism about ten feet above the floor.

Probably the most ominous note of all was the group of four airmen spreading out the last of the floor mats underneath the scaffolding and curved rail. Even the seat wasn't resting on the floor, but sat on a section of padded mat.

"Gentlemen," Fitzhugh said, "please take your seats. We have a lot to accomplish and not a lot of time to do it in."

As the SEALs sat down at their desks, Fitzhugh continued, "Today, you will be trying out the new ground trainer system. First, we will be doing individual drops. This rail system here will simulate the attitude of the seat as a jumper is dropped. The cable will slow the drop of the seat to match the fall of the system from an aircraft. Approximately three seconds after the seat is dropped, the jumper will be released.

"You can see by the curve of the rail system that the jumper will be in a facedown position when he is released. This simulator will allow you to have your arms up and set in a good modified frog position when the seat releases you. Who will be first?"

There was a stir among the SEALs, but no one immediately raised his hand. Instead, Ryan Marks asked, "What's supposed to protect you from smacking your face into the mats there?"

"Nothing," Fitzhugh said, "if you're not in the proper position. If you're in a good modified frog position, your back arched up and your head raised, your arms extended from the shoulders, elbows bent and hands palm down at eye level, you'll be fine. Smack down with your hands, and your chest and arms will absorb the drop. Screw it up and you'll get a bloody nose."

That description was pretty straightforward to all of the SEALs. But none of the men jumped up for the chance to be the first to try it. In spite of all the work the men had done up to that point, the first few to try this new system had the best chance of landing flat on their faces. That was not something any one of the SEALs wanted to do in front of his Teammates.

Always ready to set the example, Rockham started to get up, but Chief Monday cut him off. "Okay, Stadt," he said. "Get up there and show us how it's done."

Larry Stadt turned and looked at his chief.

"Next time," Monday said, "don't be late for muster."

Kurkowski bellowed out a laugh at the look on Larry Stadt's face.

"Glad you think it's funny," Monday said, "because you're next in the hot seat, Kurkowski."

Immediately shutting his mouth, Kurkowski turned to his chief.

"Thanks for volunteering," Monday said with a wide grin.

All the SEALs got up from their seats and gathered around the mats as Larry Stadt was strapped into the ejector seat. Sergeant Posey reached into a cardboard box on the ground and handed Stadt a new mouth guard in a plastic bag.

"Bite down on this for the drop," Posey said.

Stadt looked over at the sergeant.

"In case you hit your chin on the mat," Posey explained.

"Handlers clear," Fitzhugh said.

As the two Special Forces sergeants stepped back, Fitzhugh pressed one of the buttons on a controller on the end of a cable that dangled down from the top of the simulator. A less than thrilled Navy SEAL was lifted by the cable. Once the seat reached the top of the rail, it stopped, and Fitzhugh continued his explanation.

"I know we have been covering this for the last day, but now is the right time to review the signal system.

"Jumper," Fitzhugh called up to Stadt. "If you look at the panel in front of you, you will see the light system that takes the place of the hand signals you normally use for a jump. The weapons officer on the aircraft will control the signals. You will be able to communicate with the other members of your unit and the jumpmaster over the headset and microphone that is part of your helmet.

"The amber lights on the AARL itself will let you see around you, but the only thing you should be looking at is the four lights directly in front of you. There is a blue bar above three colored lights. When the yellow light on the far left starts flashing, that is your twenty minute warning."

Fitzhugh pressed a button on his controller and then continued to press buttons in sequence with what he was saying.

"When the yellow light stays on, that is your

ten minute warning. When the red light starts flashing, that's your six minute warning. When the red lights stays on, you are two minutes from the drop point.

"One minute from the drop, the blue light bar goes on. That is the signal that you are on your own oxygen. This is part of the original ACES II ejection system, and everything is done automatically.

"At the ten second point, the bomb bay doors will be opened by the aircraft's weapons officer. The green light will go on when you are to release. Pull up the yellow handles on both sides of the seat and you will be released."

Some of the SEALs had a chill go through them when the term "bomb bay doors" was used. This would be a kind of jump where they had little control over the drop. There were safeties in place for the system, but the idea of waiting to be dropped like a hunk of iron held little appeal for several members of the unit, and Larry Stadt was one of them.

"Bomb bay doors are opening," Fitzhugh called out. A few seconds later he pushed the button that lit up the green light and armed the ACES II for release.

Some ten feet above his Teammates, Larry Stadt pulled up on the handles and released his seat. The results were anticlimactic. The seat released from the simulator and started to drop, held back by the breaking system on the cable. As the seat slid down the rail, it started to turn facedown. As soon as the seat was fully horizontal, there was a loud *click* and the seat harness holding Stadt to the seat unlatched.

The big SEAL was in anything but a good modified frog position as he fell four feet facedown onto the matting. There was a loud smack as he impacted on the mat.

Stadt rolled over with a groan as Fitzhugh asked, "Is the jumper all right?"

In spite of having a very red face from hitting the mat like a sack of cement, Stadt held out his hand in a thumbs-up. Some laughter ran through the unit as they looked at their Teammate lying flat on the mat.

"Okay," Fitzhugh said. "The jumper failed to release the handles after the seat was released. Get your hands into the proper position and arch your body and everything will be fine. Next man, please."

Kurkowski's performance on the simulator was not much better than Stadt's. But he did get his hands up away from the seat handles before his harness released. And the bloody nose he got from hitting the mat stopped bleeding fairly quickly.

It wasn't until Mike Bryant got on the simulator that the system worked perfectly. He had his hands up as soon as the seat was released. Even with an excellent back arch and with his head properly raised, landing on the matting wasn't the most comfortable simulation Bryant had ever gone through. After only a few tries, three at the most for Kurkowski, all of the SEALs completed the simulation successfully.

By that afternoon, all of the SEALs had become more than competent at following the light signals and releasing from the ACES II in the proper position. Both of the Special Forces sergeants appeared satisfied with the SEALs' progress. Even ChiefMaster Sergeant Fitzhugh seemed pleased.

As the SEALs wrapped up another set of practice drops, one of the outside guards opened the side door in the hangar and called out to Fitzhugh. The black chief master sergeant handed off the training to Master Sergeant Edgars and stepped out of the building. Only a few minutes had gone by before Fitzhugh was back.

"Gentlemen," Fitzhugh said, "your ride is here if you'd like to see it."

Nellis Air Force Base was an active field, and the sounds of jets of various types landing and taking off had constantly been in the background as the SEALs trained. They hadn't heard anything to indicate something special had happened, but seeing their "ride," as Fitzhugh put it, wasn't something they wanted to miss.

All of the members of the SMD stepped out of the hangar and looked in the direction Fitzhugh was pointing.

"Holy shit," Kurkowski said, "it's the Batplane."

Taxiing toward a nearby hangar was a strange aircraft that did resemble the movie plane. As the big black aircraft turned, it looked like a wide, misshapen letter W. With the side of the plane facing the SEALs, it was obvious there wasn't a normal tail section. The whole aircraft was nothing more than a huge flying wing with a swollen center section smoothly rising up from the wings.

"Damn," Daugherty said, "it's a B-2 bomber.

The stealth bomber. That's what we're going to be riding in?"

It wasn't until that moment that Rockham was sure the unit would actually be training with a stealth bomber. The huge aircraft was one of the most expensive ever produced, and only two of them were in existence at the time. Both of the B-2s were undergoing a series of flight and capability tests.

The idea of using one of the rare aircraft as an insertion platform was developed in one of the military and intelligence think tanks. Captain Moisen and even some of the CIA executives at the Agency wanted to see if the SMD could be trained to jump from such an unusual platform. Rockham had faith in his men, and they had come through so far with flying colors.

While the men watched, the B-2 moved along the ground to a nearby hangar and disappeared from their view. They broke for lunch and joined with workers and airmen of Nellis who were talking about the unusual plane. The B-2 was known as the stealth bomber because it was supposed to have a minimal radar signature. Rumors abounded about what the aircraft was doing at Nellis. Few people knew the truth beyond the fact that the multi-billion-dollar plane was undergoing tests.

Rockham and his men not only knew at least part of the truth about the B-2 being at Nellis, they were working hard to make some of those truths a reality. After chow, the SEALs reported back to the hangar, bringing their full load of field gear with them.

With their normal weapons replaced with rubber mockups, the SEALs practiced releasing from the ACES II seats with all of their gear, including a rucksack. The backs of the ACES II seats had been cut away and most of the padding removed to allow the SEALs to sit reasonably comfortably while wearing their MT 1XS/SL parachutes. The rigs had both the main canopy and the reserve chute in the backpack. If the seat backs hadn't opened up properly, the SEALs would have had to sit on the very edge of the seats in order to fit.

The SEALs discovered there was no way to remove enough material from the bottom of the ACES II to make room for the rucksacks they would jump with. So, instead of strapping the rucks behind their legs as they normally would, they had to rerig their rucksacks so they could be strapped onto the front of their legs. Each SEAL would ride on his ACES II seat with his parachute behind him and his rucksack sitting on his lap. This was in addition to their helmets, oxygen bottles, MBU-3/P rubber oxygen masks, weapons, and all of their other equipment.

The only way to conduct a jump with all of this equipment was to go back on the simulator. But this time the SEALs were going to use a much larger system.

There was a new piece of equipment waiting for them back at their training hangar, and it wasn't the B-2 bomber. Standing just above the hangar floor was a huge boxlike structure with tall scaffolding attached to both ends. Underneath the box were two rows of ACES II seats, attached to the now familiar curved rails. The seats were all sitting on a thick tarp that was on the ground. The padded mats were nowhere to be seen.

Chief Master Sergeant Fitzhugh gave the SEALs one last safety briefing and then began the simulation. With the assistance of the two Special Forces sergeants, as well as four airmen who almost didn't speak a word the entire time, one full squad of SEALs were helped onto the ACES II seats and strapped in place.

While their Teammates watched, the SEALs were secured, then the entire box started to lift up from the ground, climbing up along cables attached to the tops of the scaffolding.

When the huge box reached the top of its supports, it was about twenty feet off of the ground. One of the airmen turned a loud compressor fan on, and the thick tarp beneath the simulator began to lump up and inflate. In a few moments it could be seen that the tarp was an air bag such as those used to protect movie stuntmen from injury in long falls.

As each SEAL in the simulator watched his signal lights, Fitzhugh ran through the program much the same as during that morning's training. This time, each SEAL had to wait for the green release signal to light up after the man behind him had dropped. The sequence of operation was for the last man in the stick to drop first. As he hit the air bag, the additional airmen on the ground would quickly help him roll off and clear the way for the next SEAL to drop. The air bag reinflated and Fitzhugh would signal the next jumper to release.

The system worked well and the men of the SMD had little trouble adapting to it. As the afternoon went by, they continued to drop in whole squads, five men on one side of the AARL simulator and four men on the other side. In the front of the simulator was the last man to drop, the jumpmaster. Mike Ferber was jumpmaster for the first squad and Chief Monday for the second.

Neither jumpmaster liked turning over control of the last few minutes of the jump to the weapons officer of the aircraft, but there wasn't any other way to work the system. Over their helmet rigs, all of the men could talk to each other or the aircraft crew, but only the jumpmasters were supposed to talk to the weapons officer.

While the SEALs were packing up their gear at the end of a very long afternoon, a high-ranking officer entered the hangar. The full bird colonel was immediately approached by Chief Master Sergeant Fitzhugh. After the two had a quick consultation, the colonel walked over to where Rockham and Daugherty were stripping off their gear.

"Attention!" Rockham called out when he saw the senior officer approaching.

"As you were," the colonel ordered as the SEALs were coming to attention. "Sergeant Fitzhugh has some great things to say about you and your men," the colonel said.

"Thank you, sir," Rockham replied. "He is an excellent instructor."

"He must be for you to have picked up techniques and procedures it took a number of experts to develop over several months," the colonel said with a chuckle. "However, that is to be expected, given the SEALs reputation for excellence. I just wanted to see you men before tomorrow morning and wish you luck on your first drop. It's scheduled for shortly after dawn, as I understand it."

"We were just being briefed on it as you came in, sir," Rockham said. "We should be in a wheels-up position by 0700 tomorrow morning. The drop takes place any time after we reach altitude and the drop zone."

The colonel made some additional small talk with the SEALs, and after speaking to Fitzhugh and the two Special Forces NCOs, he left.

"Who was that?" Pete Wilkes asked.

"That was the pilot of the B-2 you saw this afternoon," Fitzhugh said. "Tomorrow, he will be dropping you from over 20,000 feet into the Nevada desert."

1022 ZULU
33° 20' North, 44° 10' East
Aby Ghurayb Research Institute
Five miles west of Baghdad
Iraq

"Badra," Saeed Hushmand said as he walked into the office, "do you know where Abu Waheed is? I've been looking for him but no one seems to have seen him for several days now."

Badra Hushmand looked at her brother. An attractive woman, she stood out even among women in Iraq by wearing flashy Western-style clothes whenever possible. Her bright exterior lay over an intelligent and Machiavellian mind. She knew her brother was a brilliant scientist, but his knowledge in other areas of life was limited, and that was being kind. Though he was the director of the institute, his preference was to work in the research labs. It was Badra who manipulated the power base for the two.

In the political world of Iraq under Saddam Hussein, power was the means to personal wealth and glory, as well as safety. Ruthlessness with your enemies, both present and future, was the only means to move ahead in the power structure. Ambition was not something Badra Hushmand was short of; neither was the ability to deal with a perceived threat to her or her brother's position.

"He has left the facility, Saeed," Badra said. "He and the weapons technician Jaleel al-Dossadi were sent forward with Colonel Kassar's unit to field the new warhead."

"To field the warhead?" Saeed said. "But there should be no difficulty in using the weapon, as long as the proper transportation and storage procedures are followed."

"And that is why they went along with the weapon," Badra said. "I felt that the best way to ensure that the proper procedures were followed was to send our most senior technicians along with the shipment. You can't trust the military with something that important and technical."

"Colonel Kassar struck me as technically very competent, even for someone in the military," Saeed said. "And I wanted to discuss the bentonite incorporation process with Waheed. It was origi-

nally his suggestion to use that material to eliminate the clumping problem with the anthrax."

"You know that it would have just been a matter of a little more time before you had come up
with the same idea," Badra said. "Waheed was
just a technician, even though a competent one.
He is being put to good use in making sure that
the weapon is correctly handled. And al-Dossadi
is the perfect man to make certain that the fuzing
and other aspects of the warhead operate at maximum efficiency. Now, are you ready for our one-
thirty meeting with Talfaq?"

She wanted to distract her brother from further
thoughts about Waheed for the moment. His being out of the facility meant that only her brother
was there to take the credit for making a func-
tional biological weapon. If he never came back,
they had his processes and laboratory notes—
those would be enough to move her and her
brother's facility into Saddam Hussein's favor.

Saeed and Badra Hushmand might have been in
charge at the Aby Ghurayb facility, but they were
very small and impotent fish compared to Abdul
Talfaq. It was rare for the nephew of Saddam
Hussein to hold a meeting outside of his offices at
the Salman Pak biological warfare facility on the
banks of the Tigris River south of Baghdad. The
fact that he was at the Aby Ghurayb site was
enough to make the Hushmands nervous. The last
thing they wanted to do was be late for a meeting
with him.

The huge soldiers who were standing guard outside the meeting room had completed their own security sweep of the area. Since the door to the room was open, Badra breathed a sigh of relief. Talfaq was obsessed with security, and would never wait in a room with the door open—and the last thing that Badra wanted to do was make someone like Talfaq wait. He was here to meet with the Hushmands to assure himself that there was nothing to stop the immediate use of the biological version of those weapons if Saddam so ordered.

Entering the room under the contemptuous gaze of the four guards, Badra felt something very close to fear, not something she was used to in the offices of her own institute. Talfaq's bodyguards were answerable only to him. There had been more than one rumored meeting where Talfaq had never shown up, and his guards were the only ones to walk away afterward.

Two of the guards stepped into the meeting room a few minutes after Badra and her brother sat down. Their polished AK-47 rifles were held at waist level and they swept the room with the muzzles of their weapons before standing back at attention on either side of the door. Both of the Hushmands came to their feet as the guards entered, and they remained standing as Abdul Talfaq strode into the room a moment later.

Going up to the head of the large meeting table, Talfaq sat and looked at the two scientists. Nervously, the two finally sat and faced Talfaq.

"I am here to take your final assurances to President Hussein that the special weapon will do everything that has been promised to him," Talfaq said. "Out of all of the special programs, yours has been the only one to deliver a fieldable weapon. The number of those weapons is poor compared to the money and resources that this project has absorbed."

"The technical problems of properly weaponizing a biological agent have been solved," Saeed said. "It is only the production facilities that are still limited. The agent is only being made on a laboratory scale at present—it only grows so fast."

"You have had years to grow your diseases," Talfaq said angrily. "There are hundreds of R-400 bombs and dozens of missile warheads loaded with your agents. And now you tell me that only a few are worth the trouble."

"Please," Badra said, "you misunderstand. All of the weapons that have been made for you will work. They are deadly to the extreme. But some of the most technical problems have only been answered by my brother in the last few months. The very best, the most deadly and efficient agent, is the weaponized anthrax that has been loaded into a pair of warheads. And they are capable of devastating a huge area. No time or materials were wasted in creating the other weapons—they have just been improved upon."

"The process to create the free-flowing powdered form of anthrax has only just been perfected," Saeed said. "The agent has to be treated with an anticlumping agent, bentonite, while still in the liquid form. Then it can be dried and milled down to a very fine powder with a particle size of three to five microns."

"That's four times smaller than the finest human hair," Badra said.

"At that size," Saeed said, "the powder acts almost like a liquid. Properly treated with an antistatic and anticlumping agent, it will divide and drift in the air for an extended time."

"Your technical explanations are not what I want right now," Talfaq said. "In simple terms, how large an area can one warhead cover? How many casualties among the enemy forces?"

"At a thousand meters above ground-level burst," Saeed said, "in sixty minutes the warhead would cover an estimated thirty square kilometers. Casualties would depend on population density, but in a built-up area, several hundred thousand at a minimum."

"And those are just the immediate casualties within a twenty-four-hour period," Badra said. "The agent would keep spreading and maintain its virulence. Any breeze or movement would stir it back up. The final casualty count from a single warhead could easily reach a million or more."

"That is a result that would satisfy President Hussein," Talfaq said. "And it is what I planned on when I assigned Colonel Kassar to move the special weapon into the field. He has been given specific orders regarding its security and use. The location of the weapon is one chosen by President Hussein himself. It is a very secure and secret site.

If everything goes the way you say it can, just the threat of such a weapon would keep the coalition forces in Saudi Arabia."

"Serving Iraq is all we could ask for," Badra said as she turned her eyes down.

CHAPTER 8

The hard rubber soles of Dan Able's CT boots crunched as they hit the bone dry desert gravel. His rucksack had already hit the ground behind him, dropping to the end of a lowering line as Able came close to the ground. Without the heavy rucksack attached to the front of his legs, Able could hit the ground with his feet together and conduct a near perfect parachute-landing fall. The PLF had the SEAL rolling into the fall in one long continuous motion, ending up with his legs flipping over, lying on the ground. The exaggerated rolling motion absorbed the impact of landing, distributing the force over the large muscle groups of the body rather than just the legs.

The square canopies of the MT 1XS/SL parachutes the SMD were jumping with had 370 square feet of F-111 nylon fabric, making for a controllable descent. It was easy to land standing up with such a rig, and the SEALs did it often on demonstration and sport jumps. But such a flashy maneuver was not in order when the jump was for real—even in training. It was very easy to hit a rock or unforeseen obstacle and end up with a broken ankle or worse.

Dan Able wasn't a fool. If he was, he certainly wouldn't have been in the SMD or even the Teams. But he didn't particularly like parachuting. He did it because it was part of the job. He was competent, careful, and not flashy. He was also very glad to be back on the ground.

This was the third jump the men had conducted from a B-2 bomber. The first two had been done without their normal load of field equipment and weapons: a simple medium altitude HALO jump, with a freefall from 14,000 feet; then a hop-and-pop HAHO jump where the men opened their parachutes soon after leaving the aircraft.

The jumps had been successful, and a lot of people on the ground were excited about the insertion technique's possibilities. But Dan Able had the same opinion of the drops as most of the rest of his unit. A normal flight in a military transport, even with a jump involved, meant a lot of tedious time. Traveling in the dark confines of a bomb bay, even in the most sophisticated aircraft in the world, was just plain boring.

The most exciting part of the flight was when the bomb-bay doors opened up only ten seconds before the drop was to take place. The SEALs had been told that this was to minimize the radar signature of the B-2 when it effectively had its bottom opened up. Dan thought it was just to scare the hell out of them right before they were dropped.

Even though the SEALs had the final say on the drop by pulling the release handles, the whole operation had a certain dehumanizing feeling about it. Were they really becoming little more than another weapons system? Something to be dropped on the enemy like a radar-guided bomb?

Now that he had to scramble up to dump the air out of his canopy by pulling on the toggle and risers on one side of the rig, Able was too busy to continue his philosophical line of thought. And listening to Ed Lopez curse heavily in English and Spanish also distracted him from heavy thoughts.

Lopez was okay, he had just rolled into a white thornbush during his landing. No matter how hard you worked at it, there always seemed to be some unexpected hazard waiting to bite you on the ass during an operation. Or, in this case, on the thigh, since Lopez had rolled his right leg over onto the short, nasty little bush.

Minor irritations aside, the unit conducted the third jump flawlessly, landing well within the target drop zone. The men carefully gathered up their parachutes, wrapping the suspension lines in a figure-eight skein to keep them from tangling.

Able pulled the rolled-up aviator's flight bag out from where it was secured across his lap, the ends tucked under the front of his leg straps. The big, green cloth bag was opened and placed on the ground, then the parachute harness and pack tray went in. Lopez stepped over and helped Able collect his canopy by holding onto the bridle and pilot chute. Able was then able to pull the holding bag down over the canopy.

Folding the canopy and then the suspension lines into figure-eight rolls, he piled everything into the aviator's bag. Finally, the pilot chute went into the bag on top of the rest of the gear. Snapping the fasteners shut on the kit bag—the zipper was never used, so the teeth wouldn't grab the fabric of the canopy—Able was now free to help his Teammate recover his chute.

A truck and a small blue bus stood close by, with the parachute recovery team from Nellis standing by. All the SEALs had landed in the drop zone less than a hundred meters from the trucks and waiting safety ambulance. Landing close meant they not only had help to properly gather up their parachute rigs, but that they also didn't have to walk far to the trucks, their transport over to Indian Springs, less than ten miles away. There, they were expecting a helicopter ride back to Nellis.

Able thought the unit wasn't all that far from the Indian Springs Air Force Auxiliary Field. He had been concentrating on the jump and guiding in behind Mike Bryant, the lead jumper on the drop, and so hadn't seen the airfield off in the distance. That had been where the SMD conducted their certification op only the year before.

Even though the SEALs had the recovery crew

and vehicles right there on the drop zone, they only went "administrative" long enough to recover the parachutes, oxygen masks, and other jump gear. Such very expensive equipment was not expended without justification, and a training jump was not considered a good enough reason. Even the stripped ACES II seats used on the drops had their own parachutes, so they could be recovered after the drop. The SEALs did not envy the Air Force ground crew who had to chase those seats down and find them on the ground.

The men stopped operating under tactical rules long enough to collect and pack the gear. As soon as the bags of gear were gone, the rucksacks were opened and the field gear went on. Jumpsuits were stripped off and weapons made ready. Dan Able paired up with Ed Lopez and they took their position in the security perimeter around the drop zone.

Able's normal shooting partner, John Sukov, had his HST-4 UHF/SATCOM radio and KY-57 encryption set out and was establishing contact with the air command back at Nellis. Greg Rockham was using his MX-300R UHF radio to call in Shaun Daugherty and second squad. The two squads had dropped as separate sticks from the B-2 as it passed over the drop zone. Second squad had landed close by and could be clearly seen only a short distance away in the crisp desert air. While first squad held their position near the vehicles, Daugherty brought second squad in to meet at the vehicles.

The SEALs in second squad used a simple

bounding overwatch technique to move tactically across the open area of the valley. There was little more than scrub brush and gravel covering what might have been an ancient lake bed. So the SEALs moved quickly and efficiently—one element stopping and dropping prone to cover the advancement of the other element as it rushed forward. In a fast series of giant "steps," both squads of the SMD were quickly consolidated.

Rockham had everyone continue to practice assault movements across the desert as a unit. The men had all stripped off their gray jumpsuits when they had put on their tactical equipment after the landing. The desert air had been cool to begin with after a long, cold night. But the SEALs' movements across the open gravel plain and into the rocks beyond the dry lake bed was heating them up fast. The lake bed was at the bottom of a long slope leading up into the Pintwater Mountain Range of mountains about five miles northwest of the landing zone. The slope was gradual, rising only twenty meters every half mile or so. But even that mild climb was felt by the men under the bright Nevada sun.

"What the hell is going on with Rock?" Kurkowski said during a break. "He has us running all over this range like we're going to get back Kuwait all by ourselves."

"He must have his reasons," Wayne Alexander said from where he squatted down on the ground. "Chief Monday, Ferber, and the XO are all going along with this crap without question. Rock has never been a chickenshit officer before. Make-work just to keep us busy has never been his style. But why we're doing this desert maneuver stuff is beyond me."

"Maybe he just wants us to be ready to go back to Desert Shield," John Grant said quietly.

Learning the reason behind the morning workout would have to wait. Chief Monday had everyone on their feet again and the men went back to work. This time they ran breaking contact drills against an imaginary enemy.

"Peel right!" shouted Rockham as he gave the order to break contact. "Rear security, take us out!"

As the men learned where the enemy was firing from, they moved back away from that point. While the rest of their Teammates peeled away outboard along the sides of the platoon and ran back, the automatic weapons men—Wayne Alexander, John Grant, Dan Able, and Roger Kurkowski—kept up a constant imaginary barrage against the enemy's location. Then one of them would peel back and set up with his weapon to cover the withdrawal of the last man. All these movements were done with great care, so no man crossed the line of fire of a Teammate.

The rear security element for either squad—in this case, Pete Wilkes and Larry Stadt—led the way for the withdrawal. They had been bringing up the rear of their formations only a moment before. Now they were acting as the point men for their respective squads.

The movement was fast and organized, quickly taking the platoon back about 150 meters from the point of contact with the enemy. Once the platoon was withdrawn, a hasty perimeter was set up and a headcount taken. This was very serious training to all of the men, and the grumbling stopped as the work began. No SEAL had ever been left behind, and this kind of practice was one of the reasons for that. Wounded were treated at this point, and the men would redistribute ammunition among themselves as necessary. Then the platoon would reorganize for follow-on contact against the enemy.

"Okay, that sucked," said Chief Monday. "Watch your fields of fire and let's move quickly, gentlemen."

The platoon never liked it when Monday called them "gentlemen." That always meant he was disappointed. When he was gruff but smiling, that showed he was happy with their performance.

"We'll do it again," said Rockham. "This time withdraw as fire teams."

Instead of peeling back as two-man shooting pairs, now half a squad—a fire team of four SEALs—would withdraw at the same time.

The organized withdrawal of the men went on until they were all hot, sweating, and dirty. Flopping down over and over into the gravel and dust of the desert made a man look like a big dirty lump. It was great camouflage, but a miserable way to put it on.

Before the sun went up much higher in the sky, Rockham called an end to the SEALs' tactical maneuverings. By then they had worked their way back to where the transport bus was waiting. The truck with their recovered parachutes was long since gone, and it was a very happy airman driver who welcomed the SEALs onto the bus. Now that their desert exercises were done, the airman could return to a lot more comfortable location back at the base.

The ride to Indian Springs was a bumpy one. The roads that crisscrossed the Nellis range area were restricted to public traffic. The unimproved roads were little more than a set of worn ruts. The improved roads were smoother, but still nothing anyone would want to drive in a family car. It wasn't until the bus had crossed more than five miles of country roads that they reached Highway 95, a four-lane divided road that led them smoothly into Indian Springs.

The hoped-for helicopter was waiting for the SEALs. The Blackhawk rescue bird didn't have seats that were all that comfortable, but the ride was a quick and smooth one. The men all arrived back at Nellis in plenty of time to grab a quick shower and clean up before a meal and a debriefing. Now, Kurkowski and several of the other SEALs were looking forward to a night in Las Vegas. They were going to have a night of it, but not in the gambling capital of the United States.

The hangar building in which the men had conducted all of their ACES II drop training was still available. It was a secure site, and Rockham had already made arrangements to use it to brief his men on their upcoming training op. The fact that they were working so well together again told him once again that giving them some hard training was just what they had needed. Now he would give them a real problem to solve.

When the SEALs gathered back in the training hangar, the equipment they had been using for the last few days was back under the cover of big dropcloths. The line of student desks was still there, along with a pair of portable chalkboards that had been used for explanations and sketches. Now the chalkboards were both covered with a cloth and something new was in the room: a six-by-four-foot table set up next to the desks. The unusually high table looked familiar to several of the SEALs, though it was also covered with a cloth to hide it from sight.

"BOHICA," Sid Mainhart said as the SEALs took their seats.

"BOHICA?" Kurkowski said as he sat next to him. "What the hell does BOHICA mean?"

"Bend over, here it comes again," Ryan Marks said from behind him. "You've really got to start getting with the program Kurkowski or the language will leave you behind."

Before Kurkowski could come up with a decent return, Chief Monday glowered over at the men. Kurkowski wisely shut up. As they were sitting down, Greg Rockham went up to one of the chalkboards. He turned and faced his men, who were now watching him.

"Most of you," Rockham said, "realize that eventually we're going to be going back to the Persian Gulf. Iraq has not cleared out of Kuwait and it doesn't look like they're going to any time soon. President Bush has upped the stakes and given Saddam a deadline to get out of Kuwait. That deadline is later this month. When that date passes, things are going to change. The gloves will be coming off and Kuwait will be liberated. Today, tomorrow, next week, or next month, you can be sure that we're going to spend our time in the sandbox.

"The last time we were in the Gulf, we spent a lot of time sitting on our hands. That was particularly hard because we had just come off a hot operation. You may not know all the details yet, but even though we didn't find a weapon of mass destruction on that ship off the Sudan coast, we did bring back some very valuable intelligence.

"We know for certain that Saddam Hussein has modified his Scud missiles for longer range and to carry a modified warhead. This isn't any kind of educated guess. We saw the weapons, touched them, measured and took pictures of them. Then we blew them to hell.

"The longer range of the new Scud is a problem for the politicians and the war planners. The modified warhead falls straight into our laps. Saddam didn't make those missiles just to ship them out of the country. And he sure as hell didn't modify them just for the fun of it.

"Finding those warheads, whatever they may be, is a top target for the intelligence assets of the United States and the coalition forces. When they find those warheads, we will be ready to go in and take them out. We aren't going to just be sitting around waiting for the word to come down to us. We sat and waited in Saudi, and that's all we did. Now we're back here, and I mean to see that we will be prepared for action at a moment's notice. In the meantime, we will have some real good training here to make us ready to go out on a hot op.

"While we sat and waited over there, I watched a great team of men, my team, start to come apart and argue among itself for lack of anything better to do. Well, that isn't going to happen again. We have something better to do, and here it is."

Rockham tossed the cover back on one of the chalkboards while Daugherty did the same on the other. The men had responded to their commanding officer's words. They knew they had let the boredom and disappointment of not having anything active to do over in Saudi get the better of them. They were professionals and knew how to act like them. And what they saw on the boards was a professional problem, one they knew exactly how to solve.

The chalkboard on the left that Daugherty had uncovered had a number of photographs taped up on it. The largest pictures were blowups of aerial photos of an airfield that looked like it had seen much better days. There were aircraft parked on the runways, but something looked very odd about a number of them.

The chalkboard on the right, where Rockham was standing, had a number of large maps on it. He picked up a pointer from the chalk tray and pointed to a gray marking on the map. The elongated marking had a long narrow middle section with a much larger northern end. The marking was so big that it extended through two maps that had been taped together.

"This prime piece of real estate," Rockham said as he pointed to the upper map, "is Dog Bone Lake. And it's about as dry as an old bone as well. You may recognize that it's not a long way from where we did our practice jump this morning. There was a reason for that."

"And now the movie," Kurkowski said quietly.

Ignoring Kurkowski's comment, Rockham went on with the briefing.

"In the middle of the upper section of Dog Bone Lake is an enemy airfield. This field has been used as a target in the past by the planes stationed here at Nellis. Right now, it's going to be our target."

Turning to the other chalkboard, Rockham pointed to a large photo showing a complex series of runways. They were shaped roughly like a long letter H with the ends squared off and closed. There were a number of dots along a short extension angling off from the western end of the upper runway.

"This entire area has been declared cleared by Explosive Ordnance Disposal," Rockham said. "It has been used by a number of different special operations units for training. The layout is a duplication of that known to be used by the Iraqi Air Force. For the most part, the aircraft on the runway and the parking apron are stripped-down hulls of foreign aircraft, or obsolete U.S. planes. On this runway is parked a MiG 15SB fighter-bomber."

Moving his pointer to the other photograph, an

enlargement of the parking apron, Rockham pointed to a single plane among a group of four.

"Reliable intelligence reports say that MiG has been converted to a drone that can be flown by radio control. We aren't particularly interested in a giant radio-controlled airplane. Our specific target is what's mounted underneath the wings of that aircraft. On the hard points of both wings are spray tanks modified to carry chemical or biological agents.

"Our mission is to infiltrate the airfield and confirm the target. We will examine the spray tanks and the aircraft. Once we have all the technical information in hand, we will destroy the spray tanks and the aircraft with explosives.

"We will infiltrate by a night HAHO drop from the B-2 bomber. Once consolidated on the ground, we will reconnoiter the airfield and locate the target. Extraction will be by helicopter after destruction of the target is confirmed.

"This is a live-fire exercise. We will be carrying a full combat load of small-arms ammunition for our M4s. There won't be any live aggressor forces in the target area, but I can't rule out there being pop-up targets in the vicinity of the airfield.

"Live fire. That means everyone has to do their job exactly to the numbers. There won't be any room for mistakes—just like in the real world. Are there any questions?"

CHAPTER 9
★ ★ ★ ★

After Rockham's introduction to their mission, he went into a full briefing on the operation. No detail was left out as the information was given to the men of the SMD: where their insertion and extraction points were, where they would rendezvous if anyone became separated from the unit as the operation went down, radio frequencies, call signs, the simulated enemy forces in the area—even details about who would carry what gear, ammunition, and supplies.

The thick covered object with legs turned out to be a sand table with a model of the airfield objective built up on it. The three-dimensional model allowed the SEALs gathered around it to more closely examine the area they would be operating in. Where the men would go, who would do what, and what the lines of fire would be could be seen with the figures and models on the sand table.

This might have been a training operation, but it had to be treated like a real-world op. This was especially true because the men would be carrying live ammunition. The SEALs always trained as they would fight, and they fought as they trained. It was the only way they knew to get the job done right.

Training could be dangerous at any time. It was even more so when the bullets were real. An accidental discharge of a weapon could cost a Teammate his life. It had happened before in training, and every SEAL knew it could happen again. That's why practicing and rehearsing an op was always so important.

So after the men completed their briefing, received the full warning order on the op, and had time to ask questions and give their feedback to the plan, they practiced. The platoon, squads, fire teams, and sometimes just shooter pairs, moved across the fields behind their hangar. In spite of not having weapons with them, each man acted as if his Teammate's life was in his hands. Later, in the field, when they were carrying loaded weapons, each man's life would be in the rest of his unit's hands. So it was with deadly seriousness that the rehearsal went forward.

During the planning and rehearsal stages of an operation, SEAL officers listened to the input of their men—at least the good ones did. Rockham was a very good officer and leader. He knew that the men he led each had a lifetime's worth of experience and knowledge they brought to the unit. And he was not above listening to their advice and suggestions. The final decision was always in his lap—he was the unit's commanding officer, after all. But he trusted and respected his men, and they knew it.

After the rehearsals, equipment was examined and checked. Weapons were given a close going over. It was now time for John Sukov and Henry Lutz, the two EOD-trained members of the SMD, to prepare their explosive charges.

The exact details of the target that would have to be destroyed were unknown. But as experienced demolition men, both Sukov and Lutz knew what they could probably expect to find. This was the target interdiction part of the planning process. The photographs they had of the target told them the approximate size and shape of the aircraft. And the experience of the two men, and particularly their training for the Special Materials Detachment, gave them a good idea what to expect such aircraft to carry.

Sketches of the targets, layouts of explosive lines, and the location and size of charges were all prepared. For this kind of operation, speed was more important than the economy of explosives. The Teams had a habit of overloading a target— that helped guarantee its destruction. But explosives, detonating cord, and firing systems weighed something, and it all had to be hand-carried to the target. Everything they needed to use had to drop from the aircraft with them. So excess materials were held to a minimum.

Gear was packed, the men ate, and more discussions were held. As they could, the men grabbed a few hours of sleep. That was something they could all thank Basic Underwater Demolition/SEAL training for—the ability to sleep when the opportunity presented itself. They could go literally for days without sleep, and still work efficiently. BUD/S, and especially the grueling test of Hell Week, had proved that. And it also taught them to sleep when they could—you didn't know when the next chance was.

Finally, it was time to gather their gear and board the aircraft. In this case it was a lot more like loading a weapon aboard the B-2. Kurkowski still thought the huge, dull black, whale-with-wings stealth bomber looked like the Batplane, and none of his Teammates could argue against that impression.

The flight in the belly of the B-2 was long and boring. There was little enough to normally do on an insertion flight. In the bomb bays of the big aircraft there was even less entertainment than normal.

The ACES II seats were reasonably comfortable, even with the heavy load of gear each SEAL carried. At least the hardware the automatic weapons men and grenadiers were carrying were M4 carbines instead of M60E3 light machine guns or M203 grenade launchers. Both of those weapons were heavy; or at least the M60E3s were heavy.

The M203 40-millimeter grenade launchers only added about three pounds to the five and a half pound weight of the M4. But each round of 40mm ammunition weighed half a pound by itself. And a normal load of grenades could easily be thirty-six rounds or more.

So the men would be running light with weapons, and fairly lightly with ammunition. Instead of a normal dozen or so thirty-round magazines, each SEAL was carrying seven magazines, each loaded with twenty-eight rounds of ammunition for their M4s.

Even though Rockham had ordered a light load of weapons and ammo, he made up for it with a heavy load of supplies, especially water. Each man had six one-quart canteens packed in his rucksack. Some of the men liked the two-quart bladder canteens and carried one or two of them along with the normal one-quart belt canteens. But everyone had a gallon and a half of water with him. It looked like Rockham was expecting the men to be in the desert well into the daylight before they were extracted.

The squads were broken up between the two bomb bays of the B-2. The Special Forces instructors and Chief Master Sergeant Fitzhugh learned that dropping half a squad simultaneously from either side of the aircraft made for a cleaner, faster exit. There was no reason for the SEALs to argue about the procedure, and that's what they had practiced during their earlier drops.

The odd number of men in the SMD squads meant splitting a squad between the bomb bays—

one bay held a row of five jumpers, and the other held four. During the drops, the procedure went smoothly, and it was how the present night drop would be conducted.

A night drop was normally an exciting thing, and this one wasn't any different for the jumpers as they sat in their modified ejection seats. But if the actual drop would be exciting, the ride to the drop zone was anything but. The roar of the 19,000-pound-thrust General Electric F118-GE-100 turbofan engines—two of the four engines were outboard of each bomb bay—was muted by the body of the B-2 and by the headsets the SEALs wore inside their helmets.

For this high altitude drop, the SEALs wore stripped-down and recycled HGU-55 fighter pilot helmets, which connected up well with the communications system inside the B-2. They weren't as comfortable as the custom-fitted versions worn by active fighter pilots, but weren't as bad as heavy-duty drop helmets. The new MBU-5/P oxygen masks had built-in microphones. They didn't get much use, however, since few of the men had anything to say.

There was the occasional exchange of information between the SEAL jumpmaster, Chief Monday, and the two-man aircrew of the B-2. But that was about all the men had to listen to during the long wait leading up to the drop. It surprised no one when Kurkowski made a comment about the situation prior to their being loaded into the bomb bays.

"More than a billion dollars of taxpayers' money

spent to develop and build this thing," he said. "You would have thought they could spend a couple of bucks for an in-flight movie. I'm going to write my congressman about this."

"You can write?" Ryan Marks had said.

The SEALs all had a last laugh before each man clumsily clambered up a short ladder and into his ACES II seat. There were a number of Air Force ordnance men to help the SEALs into the seats and then secure them into place. The young men had said little as they connected the buckles and pulled the straps tight. They may have been thinking that the SEALs were crazy to do such a thing as being dropped like a bomb from a plane. Or they may have thought idle chitchat was not something you wanted to make with men as heavily armed as the SEALs were. Either way, the loading went quietly and efficiently.

Now, the only thing the SEALs could do was look around the dimly lit bomb bays. That activity had lost its novelty sometime during their second practice drop. The amber light preserved the SEALs' night vision—not that there was much to see.

The curved top of the bomb bays were crossed with spars that were attached to the nearly inch-thick carbon fiber composite outer skin of the B-2. Cables and conduits lined the walls of the compartment and also ran along the inside of the spars. Junction boxes, connecting rods, pipes, and tubing, some with obscure undecipherable labels on them, added to the technological maze inside the bay.

It was weird to some of the SEALs not to be

able to move around while coming up for a drop. This was more like waiting for an exotic amusement park ride to start up. The yellow flashing light of the twenty minute warning had been on for what seemed an excessively long time. It took a second look to make sure the light had stopped flashing when it stayed on to indicate that there was ten minutes to the drop.

Normally, a ten minute warning meant nothing more active than each man running an oxygen check on his breathing system. Chief Monday wanted to be sure that everyone was ready, and he knew his men well. He couldn't walk up and down the line of jumpers for this drop. But he did have an effective intercom system available to him.

"Ten minute warning," his voice blared out from the headsets. Most of the men jumped at the sudden noise. "Oxygen check. First squad, count off."

"One, okay," Rockham said.

"Two, okay."

"Three, okay."

"Four, okay."

"Five, okay."

"Six, okay."

There was a long pause after Pete Wilkes had called out his number.

"Seven?" Chief Monday said. "Seven? . . . Alexander!" the chief bellowed, "wake the fuck up and count off!"

"Seven," came a sheepish voice a moment later. "Seven, uh, okay."

The count continued to nine without another

major pause. Chief Monday called out to second squad to do the same thing, and by then all of those SEALs were wide-awake and alert. Chuckling was heard over the intercom, but it didn't sound like any of the SEALs—they were used to Alexander sleeping anywhere. Instead it sounded like the aircrew of the B-2 listening in on the intercom. They may have been just as bored as the SEALs.

There was an oxygen console as part of the AARL drop modifications. It replaced the Model 2900 system that the SEALs had always used before on high altitude drops. The hand of the freefall instructors was visible in the design of the modifications, since it used a lot of older components. The familiar blinking "eye" of the A14 regulator told each SEAL that his oxygen was flowing properly. Now, as the time for the actual drop approached, things started to get more exciting.

The red flashing light indicated the six minute warning. Another oxygen check was made as the SEALs counted off. The red light stopped flashing and stayed on at the two minute warning. Then the blue light came on and each SEAL activated his bailout bottle of oxygen.

As he felt the surge of oxygen from the steel bottles on his rig, Mike Bryant disconnected his hose from the A14 manifold. The drop was only seconds away, and as his heart started racing he wondered if the rest of his Teammates felt the same way. They sat in the row in front of him. As the lead jumper for his squad, he would be the first one dropped from the plane. His position was at the rear so he couldn't collide with another jumper.

The roar of the engines sounded out, echoing in the compartment as the bomb bay doors opened. Below his feet there was nothing more than 26,000 feet of air. Bryant grinned widely beneath his oxygen mask. He suddenly had an urge to scream a "Yee-haw!" cowboy yell as his seat dropped—like the Slim Pickens character in the movie *Dr. Strangelove* when he fell from a bomb bay riding a nuclear weapon to the end of the world.

Kurkowski might have appreciated the gag, but Bryant was pretty sure Chief Monday wouldn't have. Then there was no more time for thought, only actions. The green light came on and Bryant pulled up on the yellow and black release handles. The ACES II seat dropped away from the B-2 and Bryant was alone in the sky.

Immediately letting go of the handles, Bryant put his arms up against the rush of the wind. There was a small set of perforated wind deflector panels that extended down into the slipstream from the front of the bomb bays when the doors were opened. The panels helped improve the airflow around the open bay compartment and made the release of weapons—or in this case, the drop of the SEALs—much smoother.

Only a few seconds from release, Bryant felt the securing straps release as his seat's drogue chute pulled it from him. He was now falling free in the sky, moving in a perfect modified frog position with his arms out in front of him, his legs bent at the knees, and his back arched. Stable in the air, Bryant pulled his chute release.

There was a flutter and snap as the canopy opened over his head. Looking up, Bryant couldn't see the canopy clearly except where it blotted out the stars. But it felt open and smooth. Pulling on the toggles, he turned into the wind on the first leg of the zigzag course of their long drop. That was the last thing that went completely right for Bryant during the drop.

Within a few moments of his canopy opening, Bryant began to feel light-headed and a little dizzy. He had undergone enough high-altitude and closed-circuit diving training to immediately recognize the first symptoms of hypoxia. Something was wrong with his oxygen system. He wasn't getting the oxygen his brain needed to stay alert, or even conscious.

Each of the SEALs had their MX-300R radios hooked in to their headsets and oxygen mask microphones. The radios were for emergency use, and this qualified as one. Mike Bryant was in trouble and he had to let his Teammates know it.

"Bravo leader, Bravo leader," Bryant said after keying his radio mike. "I am going to sleep. Repeat, I am going to sleep."

Rockham responded to hearing his call sign over the radio. But there was nothing he or any of the SEALs could do to help their Teammate. Bryant was on his own until they reached the ground. The only thing that could be done was for the stick to track on him, following Bryant's chute until he was on the ground.

"Roger that," Rockham said. "We'll see you on the ground."

Bryant knew he had less than half a minute to react to his situation before he went under. Pulling down on his steering toggles, he set his canopy to half-brakes. This slowed his forward movement to around ten miles an hour and decreased his rate of descent. Crossing his arms, he locked his hands underneath his armpits. As the night suddenly got darker, Bryant passed out from lack of oxygen.

Winds blew across the flight path of the SEALs as they tracked their unconscious Teammate. The flashing SDU-5/E strobe lights that each man had strapped to his helmet gave a guide for the rest of the SEALs in the stick to follow. Red caps over the lens of the strobe lights dimmed the bright flashes. The lights couldn't be seen from the ground except through night vision devices—such as those carried by the ambulance and parachute recovery crews at the targeted drop zone.

The crews heard the emergency call over the radio and looked into the sky to try and follow the SEALs' parachutes to the ground. The crosswinds caused Bryant's canopy to slip across the sky. He was at the mercy of the winds, but his Teammates stayed with him all the way.

The plan was for the SEALs to travel about ten miles across the ground before touching down. Second squad had dropped when the B-2 crossed back over its flight path. The two wedges of parachutists were to have flown in to the drop zone, turning into the wind on either side of the designated zone and touching down within a hundred

meters of each other. Now, with Bryant uncon-
sciously sailing across the sky, it didn't look like
first squad was going to set down anywhere near
the planned drop zone. Unable to help the situation, which they heard clearly over their radios,
second squad continued on the originally planned
flight path.

CHAPTER 10

★ ★ ★ ★

1012 ZULU
36° 48' North, 115° 28' West
Three Lakes Valley
Nellis Air Force Range
Nevada

As Bryant's parachute canopy carried him across the desert sky, he gradually drew closer to the ground and the denser air below 10,000 feet. When he was only about a thousand feet above the ground his eyes fluttered and then sprang open. The young SEAL didn't know where he was for a moment. Then he saw the ground coming up below him.

"I'm up," Bryant said into his microphone.

"Turn into the wind," Rockham said into his own radio. "Track to your left."

The ground was coming up fast, but Bryant felt suddenly energized, despite the situation. He knew that was a by-product of the hypoxia. Had he been above 28,000 feet when his oxygen cut out, the chances were he would have fried some brain cells for lack of oxygen before reaching the ground. Right now, however, he felt fine as he dropped his rucksack on its lowering line. Then he lined up his chute into the wind before pulling his toggles all the way down for a flare.

In spite of feeling up, Bryant wasn't going to be stupid about his condition. The ground was an unknown factor, so he went into a classic PLF as his boots hit the gravel. The rest of the stick hit the ground within fifty meters of him.

Once on the ground, as soon as he had collapsed his chute and shed his jump rig, Jack Tinsley, first squad's corpsman, ran to where Bryant had landed. The SEAL was easy to spot, even in the darkness, from the crowd gathering around him. Greg Rockham was Mike Bryant's shooting partner as well as his commanding officer. Rockham had been first at the downed man's side, almost running as he dumped his canopy.

After Bryant landed and collapsed his parachute canopy, a wave of dizziness swept over him when he straightened up to a standing position. As he was trying to shed his harness, the young SEAL was overcome with dizziness and fell flat on his back.

As Rockham pulled away Bryant's harness and gear, Tinsley knelt down to check on his Teammate. The entire unit was now on the ground with their parachutes and harnesses off and secured. They would be "going administrative" until the chutes were picked up. In spite of not being on a combat footing, the men quickly set up a security perimeter around the landing zone.

The SEALs weren't in as bad shape as they could have been. In spite of having to follow Bryant during the jump, they were only about six miles from their planned drop zone. Bryant regaining consciousness and being able to steer his rig had landed the stick on the very southern end of Dog Bone Lake.

The operation could go ahead without much trouble—if Mike Bryant was okay. Rockham didn't want to call for emergency extraction or a medevac if he didn't have to. The SMD was still a new unit, not even a full year old yet, and any inability to complete even a training operation would look bad for them. But if his lead corpsman said that his man was in trouble, Rockham would shut everything down in an instant and do whatever was necessary to get his man to proper treatment.

The lack of oxygen that had caused Bryant to pass out on the jump could be a simple thing to recover from. Just coming down to the lower altitude had been enough to bring Bryant around. But the situation could be life threatening, depending on how long the brain had been starved of oxygen. The possibility of brain damage was a real concern.

Several of Bryant's Teammates gathered around to lend any assistance that they could. Mike Ferber was kneeling at Bryant's right side as Tinsley began examining the downed SEAL. Wayne

Alexander had come up behind Ferber and was looking on with concern. And the short SEAL had reason to show concern.

In spite of being conscious, Bryant looked to be in less than great shape in the subdued red beams of several flashlights held by his Teammates. As he reached across and turned the SEAL's face toward him, Tinsley placed the fingers of his left hand underneath the corner of Bryant's jaw. The corpsman felt a strong and regular pulse, one that was running a little fast.

Pulling a penlight from his pocket, Tinsley shielded much of the beam with his hand as he shined the light into Bryant's eyes—first one and then the other. In the dark, desert night, even the dim light was blinding to Bryant, who groaned. The prostrate SEAL cursed and turned his head, raising one hand as a shield to the light.

The pupillary response looked good to Tinsley, but it was how Bryant thought that was of real concern now. Did the man know where he was and who was around him?

"Do you know who that is?" Tinsley asked Bryant as he pointed to Ferber.

Bryant didn't see Ferber at first. He saw Alexander standing behind the corpsman and holding a red-lensed flashlight. And the flattened SEAL was starting to get upset at all the attention as he recovered from what could have been described as a fainting spell.

"Yeah," Bryant answered, "an asshole with a flashlight."

That was not the answer Tinsley was expecting. As Ferber turned his head to look at who was standing behind him, Tinsley also looked up at Alexander.

"Hey," Alexander said defensively, "the man's delirious, that's all."

Looking back at Bryant, Tinsley asked, "Do you know who I am?"

"Yeah," Bryant said. "You're an even bigger asshole if you shine that light in my eyes again. I'm fine. I was just dizzy for a moment, that's all. Now can I get up?"

Tinsley turned to Rockham, who was standing behind Bryant's head. "He's fine," he said. "He should be able to continue with the mission without any trouble."

"You're damned right I can continue with the mission," Bryant said. "No way am I going back with the chutes."

"We'll medevac your ass out of here if Tinsley says so," Rockham said sharply. "Now gather up your gear and take it easy for the time being."

While Rockham was talking, Tinsley reached into one of the pockets on his aid kit and pulled out a packet of pills. Holding them out to Bryant, he said, "Here, take these with a good swallow of water."

"What the hell are they for?" Bryant said as he took the packet.

"They're Motrin for your headache," Tinsley said.

"What headache?" Bryant said as he started to

get up. Halfway to the sitting position, he groaned and grabbed at his head. Rockham had quickly stepped in and supported his shooting partner as he tried to get up.

"That headache," Tinsley said.

"Okay, okay," Bryant said, "I'll take the pills. Do I have to call you in the morning?"

"I don't make house calls," Tinsley said with a chuckle.

By then the ambulance and ground crew had arrived. Tinsley was able to tell the Air Force doctor that Bryant was okay and didn't seem to have any aftereffects from his hypoxia. But the medical officer wanted to check the man out for himself.

Finally, when the necessary checks had been made, the officer declared Bryant fit to continue with the operation. That was a relief to both the SEAL and his Teammates. With the chutes collected and packed away, first squad broke open their rucksacks and put on their field gear. It was time to continue with the operation, and they were already well behind schedule.

Pete Wilkes was going to take point for the squad while Bryant brought up the rear security position. They had a bunch of miles to cross and not a lot of time to do it. Prior planning had accounted for some slack in the schedule, in case one of the squads landed off-target. But almost six miles was going to be a good trot for the SEALs to reach the rendezvous point with their Teammates. If they didn't get there, second squad would fall back on the alternate plan and carry forward the operation without them.

The Motrin was taking care of Mike Bryant's headache, but it wasn't doing anything for the mild nausea he felt as the squad moved across the dry lake bed. Now he just had to gut it out along with his Teammates. They were a long way from the initial rally point, where they were going to meet up with second squad. To meet the planned schedule for the operation, they had to make all possible speed while maintaining a tactical formation.

The ground surface was a rough sand mixed with gravel and larger rocks. The scattered scrub brush tended to be dry, thorny, and brittle— which was how several of the SEALs felt during their forced march.

Rockham had planned to take his men out for a run, but he hadn't meant it literally. The squad was moving forward across the desert at a brisk pace. They took their cue from Bryant, since he could be expected to be their slowest member. Bryant had set out walking at about an eleven minute mile and just kept going.

This was what they trained so hard for, why the Teams stressed physical fitness above all. It didn't matter how well trained you were or what kind of high-tech gear or weapons you had with you if you couldn't get it or yourself to the target. Being able to run fast and for long distances wasn't enough. It didn't matter how fast you were if you couldn't carry the necessary amount of equipment.

Wayne Alexander was the master of the weighted run. During their training, the unit sometimes went out for a two or four mile run wearing rucksacks with about forty pounds of sandbags in them. Alexander couldn't come in first on the speed runs, but he could hump a ruck forever. Now, as the fireplug of a man just kept going, he was proving this once again.

The cold night air of the Nevada desert in January was a blessing. The SEALs had left their jumpsuits back with their rigs, to be returned to the air base rather than buried in the desert, as they would have been on a hot operation. Now, with their gear bouncing against their bodies, the men of first squad were plenty warm as they ran.

The stars and a sliver of moon shone down on the line of men crossing the desert. It was a dry lake bed they ran on, but they left moist spots behind them as the sweat ran off their bodies. Now, Rockham's insistence on six canteens per man was making a lot of sense. Water was swallowed in volume as the men hydrated themselves during very short breaks where they just walked. Then they resumed running.

The pace was not particularly fast. They knew it wouldn't do any good to get to the rally point only to be too exhausted to move to the objective. So instead the thud of the men's boots on the desert floor was constant and unwavering.

Finally, the location of the rally point was ahead. But no one could be seen from the other squad. Checking his map, Rockham was certain they were at the right coordinates. They had arrived later than he'd wanted, he reasoned, and the second squad might have already moved out to the operational rally point. There, the assault against the airfield would start.

Over the sound of the men's breathing, a voice called out.

"Five," it said.

"Four," Rockham answered back.

From a depression nearby, ponchos and ground sheets lifted up from where the men of second squad lay hidden beneath them. It had been Shaun Daugherty who called out the challenge. Rockham had answered with the password—a number that when added to the challenge made the number nine.

"Sorry we're running a bit late," Rockham said with a grin to his second in command.

"We know," Daugherty said. "The pilot told us there was a problem with your jump over the intercom. He had been monitoring your radio frequency and heard Bryant say what was going on. How is he anyway?"

"He's fine," Rockham said. "Could use a little more time on runs is all."

"Well," Daugherty said, "we figured you might be a little behind schedule, so we decided to wait for you."

With the two squads back together, the men prepared to move out to the operational rally point. From that position, overlooking the target area, they would launch the actual infiltration of the airfield and approach their target. At the ORP, they would take a longer break and rest a moment before pushing ahead with the op.

They were still within their time window, past the optimum time to launch but not so late that the sun would come up while they were on the airfield. Once at the objective, they would have to move quickly, but they had intended to do this from the beginning.

The airfield complex was a large area. The main runway, running east to west, was over half a mile long. The secondary runway, which ran up to the northeast, was almost half a mile long. There were over a dozen target planes scattered about the facility. Their specific objective, the MiG fighter-bomber, sat parked on the parking apron of the shorter runway.

Even though the SEALs knew there wasn't anyone in the target area, especially not during a live-fire exercise, all the men moved carefully and with focused determination. This was their kind of op, a quiet infiltration and target interdiction. They had been told there could be sensors planted throughout the area. They hadn't been told what kind of sensors—noise, heat, movement, or vibration—only that they could activate pop-up targets that they would then have to engage.

The two squads moved across the airfield using the traveling overwatch technique. They knew there was a possibility of contact with an enemy, in the form of the pop-up targets, but they still had to advance fairly quickly to help give them time on the target in case the unexpected happened. You were never sure of what the unexpected could be, but a good leader always planned for something to show up.

While second squad dropped back, first squad went ahead on point. Second squad was still moving forward, but trailed first squad by about fifty

meters. In this position, they could support the
lead squad with their firepower. Both squads kept
moving ahead to approach the final objective
quickly, crossing the airfield in a staggered file.
The men were spaced a few paces to each side of
one another, walking with their weapons at the
ready and facing outward from the line of march.
It was a flexible formation that could quickly
move into a wedge V or other shape to react to a
situation.

As they approached the target objective, the
SEALs slowed and moved even more carefully. If
there were sensors about, this was where they had
the greatest chance of running into them. Signals
were given by hand and arm movements only, no
talking, a mode of operation that had earned the
SEALs a fearsome reputation. They could move
silently and efficiently over long distances—com-
municating with each other without ever speaking
a word. And they could lash out with a thunder-
storm of firepower in instant reaction to a threat.

Mike Bryant had recovered from his hypoxia
symptoms before the SEALs came to the airfield.
For the final approach he switched places with
Pete Wilkes, and was now on point for the first
squad. This was where Bryant felt most at home,
and most alive. He moved ahead of his Teammates, determining the actual line of march for
the unit and trying to detect trouble well before it
might become a problem.

Within a hundred meters of the apron, where
the objective lay in plain sight, Bryant dropped to
one knee and raised his clenched fist in the air.

Everyone in the patrol stopped, dropped to one knee, and passed the signal down the line.

In the desert starlight and remaining moonlight, Rockham could see his point man kneeling and looking back at him. Bryant first pointed to his eyes to indicate that he saw something. Then he held a hand over his face to show that he had seen the enemy. Finally, he held out a cupped hand with his fingers open and facing down, the signal for a man-made structure. In this case, he had seen the target and identified it.

Rockham returned Bryant's signals and watched them get passed up the line so every man knew what was going on. Turning to face the second squad, he passed the same signals along and got his response passed back from them. Now he had a new message for second squad, holding up his hand and swinging it in a circular movement over his head. It called on all SEALs to rally up, that the second squad should close with the first.

The message was returned, and second squad moved in. Rockham held the edge of his hand to his face, telling Daugherty to set security with his men. Instead of pointing as he normally would to indicate where the second squad was to set their security, Rockham held out both his arms, curving them forward.

Understanding the message, Daugherty signaled his squad to split into two elements, move out, and encircle the front of the target area for security. While first squad was examining the target and setting the demolition charges, second squad would have spread out in a semicircle with the target at the center, their weapons pointed out and away from their Teammates.

With second squad maintaining security, first squad moved up near the apron, where three aircraft sat. Wings were laid out on the ground and not attached to the fuselage, which puzzled the SEALs. But then sitting back from the other aircraft, they saw their target—the MiG 15.

The open-scoop funnel nose and swept-back wings of the MiG 15 matched the pictures the SEALs had studied. The short little jet looked a lot like the North American F-86 Sabre jet of the same era. But the F-86 had its horizontal stabilizers attached to the body of the aircraft. The MiG 15 had its horizontal tail parts mounted high up on the vertical fin, just as the aircraft in front of them had. The Iraqi Air Force markings on the tail of the MiG were a nice touch.

The other aspect of the MiG of particular importance to the SEALs were the two bomblike devices hanging underneath the wings of the stubby jet. The devices were considered ordnance for the purposes of the present mission and would be treated as if they were live bombs. Painted black and with sharp pointed noses, they were secured to the wings, hanging on the same hard points any other aircraft weapon would use.

The SEALs saw all this at a distance. Now they had to approach the target to continue the mission. While the second fire team set up to cover their approach, Rockham and Bryant moved toward the target. Half of the second fire team faced the target, while the other SEALs faced outward, covering their area of approach. Now the first fire team could move in and complete the mission while completely encircled by their Teammates. At no time during the maneuvering and communications had anyone spoken. And more important, at no time had a single SEAL moved into another Teammate's line of fire. They could unleash an unbelievable firestorm of destruction in an instant.

Because of that destructive power literally at their fingertips, and the dangers of their everyday operations, safety took on the weight of a religion in the Teams. And the men of the SMD were the equivalent of high priests in the Church of Heavenly Safety. If a man accidentally swept a Teammate with the muzzle of his weapon, the infraction could get him tossed out of the unit, if not out of the Teams entirely, and sent back to the Fleet Navy.

CHAPTER 11

★ ★ ★ ★

1203 ZULU
Grid Coordinate PA396848
Dog Bone Airfield
Nellis Air Force Range
Nevada

With security set around the target, it was time for the demolition team to get to work. The operation had been relatively successful so far, and Rockham intended to keep it that way. He had already built a surprise into the mission for the rest of the men, and didn't particularly want any surprises pulled on him.

Dan Able and John Sukov came up to examine the MiG and the ordnance hanging under its wings. While Able took off his rucksack and started pulling packages out of it, Sukov went over the MiG, examining it for booby traps and any other visible threats.

The weapons beneath the wings looked like five-foot-long, eight-inch-thick bombs. There was an odd scooplike opening under the nose of both devices, and the four-bladed finned tail had an open hole in its center. The bomblike weapons hung from quick-release shackles, with a fairly complex set of cables running from them up into sockets in the wings. Rockham knew that what Sukov was looking at was a jury-rigged simulation for his mission, but the ordnance people had done a very good job of it. They looked real, and could be something his people might have to face in the future. But that was a worry for another time

At the objective, Rockham and Bryant also had their own specific parts of the mission to carry out. Information had to be collected on the weapons, the aircraft carrying them, and the airfield that was being used to launch them. Once analyzed and collated, this field information would become hard intelligence for possible future operations.

Unwrapping a package of photographic equipment he had in his rucksack, Rockham prepared to take pictures of the MiG, overall shots as well as close-ups. The dark night meant he had to use long exposures, and he had a light, collapsible tripod and shutter cable to help him make clear photos.

In case the photographs didn't come out, Mike Bryant was making quick sketches of the MiG and its ordnance loads. He paid close attention to the markings on the bomb—three green rings near the nose—and the cabling that connected them to the aircraft. While they worked, neither Bryant nor Rockham touched any part of the aircraft, or crowded Sukov. Until Sukov declared the MiG safe from booby traps, the rest of the SEALs would keep their distance.

With his packages laid out, Dan Able ran detonating cord trunk lines along the ground. The lines would be used to initiate all the explosive charges at once, so Able ran them the length of the aircraft—from nose to tail, underneath the body of the plane. Since he was carrying lightweight detonating cord, he doubled the lines he laid out.

Even though the cord had a breaking strength of 170 pounds, Able handled it with care. The cord would detonate at a rate of 21,000 to 23,000 feet per second—a four-mile length of detonating cord would all go up in a single second. It was safe to handle, but if he didn't treat it with respect, it could blow his hands off before he ever knew it.

Respect was also foremost in John Sukov's mind as he examined the MiG. Once he was done looking for the obvious—and sometimes subtle—signs of any booby traps, he concentrated on the weapons hanging underneath the wings. These were aerosol spray tanks that could spread a wide variety of liquid agents. Specifically, they were stripped-out Aero 14B GB or VX gas spray tanks that had been in the active U.S. inventory in the 1960s.

The opening under the nose of the weapons were air scoops that powered a turbine inside the nose of the tank. The pilot of the aircraft could turn the tanks on and off at will, the system being entirely self-contained. Not only could nerve gas be sprayed from such a tank, but the tank could also handle liquid biological agents.

At first Sukov tapped the bodies of the spray tanks. When he heard a hollow sound, he tried raising them a little against the bomb shackles to determine the weight of the device. The light weight, together with the hollow sound, told him the tanks were empty. It would be safe to blow them in place.

Ducking down under the wing, Rockham took his close-ups of the spray tanks. He was bracketing his exposures to ensure that the pictures would show good details. It was just exposing film, and Rockham had brought half a dozen rolls of it. When he stopped taking pictures, Sukov leaned close and whispered into his ear.

"These are what we came for. They're both empty, and there's no sign of any simulated agent around. I think they're safe to blow."

Trusting the opinion and knowledge of his men, Rockham gave Sukov the okay to prepare the demolition charges. As he got out from under the wings of the MiG, Rockham was scribbling notes in his photo log. Signaling Bryant to come over to him, he split up the number of exposed film canisters between himself and his shooting partner. With the information they had gathered as safe as they could make it, Rockham finished up the roll of film in his camera by shooting panoramic shots of the parking apron and the airfield around it.

Taking his rucksack off again, Rockham secured his camera in the bubble wrap he had first packed it in. It was a low-tech, lightweight way of protecting the equipment, and it worked fine. Not everything the SEALs used was exotic or expensive.

While Rockham had been finishing his pictures and packing up his camera, Sukov and Able were preparing to destroy the target with explosives. They were conducting what was called a hasty demolition. Time was limited, and the economy of explosives was secondary to the speed of the operation.

Sukov was carrying one of the unit's two HST-4 SATCOM radios in his rucksack. Henry Lutz, the radio telephone operator of second squad, had a duplicate of Sukov's equipment. The radio, batteries, and antennas didn't weigh more than twenty pounds. The KY-57 encryption system and all of its accessories and spare batteries for everything added almost ten more pounds to Sukov's rucksack. So the bulk of the demolitions had been carried in by Dan Able.

For demolitions, the SEALs had chosen Mark 20, Mod-3 demolition charges. The rectangular green cloth bags filled with two pounds of C-4 explosive were the direct descendants of the Hagensen packs that the predecessors of the SEALs—the Naval Combat Demolition Units—had used to blast the beaches at Normandy in World War II. The charges had worked then, and were just as flexible and useful now.

Each Mark 20 charge had a forty-two-inch length of cord with a flat metal hook on the end, to help the operator secure the charge to the target. There was also a five-foot lead of detonating cord attached to the charge to allow it to be tied into a trunk line quickly. Normally, the Mark 20 charge was part of the Mark 135 demolition kit. But Sukov and Able had removed the charges they would need from the haversack of the big 135. The separate charges made for a much more flexible package to carry in a rucksack.

Moving smoothly and efficiently, Sukov placed a pair of Mark 20 charges on each of the spray tanks. Another pair of charges went on either side of the plane's tail, up tight against the fuselage. Since Rockham and Bryant had sketched and photographed the cockpit controls and layout—what there was of it in the stripped MiG—Able placed a pair of charges on top of the instrument panel. Sukov finished placing his pair of charges deep inside the tail of the plane, where the turbine sections of the engine would be. Up in the nose of the MiG, Able was slipping his last charge pair as far into the intake as he could, to destroy the intake compressor of the engine.

When all of the charges detonated, twenty pounds of C-4 explosive would rip the aircraft apart. There wouldn't be much of anything useful remaining of the aircraft, or the weapons it carried.

Carefully pulling the leads from the Mark 20 charges down to the detonating cord trunk lines, Sukov and Able tied the lines in place with long-practiced knots. Reaching into his rucksack, Sukov pulled out a Kevlar pouch holding the firing assemblies. They were a length of M-700 time fuse crimped to an M7 nonelectric blasting cap, an M60 weatherproof fuse lighter on the other end of the fuse. Both assemblies had been water-proofed and dried.

Prior to assembling the firing systems, Sukov and Able had burned test lengths of the M-700 time fuse. The coil they were using burned at a rate of forty seconds a foot, varying only a few seconds between lengths. The assemblies both held 22.5 feet of fuse, a fifteen minute time delay.

After attaching the M7 blasting caps to the detonating cord trunk lines, Sukov and Able double-checked each other's work. Looking up at Rockham, each man raised an extended thumb to indicate they were ready. From start to finish, they had all spent less than fifteen minutes at the MiG. The information they had been sent to gather had been collected and the aircraft rigged for destruction. All that it took now was a signal from Rockham to pull the fuse lighters.

When he saw the all-ready signal from his demolition team, Rockham signaled the rest of the squad to rally up by swinging his arm in a circular movement over his head. When he saw the signal returned, Rockham turned in the other direction and waved his hand forward. Then he held his weapon up over his head, parallel to the ground. That was the signal to Daugherty and second squad to advance in a staggered column formation, the same formation they had used to approach the target site. After he saw the signal returned, Rockham turned back to where Sukov and Able knelt next to the fuse lighters.

Slinging his M4 over his shoulder, Rockham

made a slashing chop with his right hand into the open palm of his left hand. Repeating the chop three times, he gave the demolition team the unit signal to fire their igniters. Both Sukov and Able simultaneously pulled the rings on the ends of the M60 fuse lighters. Holding the lighters until they could see smoke rising from the burning fuses, both SEALs ensured that the time delay on the firing assemblies had been properly started.

Getting up from where they had knelt, Sukov and Able rejoined Rockham and moved out as the fuses burned behind them. The area they were in was void of any living human presence. Even the normal desert life was scarce in the cold winter night. Safety precautions had been taken so no civilians could accidentally penetrate this deeply into the restricted space of the Nellis range area.

The SEALs began to withdraw from the target area, leaving the live explosive charges behind them. The fifteen minute delay in the firing assemblies were more than twice as long as they needed to patrol to a safe distance. They were once again moving in a staggered column formation, this time first squad was trailing second as they moved across the desert gravel and sand away from the airfield.

Afterward, no one in the patrol could say what it was they had done to activate the system. Suddenly, about ten meters to the left of the SEALs' formation, a pop-up target snapped up from the ground.

"Enemy left!" Kurkowski shouted.

The silhouette was immediately taken under fire by Kurkowski and Sid Mainhart on the left flank of second squad. As the short, controlled bursts of automatic fire struck the target, it fell down under the onslaught.

The other SEALs reacted to the fire. The target was down but there could easily be others. Live demolitions were burning behind them, so that avenue was closed. They were not in a channel-ized area. Instead, the platoon was in an open field. Rockham immediately issued verbal com-mands as the SEALs began their practiced imme-diate action drill.

"Twelve o'clock," Rockham shouted, "two hundred meters, wedge formation, follow me."

The staggered column of SEALs immediately broke into a wedge formation. Rockham took the point as second squad made the left arm of the wedge. First platoon made the right arm, and the SEALs moved forward as their platoon leader moved up to the apex of the wedge. They had a full field of fire to their front, and either squad could concentrate on either flank.

Now, the SEALs moved at a crouching run be-hind Rockham. They would go forward two hun-dred meters and rally. Any new targets coming up would be taken under fire by the men who first saw them.

"Target left," Ryan Marks called out close to the front of the wedge. As he spoke, the big man opened fire on another pop-up target, this one about fifteen meters away.

Even as his target went down, more began pop-ping up. The reaction to the situation by the highly trained SEALs was controlled, and violent.

Heavy fire was brought down on the targets almost as soon as the silhouettes rose from the ground. In scant seconds they were pounded back down. Meanwhile, the formation kept moving forward.

Besides reacting to the situation around them, Rockham kept the burning fuse delays on the charges behind him in the back of his mind. The men reacted like the professionals they were. There wasn't any unnecessary fire from the formation, no long, wasteful automatic bursts to spray the countryside. Instead, fire discipline had the SEALs all putting out short, controlled bursts of two or three rounds for every pull of the trigger.

It was as if the SEALs' weapons had mechanical limiters on their automatic mechanisms. Some military units did limit their weapons so they could only fire in three-round bursts. But if the SEALs needed it, they could hold the triggers back on their M4s and put out a stream of 5.56mm projectiles at a rate of 700 to 900 rounds per minute. That fire only lasted for the twenty-eight rounds each magazine held. But the SEALs could change magazines on the run, which they were doing now as they moved across the desert.

The targets stopped popping up as the formation crossed more than a hundred meters of ground. Whatever triggering mechanism they had come across, they seemed to be past it now. But they all continued to move at a trot, following Rockham to his indicated rally point.

Eventually, Rockham slowed to a walk. He turned back to the men and indicated the rally point by circling his arm and hand over his head with his finger extended. Then he pointed to a small clump of rocks off to the right. That would be their rally point. Each man pointed to it with his nonfiring hand. Their weapons remained pointing outward to either side as they moved forward. They had just effectively fought their way through an enemy formation.

As the men circled around the rocks, they formed a security perimeter with Rockham and Sukov at the center. As the RTO of first squad, Sukov always tried to stay within Rockham's immediate reach, even when he wasn't actively using the radio.

Without being asked, Chief Monday conducted a quick head count of all the members of the patrol. At the same time, he performed an ammo check from each man.

"All present and accounted for," Monday said quietly to Rockham. "Ammo count is satisfactory."

If they had just come out of a real firefight, a lot more ammunition would have been expended. Now would be the time to redistribute the remaining ammunition evenly among the men. That wasn't necessary, and Rockham wanted more space between the unit and the airfield.

"Move out in one minute," Rockham said. "Wedge formation."

"Bryant, on point," Chief Monday said as he passed Mike Bryant kneeling in the sand. "Move out in one minute."

Bryant simply nodded as his chief continued on down the line of men. With Rockham pointing out the direction of travel, the men formed up and started traveling back along their planned exit route.

There were no further incidents as the platoon continued to move in their wedge formation. They were more than a kilometer from the airfield when Rockham again signaled a halt and had the men move into a security perimeter. As he looked at his watch, he counted down the seconds. He then looked up and back at the airfield.

There was a resounding *thud* as the twenty pounds of C-4 explosive blasted the MiG into a memory. The men all heard the explosion and felt the ground shock through the soles of their boots a moment later. As some of the men looked back, pop-up targets suddenly snapped up all over the airfield.

"I guess this means we woke them up," Rockham said quietly.

A soft chuckle came from a few of the men at their leader's words. But none of the SEALs relaxed their vigilance. Just because the explosion raised all of the targets back at the airfield didn't mean there weren't more of them to be found. Each one represented an enemy troop, and they had to be dealt with quickly and finally.

The SEALs went back on line and moved out in a staggered file formation, the two squads separated by fifty meters. They would continue on their present heading, following their exit route to the first lay-up point. It was at the LUP that they would be able to break for a moment and rest before heading out to their primary extraction point.

CHAPTER 12

★★★★★

1518 ZULU
Grid Coordinate PA377831
Dog Bone Lake
Nellis Air Force Range
Nevada

The SEALs had reached their primary extraction point on the western side of Dog Bone Lake, almost six kilometers from the airfield where they had destroyed the MiG 15. Traveling hard and fast, they had reached the coordinates well within the planned time frame. For a training operation, the men had been running their asses off all over the ancient lake bed.

Even with first squad having had to run across the desert to join up with second squad before the operation started, they had kept to the timeline of the mission. The value the Teams placed on physical fitness had been proven worthwhile once again. It wouldn't be the last time.

They had occupied their lay-up point, to rest and

reorganize after moving all the way across the lake bed from the airfield they had attacked. The area was still considered enemy territory, and the men had to treat it as such. The location of the LUP was inside a gully, just a hundred meters down from a jeep trail, an unimproved dirt road that serviced the target areas of the lake bed. The gully had been selected from the maps and aerial photos Rockham and the men examined during their briefing for the op. The exact location of the LUP was chosen when they scouted the area after the direct-action part of the op was over.

Bryant and Rockham had already gone up to the jeep trail and checked it for signs of traffic. A secondary rally point up higher in the mountain to their west had been chosen and everyone notified as to where it was. That was a normal part of the LUP routine. If discovered by an enemy force, they could break up to escape and regroup later. The landing zone for their extraction helicopter was in the lake bed in front of them. It should have been an easy out after what was another successful operation.

Having set up another circular security perimeter, the men were relaxed but at full alert status; none of the men were sleeping. This was also normal procedure just before and after sunrise and sunset. The sun would be coming up shortly, and the eastern horizon was starting to glow with colors that would soon prove gorgeous. The beauty of what they saw wasn't lost on the SEALs, even as they held their weapons at the ready.

Having set up his HST-4 SATCOM radio up

near the center of the gully LUP, John Sukov had
made contact with Air Command back at Nellis.
Rockham took the handset from the RTO and
was having what seemed like a long conversation
with command headquarters. The message should
have been a brief one, just giving a situation report and calling for extraction. The next radio
contact would have been line-of-sight with the extraction bird.

"Roger that," Rockham said into the radio
handset. "Bravo leader out."

After giving the handset back to Sukov, Rockham crouched down in the center of the LUP,
where he could talk quietly to all of the men at
once. What he had to say was not what the men
expected to hear:

"Okay, we've had a successful operation and
are ready for extraction. The trouble is, the extraction bird is not coming in."

The men were silent as the news settled in.

"So much for Vegas tonight," Kurkowski said
quietly.

"You'll still have your chance to blow a pay-
check," Rockham said, "it's just going to take a
little longer. Now, dig out your maps."

Each SEAL had been given a special survival
map of the area as part of their special equipment
for the operation. The maps were the standard
evasion charts used by military pilots, 1:250,000
scale maps printed on a strong polyester material
that didn't stretch, crack, or easily tear. It could be
folded up to fit inside an aircrew flight suit—the
same kind of suits the SEALs were wearing as uni-

forms. The EVCs the SEALs were now looking at were Fallon/Nellis training charts, not something that they had expected to use.

"We are here," Rockham pointed to the map, "at grid coordinates 377831. Our emergency extraction point is Pintwater cave at grid coordinate 277728. That's only about fifteen klicks away in a straight line on a compass heading of 205 degrees. That's the good news. The bad news is that we aren't going to be traveling in a straight line. The cave is on the far side of this mountain range. So we could be traveling twenty klicks or more to get to the site. We have forty-eight hours to get there, and we will be running an E and E tactical movement all the way."

A tactical movement meant that the men would be running as if in enemy territory. They would stay in formation with their weapons ready as directed. And they had two more days in the desert. E&E—escape and evasion—meant they had to live off the land while avoiding contact or leaving a trail. They had to try to eliminate all signs of even having been in the area. Now, instead of a direct action mission, they were on a desert survival course.

The men had no way of knowing that Rockham had actually dropped a full day off the survival portion of their mission. He wanted the men to have something to stretch their abilities against. Again, he'd decided that working against the desert environment and their situation was the best way to pull everyone together as a close-knit team.

With first squad's run across the desert and all the unit's movements since, Rockham didn't want to return to base with exhausted men on his hands, so he had rearranged the pickup time a full day earlier than originally planned. That also meant they would have to travel at least partially during the day to make the pickup time. Other plans had also been rearranged for the shorter timeline.

"It may not feel like it right now," Rockham said, "but we're still pretty lucky. It's the middle of winter out here and still cool in the mornings. Even this afternoon it's just going to get warm and not really hot. But that sun will be beating down on us, and we're not going to be crossing the best terrain in the world.

"Right now, it's 0615 hours. We'll rest up here for another thirty minutes. Then we move out to the southwest. There's going to be a water drop for us at 1200 hours at coordinates 341784. That's five and a half klicks southwest of here at a compass heading of 286 degrees. The location is a dry streambed south of that 4,000-foot peak."

Rockham pointed to the peak easily visible in the growing light. The rocks glowed in the rosy dawn and looked to be only a few miles away. All the SEALs knew that distances could be deceptive in the desert.

"It's going to be some pretty rough going to get to that location. I intend for us to be on site by 1100, so we're in for some hard climbing. Use your time now to tank up. Drink at least a canteen of water even if you don't feel you need it. Drink all you can, then a little bit more. Everyone has to stay hydrated. We'll conserve sweat, not water.

"John," Rockham said to John Grant, nearby, "you grew up in Arizona, didn't you?"

"At Gila River outside of Phoenix," Grant said in his deep, sonorous voice, "about 350 miles southeast of here."

"You're going to be point on this march," Rockham said. "Your experience will be a big help to all of us.

"We need that water drop," Rockham said to the men. "That's why we'll be moving in the cool of the morning. If we can get into position early enough, we'll make up a LUP near the drop site and rest up for the afternoon. Right now, we're on fifty percent watch. Drink up and take it easy, otherwise you'll wish you had later on."

Traveling across the front of the Pintwater Mountain Range was just as difficult as Rockham had predicted. The platoon moved up the foothills of the mountain to a point above where their water drop would be made. Now it was a matter of crossing the mountain while not silhouetting themselves against the backdrop of the rocks.

The rocks were red and dust-covered. The whole area seemed to be colored in shades of gray and red. There wasn't even much sign of color in the bushes and scrub plants. They were mostly gray or tan, with some brownish-green leaves covering up where the thorns were hidden.

Rocks twisted and slipped underfoot, so the SEALs always had to be wary of where they set their feet. Dust rose at almost every footstep. Even with the care they took while moving, the dust was scuffed up, and the men could all smell it and taste it.

The morning was still cool, but the unrelenting sunshine was going to change that within hours. When they could, the SEALs moved through the shade of a ridge line or rock formation. But there was little shade on the east face of a mountain in the middle of the morning.

John Grant was doing a great job of leading the men over the rocks. The SEALs moved in a single file formation, flexing and breaking as needed to go around obstacles. Mike Bryant offered to trade off the point man position with Grant to give the big man an occasional rest, but the stoic Native American just kept moving forward, his M4 up and at the ready. It was as if he was home and moving through his backyard; which Bryant realized was actually close to the truth.

They had taken a few breaks along their line of march. Rockham would signal for a rally point, and they'd grab a few minutes in whatever shade was available. Talk was still limited. They were on a tactical move, and hand signals were the primary means of communication. Rockham had just raised his hand above his head and circled his arm to indicate another rally point and rest stop. Pointing, he had the men move to the southern side of a steep gully. The sides rose above a rock-strewn sand and gravel bed, a turn in one side leaving part of the gully in shade.

They had reached grid coordinate 331811, about two and a half klicks from their objective. It was about 0930 hours, and in spite of the rough traveling, they had made very good time. They still had a maximum of two and a half hours to cover the remaining distance to meet their water drop on time. Rockham wanted them to use two hours, at most, to cover the distance.

Sid Mainhart was the youngest member of the SMD. Though a fully qualified operator, he still lacked a lot in the way of field experience. His duty tour aboard a nuclear submarine gave him a lot of knowledge his Teammates lacked; how to handle himself well in the field was something he was still working on. He had been raised a city boy in New Jersey, what did he know about wandering the desert?

There was a nice, flat rock up against a larger boulder on the side of the gully where the SEALs were taking their break. Mainhart saw that it was in the shade of the boulder, so it seemed a good seat, with a backrest to boot. Settling down on the rock, he let out a soft groan as got off his feet.

Leaning back against the boulder, Mainhart sighed and closed his eyes. The rock only moved a little bit so he wasn't worried about losing his seat. His weapon was across his lap, the muzzle up and pointed in a safe direction. Muzzle consciousness was something that had been pounded into him from his earliest days at BUD/S. Knowing where the muzzle of your weapon was pointing at all times was only one aspect of being in the Teams. Constant awareness of your surroundings was another means to safety.

"Mainhart," Mike Ferber said quietly. "Hey, Sid!"

"What," Mainhart said without opening his eyes.

"Damn it, sailor," Ferber growled sharply, "look at me when I'm fucking talking to you!"

That snapped Mainhart's eyes open. "Mike—" he started to say. Ferber was the first squad's leading petty officer, second only to Greg Rockham in the squad's chain of command.

Ferber cut him off. "Keep your eyes on me," he said in a commanding tone. "Keep your hands on your weapon. I want you to lean forward and get up slowly."

The young SEAL was now very concerned with just what the hell was going on, and he wasn't about to disobey Ferber. He kept his eyes locked on Ferber's as he slowly leaned forward and sat up. With his M4 carbine solidly in his grip, Mainhart got to his feet. There wasn't a sound from the rest of the SEALs as several of them watched the drama unfolding in the shadows of the gully.

"Step over to me," Ferber said.

Mainhart was more than a little nervous. Just what in the hell was wrong, and what was behind him? If he had sat down on a rattlesnake or something, it would have made some noise by now, wouldn't it?

He stepped over to where Ferber was sitting only a few feet away.

"I never did think it was a good idea to startle an armed man," Ferber said quietly. "Turn around and take a look at your rock."

Mainhart looked back, and only a foot away was the biggest, blackest tarantula he had ever seen. In fact, it was the only live tarantula he'd ever seen. Apparently, the large spider had been taking cover under the edge of Mainhart's nice flat seat. Tarantulas were normally nocturnal and didn't get around much during the day. The cold nights of the Nevada winter had made the little predator a lot more active during the warmer days. By sitting down and moving the rock, Mainhart had disturbed the arachnid, and it crawled out to keep from being squashed.

"Shit," Mainhart exclaimed as he looked at the biggest spider he had ever seen in his life. He leaned a little closer to take a better look, fascinated at what he saw. None of the SEALs watching had a chance to warn him.

The hairy little black horror squatted down as Sid's shadow passed over him. The eight eyes of the big spider could see movement very well, and the shadow had startled it. Suddenly, there was a loud hissing sound and the spider jumped forward.

As Mainhart almost fell backward, he instinctively snapped up his M4. Before he could even thumb off the safety, a K-bar knife spun through the air and pinned the struggling arachnid to the ground as it landed.

Quickly getting hold of himself, Mainhart looked up to see John Grant stepping forward to where the knife stuck into the spider. The big Native American pulled the blade out and dropped a rock on top of the still twitching arachnid.

"Try to keep the noise down, okay?" Grant said. "We are supposed to be in a tactical situation here, you know."

With his mouth gaping open, Mainhart watched Grant wipe off the blade against his boot and sheath the knife back on his rig. Then he just walked back over to where he had been sitting, about eight feet away—as if throwing a knife and hitting a playing-card-size target happened every day.

"Not too shabby," Kurkowski said as Grant sat down next to him.

Grant just looked at him without expression.

"Hey, John," Monday said from where he sat under a big shrub with yellow flowers. "You're supposed to be the big expert on the flora and fauna out here. What the hell is this thing?"

"That's a screwbean tree," Grant said. "It's a kind of mesquite."

"Tree?" Kurkowski said. "Ugly bush is more like it. Look at the spines on that thing."

"They grow bigger," Grant said. "They were an important food source for my ancestors out here. Those tight little spirals growing on it are the pods. They taste sweet."

"Sweet, huh?" Monday said. He reached up and pulled off a couple of the pods. The seeds looked like tightly wound coil springs, and the SEAL chief had to use his knife to cut one open.

Putting the interior of the pod in his mouth, Monday chewed thoughtfully on it. "Hey, this isn't bad at all," he said. "It is sweet."

"They can be boiled down into a sweet syrup too," Grant said.

Reaching over to where some big grasses were growing, Grant pulled off a handful of the seeds strung out along the top of the plant. He popped the grains into his mouth and started chewing.

Watching what his Teammate was doing, Kurkowski wasn't going to be outdone in survival eating. And he wasn't going to miss out on a native treat. If the screwbean pods were sweet, the grains must be great, he thought. He stripped off a handful of seed grains and started chewing.

"Blech!" Kurkowski said as he made a face and spat out the grain. "These things taste terrible."

"They're much better cooked," Grant said quietly as he kept chewing. Then he also spat out the mess and looked over to where Kurkowski was sitting. A wide, bright smile spread out across Grant's dark red face. "You did know that Indians are known for their sense of humor, didn't you? It's good to play a joke on the white invader."

Seeing the expression on Kurkowski's face, all of the SEALs cracked up.

"Break's over," Rockham said with a smile. "Grant, you're on point."

CHAPTER 13

★ ★ ★ ★

Crawling up across the rocks, Bryant slipped up to where he could just peek around the rock in front of him. From his vantage point, he was able to look down into the large gully where they were supposed to receive their water drop. He was running point for the rest of his Teammates in the LUP behind him. He had low-crawled up to the side of a tall peak to get a protected view of the gully. He felt the need to be extra cautious in approaching a point that others knew the SEALs would be arriving at. It turned out his suspicions were correct.

The gravel floor of the nearly hundred-meter-wide dry streambed didn't hold any live enemy forces. He hadn't expected live aggressors on a live-fire training op, but there was a grouping of close to a dozen of the pop-up targets that represented the enemy, and they were active. As he continued to watch, Bryant saw some of the targets drop down and others cycle to the up position. That must be to simulate enemy movement, he thought.

Turning back to where the others were waiting, Bryant held his free hand in front of his face, fingers spread. Then he held up his hand and spread his fingers, closing and opening his hand twice, then holding up two fingers. Finally, he pointed back down into the gully on the other side of the peak.

To Rockham, his point man's message read: enemy in sight, twelve possibles, down at the objective. The SEAL officer had known there would be an enemy force at their supply drop. He'd had set up the incident himself, with the cooperation of the Air Force range crews. But it would turn out that a surprise awaited them that was more than he'd expected.

Holding his smile to himself, Rockham was inwardly pleased with the professional actions of his point man and the rest of his unit. They had moved at a steady pace across the mountain. It would have been easy for the unit to walk into a simulated ambush. Then they would have had to withdraw and set up another supply drop at best, later in the day.

Now the platoon fell into its practiced standard operating procedures for an enemy sighting. In this situation, they had the element of surprise, since Bryant had spotted the enemy while under cover.

Turning to the men, Rockham put up his non-firing hand, palm out, fingers spread. He turned to make sure all of the men could see the signal to freeze. Everyone stopped moving.

As the patrol leader, it was Rockham's job to assess the situation, determine the enemy strength, and balance the next action against the patrol's mission. He slipped up to where Bryant was still down in the prone position, watching the targets.

Both Bryant and Rockham were lying prone on the flank of a small peak that stuck up at the end of a ridge line. The ridge and peak split an ancient watercourse that drained down from the mountain range to the west of them. The gravel plain itself was about a hundred meters wide and more than twice that long, running northwest to southeast. The base of the peak spread out almost a hundred meters to the front of where the two SEALs lay in concealment.

Rockham could see the targets clearly in the middle of the plain. The edge of the group was about 150 meters in front of him. Having made a count of the "enemy," Rockham slid carefully back down to where he had left the rest of the platoon.

Now he had to decide whether to attack the group of enemy troops or bypass them. Since they had to have the supplies coming in to the drop zone, and they outnumbered the enemy forces, he decided to attack. The drill was to go into a hasty ambush position up on the flanks of the peak in front of them.

Rockham repeated the enemy signal, putting his hand over his face and spreading his fingers. Then he flashed the "twelve" signal with his hand, closing and opening his fist and holding up the correct number of fingers and gave the action signal. Pumping his arm up and down, he backed up in the direction of the enemy. Pointing with a sweep of his arm, he indicated the fields of fire for the ambush.

Without a word, the men moved forward, activating a long-practiced drill. With Rockham at the center, first squad moved to the right while second squad moved to the left. Everyone slowly moved up to the top of the rise in front of them.

To ensure complete coverage of the kill zone for the ambush, second squad had to set up on the eastern side of the peak. With the peak between the two squads, second squad couldn't see any signals Rockham might put out. The lack of visibility wouldn't affect the execution of the ambush. In fact, the SEALs could rarely see each other during this kind of action in a real-world operation. The vast majority of SEAL actions took place at night, so the men practiced and drilled constantly, to the point that they didn't have to see each other to know their jobs.

The platoon would quickly move into position to conduct a hasty ambush on the enemy in the gravel field. Only Rockham would open fire to initiate the ambush. Only if one of the men knew that his movement had been detected by the enemy, or that the platoon was in immediate danger of being discovered, would that man initiate fire. And if one man fired, the entire platoon opened up. This was the application of overwhelming firepower that had worked for the Teams since the jungles of Vietnam.

The SOP was that each man armed with a rifle would fire one full magazine and reload. If there were belt-fed automatic weapons set up for the ambush, they would fire one full belt and reload. The men on either flank would throw a single hand grenade. Grenadiers would fire a single high-explosive 40-millimeter grenade and then empty a magazine from their rifles.

In less than twenty seconds the killing field in front of the SEAL platoon would be raked with almost four hundred rounds of rifle fire, four hundred rounds of machine gun fire, and thousands of fragments from exploding grenades. Ambushes were practiced often, so that the men could apply such firepower effectively, safely, and with devastating results.

Waiting a few minutes to allow his men to all reach their positions, Rockham settled the stock of his M4 deep into the pocket of his shoulder. The coated tubular stock felt warm against his cheekbone. He peered through the open circular rear sight and bracketed the horns on either side of the front sight post evenly in the circle of the rear aperture.

Pushing off the safety with his thumb, he moved the control lever past the semiautomatic position so it clicked quietly into the full automatic position. The ridged plastic cylinder of the front handguards gave a good grip for his left hand to pull the weapon back into his shoulder. Finally placing his right index finger on the curved metal of the trigger, he started to squeeze.

The smell of the eons-old dust was thick in his nose as Rockham began to fire. With his shots, the men would unleash their firestorm of high-velocity steel into the targets. Suddenly, Rockham's concentration was shattered by an irritating beeping sound.

Without conscious thought, he clicked the safety back on his M4 carbine. The muted noise of his beeper going off was coming from the upper front pocket of his dirty flight suit. Up and down across the peak, beepers went off in pockets, pouches, and a few rucksacks.

Standing up, Rockham turned to his squad. As far as he was concerned, the exercise was over. Pulling out his beeper, he looked down at the small green strip of its LED screen. The number 8 was spread out across the screen, repeated in a long line of digits.

"Sukov!" Rockham shouted. "Set up the SAT-COM. I want contact made with JSOC as quickly as you can do it. Chief, rally the platoon down on the south side of this peak."

With the peak a convenient rise, Sukov moved to set up his helical antenna on its highest point. Shucking his rucksack as he moved forward, he pulled it around in front of him. The spindly helical antenna sat on its own folding tripod. The rest of the antenna consisted of a large X of four curved elements over a wide eight-pointed star of extendible rods connected at their tips.

Breaking out his compass, Sukov set his helical antenna to the right azimuth so he could communicate with the satellite they had been assigned to use. At the same time, Henry Lutz was doing the same thing, only on the other side of the peak. If for some reason Sukov couldn't make contact, Lutz would be in position to try it himself.

While the two radio operators set up their gear, the rest of the platoon remained on watch. With his sniper-trained eyesight, Ryan Marks noticed two small specks of movement across the sky miles to the southeast of the SEALs' position. As he watched, Marks could see that the specks were moving directly toward them.

"Skipper," he said as he pointed at the growing dots, "take a look. Someone's coming, and they're coming this way fast."

The dark spots in the sky were growing larger and more distinct by the second. They soon resolved into a pair of UH60A Blackhawk helicopters.

"Lutz," Rockham called, from where he was standing next to Sukov, "see if you can get those birds on the local rescue frequencies."

Switching over from his helical antenna to a simple whip antenna, Lutz started going over the preset radio frequencies the SEALs had been given for the operation.

"Boss," Sukov said, "I have JSOC on the KY-57."

The KY-57 would give the SATCOM radio the

capability of sending an encrypted secure voice signal to the Joint Special Operations Command headquarters in Fort Bragg, North Carolina, more than two thousand miles away.

While also staying alert to the situation around them, the rest of the platoon could see that Rockham was having a conversation with somebody on the other end of the SATCOM. Lutz, meanwhile, was talking to the helicopters coming in over Dog Bone Lake and only a mile or so away from the SEALs' position.

"I don't think we're going to Kansas, Dorothy," Mainhart said, kneeling next to his partner.

"Yeah, and I'll bet our trip to the Emerald City is out too," Kurkowski said a with a wistful look.

"Hey, you know the rules," Bryant said. "All training missions are designed to hold an absolute minimum possibility of fun. It's in the Navy regulations."

"At least it doesn't look like we'll be spending much more time in the desert," Mainhart said.

The two helicopters were now only a few hundred meters from the SEALs' position. The gravel plain of the dry watercourse had been chosen for a water drop. Now it looked like it was going to be a landing zone for a set of pickup birds. The area was the size of two football fields, so there was little chance of the two big Blackhawks interfering with each other on landing.

Pulling an M18 green smoke grenade from his rig, Mike Ferber threw out the heavy canister after pulling the safety pin. Green clouds of smoke billowed from the top of the burning canister, spreading out and rising from the red gravel plain. Popping smoke allowed the helicopters to tell the direction and roughly the speed of any ground winds. This was especially important for a landing halfway up the side of a mountain, where the winds could be treacherous.

Markings on the birds were visible to all of the SEALs—these were Air Force rescue helicopters from Nellis. The pilots and crew of the Blackhawks were more than a little experienced with operations in the mountains. Walking out into the gravel, Ferber stood to the right front of the lead bird, where the pilot could see him clearly. Guiding the helicopters in to a landing took a minimum of hand signals. Quickly, the SEAL had his arms pointing down and crossed in front of his body as the big helicopter took the signal and set down in huge clouds of red dust.

One of the ground crew unsnapped himself from the open side door of the lead bird and jumped down to the ground. The pilots never shut down their engines, only throttled back. The noise from the turbines made conversation difficult.

Trotting up to Ferber, one of the aircrew shouted, "We're here to pick your people up and get them back to Nellis!"

"Roger that," Ferber said.

Turning away from the crewman, Ferber trotted back up to where Rockham was finishing his radio conversation with JSOC.

"They say they're here to pick us up for transport back to Nellis," Ferber hollered up to Rockham.

"Get with Chief Monday and see to it that everyone gets aboard," Rockham said. "This exercise is over. We've been recalled."

It took a matter of moments for the SEALs to follow long-established procedure and file aboard the helicopters. Though there was room enough to have crowded the entire platoon into a single bird, it was a lot easier on everyone involved to use two. First squad boarded the lead helicopter, while second squad got on board the trailing bird. The longest time taken for the loading was that used by Sukov and Lutz to pack up their communications rigs, and even that only took a couple of minutes. Within fifteen minutes of sighting the helicopters, the SMD was airborne and on their way back to Nellis.

Once back at the base, things didn't slow down. Even over the secure line with JSOC, Rockham had only been given limited instructions. The helicopters had been on the ground for less than a minute when vehicles showed up to transport the SEALs. Rockham gave quick instructions to Shaun Daugherty, Chief Monday, and Mike Ferber, before he was driven away. The rest of the unit climbed aboard the trucks that were waiting for them.

Traveling across the tarmac, the trucks carrying the SMD moved to the big secure building where they had stored the bulk of their equipment. They were to gather everything and pack it quickly for transport. While the rest of the SEALs started stripping down their gear, Chief Monday sent John Grant and Henry Limbaugh back to the transient quarters to pick up everyone's personal gear.

Though the SEALs remained dusty, their gear was quickly stripped down and cleaned. When Limbaugh and Grant returned less than twenty minutes later, they had more than their Teammates' personal gear. The two had stopped off at a mess hall somewhere along the line and gathered hot food and drinks.

The drinks tasted good to the parched SEALs. The food was just barely warm and they had to eat it on the run from plastic plates, but it tasted a hell of a lot better than the single meal, ready-to-eat field ration they had consumed that morning. Monday didn't bother asking Grant how he had convinced the Air Force mess sergeants to give him such a big take-out meal. He just hoped he wouldn't hear about it later.

When Rockham showed up less than an hour after he left, the men had already packed the bulk of their equipment.

"Saved some chow for you," Monday said as he handed Rockham a plastic box.

Flipping the lid back, Rockham stuffed some food into his mouth as Monday gave him the concise version of what had been done to that point.

Accepting the sitrep along with a cold soft drink, Rockham briefed the men on what he had been told over a secure phone line.

"We've been activated for a hot op," he said after a long gulp of Pepsi. "Transportation has been laid on for us to be in the Gulf roughly by this time tomorrow. Schedules are very tight and we don't have any leeway at all. So everything has to be done just about at a dead run.

"There's a C-141 being diverted from its flight path right now to come here and pick us up. It should arrive within an hour. Every piece of gear we brought with us is to be on board that aircraft so that it can be wheels-up by 1530 hours.

"As far as just what the specifics for our operation are, you know as much as I do. Hopefully, we'll get a briefing once we get back to Little Creek. We're not being held in the dark without reason—this one is big, and security is covering it like a blanket.

"Something is very much in the wind right now over in the Gulf. The UN deadline for Saddam to get out of Kuwait is coming up on the fifteenth, that's only next Tuesday. Personally, I don't think this administration is going to cut him a lot of slack on the deadline either. Right now, long-range transport is next to impossible to get. Somebody with some real clout bumped people and gear to get us that space on the C-141.

"Time is working against us on this one. We are going to be on the move for a while. There isn't even time for us to take a break so we can hit the showers. The best we'll be able to do is scrub up in the head facilities in the hangar here. Did anyone grab my personal gear with all the rest?"

"Your seabag is over here, Rock," Ferber said as he pointed to the gear pile.

"Outstanding," Rockham said with a grin. "Now all I need to find is a fire hose and a bar of soap."

CHAPTER 14

★ ★ ★ ★

2215 ZULU
Langley Air Force Base
Hampton, Virginia

The flight on the C-141 Starlifter from Nellis to Langley Air Force Base outside of Norfolk had been a long one. The freight the SEALs brought on board was packed in thick-walled cardboard boxes strapped to pallets. The handful of other passengers on the plane probably wished the SEALs had also been packed up as well. They certainly smelled like they should have been in boxes—long pine ones.

All the SEALs stank. Even the cavernous interior of the Starlifter felt like the close confines of a locker room when the smell filled the air. Not that the SEALs cared. They had just come in from a field exercise and were tired, dusty, and wearing uniforms that had seen cleaner days. They were also almost all sound asleep within ten minutes of takeoff.

Joining in with his men, Rockham also slept on the plane. Worrying about what was coming up for his unit wasn't a useful way to spend the time. He had no intelligence reports or other data to study, so catching up on sleep sounded like a fine idea.

Flight time for the C-141B was a little over four and a half hours. By the clock, the men only spent about an hour and a half in the air, because they crossed through three time zones. As far as their bodies were concerned, they were getting close to being beat up.

Physical discomfort is something SEALs ignore as part of their day-to-day activities. They don't like being uncomfortable, they just ignore it. So when Rockham pried open what felt like sand-encrusted eyes, he blinked and looked around at his men in various stages of waking up.

As he rubbed his hands on his face, he realized that his eyes were crusted over with sand. A fast wash-up in the limited facilities at the Nellis hangar hadn't been sufficient. That, and the dust that rose up from his uniform had settled back down on him while he was sleeping.

Looking over at his men, he realized they all looked the worst for wear. He knew some of the old blue-water Navy types considered the SEALs to be little more than pirates—to be kept under glass and only let out in time of war. But there was no reason his men had to actually look like pirates. Their dirty flight suits didn't suggest that they belonged to the Navy. But their appearance would attract attention. He knew he had to make arrangements for them to get to showers and fresh uniforms as soon as it was practical.

Finally, the big transport plane set its wheels down at Langley Air Force Base. It would only be a twenty-four-mile drive to Little Creek, but Rockham knew there was no way for him to get his men there and back before the C-141 lifted off to continue its flight to the Persian Gulf. The crew chief had told him they would only be sitting at Langley long enough to service the plane and load some more cargo and passengers on board. They had a scheduled takeoff at 1930 hours local time.

It was late in the afternoon in the Norfolk area, and the local rush hour was well under way. Traffic would be heavy between Hampton and Norfolk, and the Hampton Roads bridge-tunnel across the mouth of the James River would be clogged. Whatever he could do for his men, he would have to do it locally.

When the C-141 pulled up to the unloading area, the first thing Rockham saw when he stepped out of the side tail door of the aircraft was a gray-painted Navy 1¼ ton cargo truck with a secured container strapped to its bed. It was just one of thousands of similar vehicles in the Norfolk area, and it didn't stand out at all. The man standing next to the open passenger door of the truck, however, was someone Rockham recognized immediately.

Walking across the tarmac, Rockham stuck his hand out to Lieutenant Keith Whitlow, one of the intelligence officers from Special Warfare Group Two.

"Keith, good to see you," Rockham said as he shook the other man's hand. "What are you doing here?"

"Thought you could use a friendly face among all these Air Force types," Whitlow said.

The green holster on Whitlow's right hip was not something even a SEAL normally wore while out and about in the civilian world. That was a big clue to Rockham that Whitlow was here on official business.

"You have something for me?" Rockham asked.

"Yes," Whitlow said. "A secure briefing folder and transport for your extra gear. We've also laid on some space in the local Transient quarters. There's a bus in back of this hangar to take you and your men there to get cleaned up and presentable enough for the Air Force. Chief Granville here brought you and your men some fresh uniforms from Team Two."

Sitting at the wheel of the cargo truck was the chief storekeeper from SEAL Team Two. Chief Granville knew all of the men of the SMD well enough since SEAL Team Two directly supported the much smaller unit.

"Got fresh jumpsuits, socks, and underwear here," Chief Granville said as he stood up in the open door of the truck. "Took the sizes from your men's records, so everything should fit. They'll have to switch the patches from the outfits they're wearing, though. We can take all of your extra gear back with us as well, as soon as that Air

Force crew gets done playing with their forklifts."

Not having to worry about two complete issues of equipment to transport was a welcome relief to Rockham. The fact that he could let his men get cleaned up and in fresh clothes was even better.

"Chief Monday," Rockham called out, "have second squad fall in on the back of this truck. There's a fresh issue for them here. They can grab a ride on the bus behind that hangar there. It will take them to shower facilities. You've got thirty minutes. Once they're done, they can rotate back here and relieve first squad."

"Aye, sir," Monday said, and turned to start issuing orders to the men gathered behind him.

First squad fell to work helping direct the Air Force crews as to which pallets should be removed from the back of the C-141 and placed in the secured container on the back of the cargo truck. Second squad grabbed up the care packages from inside the container and took them along with them to the gray-painted Navy bus waiting off the tarmac. The idea of a fast shower and shave visibly raised the morale of the men.

While the men were doing their work, Rockham and Whitlow moved to sit inside the now vacant cab of the truck. Pulling up a briefcase and unlocking it, Whitlow handed Rockham a large envelope, heavily sealed with tape. After signing a receipt, Rockham pulled out his pocketknife to cut the sealing tape away. Whitlow reached out a hand and stopped him.

"Rock," he said, "I haven't been cleared for whatever is in that envelope—only you and your men have. That material came down from D.C. this morning by helicopter, I'm just the local courier for it. Whatever the specifics are for your mission, it looks like it's going to happen fast. Good luck."

Whitlow shook Rockham's hand and stepped out of the truck. "By the way," he said, turning back. "I figured you might need this." And he handed him the briefcase he had used to carry the envelope. "The combination's 7504," Whitlow said with a smile. "Bring it back when you're done."

"Thanks, Whit," Rockham said.

Twenty minutes later the bus had returned with a much cleaner looking and better smelling second squad aboard. Shaun Daugherty, part of his red hair still wet and shining in the sun, walked over to the cargo truck where Rockham was sitting in the cab and opened the door.

"Ah, the true saviors of humanity," Daugherty said, "whoever it was that invented the hot shower."

The smile slipped off the young SEAL officer's face as he saw the red-bordered TOP SECRET cover on the binder Rockham held on his lap inside the open briefcase.

"Well," Rockham said as he closed the binder and then shut the briefcase, "maybe it's time that I tried out one of those myself. Here's some light reading for you. I suggest you don't let this out of your sight."

Handing Daugherty the briefcase, Rockham joined the rest of first squad as they boarded the bus to take a turn at the showers.

Daugherty was right, Rockham thought later. One of the great things in modern life was the hot shower. That, and clean clothes. He now felt refreshed and a whole lot cleaner than he had for several days. His thinking was sharp, though that carried a drawback with it.

The SMD was under isolation conditions. They couldn't speak to anyone about their situation, where they were going, or what they were going to do when they got there. Any contact with the world outside of their group was to be held to a minimum. That made for some very disgruntled Air Force people who had just tried to engage the SEALs in some light conversation. That kind of detachment left a lot of people thinking that being in the Teams made you some kind of military snob. The situation didn't sit particularly well with the men, or with Rockham for that matter.

He was not much more than thirty miles from home, and couldn't speak to his wife or son. None of the married men in the unit could contact their families either. It gave him little comfort that he wasn't alone in his situation.

As far as Sharon Rockham knew, her husband was at least inside the continental United States. That was only going to remain true for the moment. Within a short time, Rockham and his men would be far out over the Atlantic, on course for the Persian Gulf.

When the bus pulled up to the hangar, the C-141 was still standing on the tarmac with airmen hustling around it. Rockham's crew was lounging around the hangar, keeping the plane and their gear within sight. As first squad came off the bus, Daugherty was waiting at the door when Rockham appeared.

"Interesting idea of reading there, Rock," Daugherty said as he handed Rockham back his briefcase.

"Not a hell of a lot more than contact orders for when we get to the Gulf," Rockham replied, taking back the case.

"Well," Daugherty said, "there's a hell of a lot more here than just what's in those mission orders. Fleming came through while you were out scrubbing up. We got chow here."

It wasn't much of a surprise to Rockham that there were containers of food from their old Teammate. Their old platoon mate always seemed to come through with the best chow around. How Ken Fleming had found out that they were even on the base, he had no idea. Probably Chief Granville had something to do with it. Either way, the morale of the unit had gone up another notch higher than it had after the hot showers.

Though Fleming wasn't in the platoon anymore, he made sure that his presence was known, and the men were glad of that. The chow from the Iceberg's boxes was a hell of a lot better than lukewarm Air Force grub snatched up on the run. Cold beer wasn't on the menu, but soft drinks, great sandwiches, fruit, pastries, and pies were.

The news from the crew chief that the flight was delayed was easier to deal with on a full stomach. Mechanics were armpit deep inside of one of the four Pratt & Whitney TF33-P-7 turbofan pods on the C-141, and they looked busy to Rockham. Within a couple of hours the mechanics were satisfied and the Starlifter was ready to continue on its way.

The trip across the Atlantic was as uneventful as only a long distance military transport ride can be. It was going to be a long fifteen hours to cover the nearly 7,000 miles between the East Coast of the United States and the small island nation of Bahrain in the Persian Gulf.

With all of the other passengers aboard the aircraft, Rockham wasn't able to give his men even a short briefing on where they were going or what they were going to do when they got there. He didn't even know himself. There had not been a hell of a lot of information in that folder—just orders and priority authorizations for the unit. The only solid information he had was that they would meet further transportation in Bahrain.

With the priorities Rockham had in hand, he could commandeer anything the Navy had available. One thing was for sure: someone wanted them in the Gulf area, and they weren't going to be bumped from any transport before they got there.

The biggest thing that happened on the flight was when they took on a full load of fuel from a tanker out of Sigonella, Italy. The KC-135 Stratotanker met up with the C-141 somewhere over the middle of the Mediterranean. After a deep drink of aviation fuel, the KC-135 headed off to deal with other flights while the C-141 continued on its way.

Having been on this same flight twice before, Rockham and his men felt they could qualify for frequent-flier miles. But there wasn't any other class they could have upgraded to even if they'd been able. The Starlifter was built to move cargo and personnel in large amounts; it wasn't built for general comfort.

Rumor had it that there were some VIP modules built for the C-141 that made for comfortable traveling arrangements for high ranking officers and politicians. If such a thing did exist, you couldn't have proved it by Rockham or his men. They were almost literally rubbing shoulders with officers carrying stars on their shoulders. And the generals were riding in the same seats as the SEALs.

Comfort wasn't much of a problem for some members of the SMD. True to form, Wayne Alexander was sound asleep soon after the C-141 lifted its wheels off American soil. By the time they were far out over the Atlantic, Alexander was snoring loud enough to drown out the engine noise of the turbofans. He did wake up with a snort when Chief Monday broke out further examples of Ken Fleming's generosity and skill in the kitchen.

After crossing eight time zones and flying a third of the way around the world, the SEALs were back in the Persian Gulf. Running slower than their earlier flights had, it was fifteen hours after takeoff when the crew chief came around and told everyone to make sure their seat belts were secure for landing. The skies over the Persian

Gulf were busy, especially over the island nation of Bahrain. There was a huge airfield on the island, and a large portion of it had been turned over to air elements of the coalition forces.

It was early evening in Bahrain when the C-141 landed, 2130 hours local time, 1730 ZULU. The night before, the SEALs had been in the Nevada desert, and now they were on the far side of the planet from Nevada and at another desert.

"Man," said Ryan Marks, "back again."

"One of these days," Kurkowski said, "we're going to land at a neat desert oasis like the ones I've seen in the movies all my life."

"Hey, Kurkowski of Arabia," Alexander growled, "lend a hand here with the gear."

With his men seeing to the moving and securing of their equipment pallets, Rockham entered the busy military terminal to see if their contact had arrived. They still had a long way to go, and he was tired of traveling already. He didn't know quite what to expect; it was certainly not what he received.

"Are you Lieutenant Rockham?" a thickly accented voice drawled.

Rockham hadn't heard anyone with a Cajun accent like that since his last blowout in New Orleans. Turning, he saw a tall man in a naval aviator's flight suit, which was about the only military thing about him.

The alligator cowboy boots were an interesting touch, They went well with the mirrored aviator sunglasses hanging from a pocket flap. The big, tan Stetson hat just topped off the picture of someone who didn't look like they were in the same Navy as Rockham.

"Okay," Rockham said slowly, "I'm Rockham. And you are?"

"Lieutenant William Coudree at your service, sir," the man said as he tipped his Stetson back on his head. "I'm your ride out to the *Midway*—the carrier, not the island."

Oh, this is going to be lots of fun, Rockham thought.

"Let's go get your baggage sorted out and moved to your ride," Coudree said. "I've been cooling my heels here for hours waiting on you. I hope birds haven't nested in my engine by now."

"Sorry," Rockham said, "we were late getting out of the States."

"Just like the Air Force," Coudree said as he headed for the door. "They make even a simple transport run seem like the bombing of Berlin, and then they show up a day late and a dollar short. Oh well, can't be helped I suppose. I was just told to get you out to the *Midway* as soon as you showed up. Time to get going."

Trash-talking the Air Force didn't quite seem like the right thing to do in a military terminal filled with personnel from that particular branch of the service. But Coudree didn't seem like the kind of person to care much about what other people thought.

Rockham couldn't help but smile at the colorful pilot as he followed him out to the runway. When they got to the C-141, the rest of the SEALs already had their gear unloaded and organized off the flight line. The pallets were sitting next to the runway apron, while ground crews moved more materials off the big transport.

"Damnation," Coudree exclaimed, "you boys don't travel light, do you? Can't be helped I suppose. Hey, Chief Boyd! Drag your carcass over here."

In answer to Coudree's yell, a tall thin man in a flight suit walked toward them. Calling the man thin was being kind; cadaveric would have been closer to a proper description. He looked like a practice body for the unit's corpsmen. The flight suit hung from his bony frame like a wet paper bag. And if you went by the man's expression, it seemed the world was about to end.

"This is my crew chief, Chief Boyd," Coudree said. "Chief, these are the men we were told to fetch. Think you can get them and that pile of hardware on board fast?"

Taking a long, slow look at the men and their pallets of equipment, Chief Boyd studied the situation for what seemed a very long time. Finally, he nodded.

"Yup," he said.

"Great, then snap to it, Chief," Coudree said. "The sooner we get this all shoveled aboard, the sooner we can get back out over the water."

Coudree and Boyd headed off, making an interesting team to watch, Rockham thought.

"You have got to be kidding," Daugherty said. "These guys are going to fly us out to an aircraft carrier in the middle of the Persian Gulf? They don't look like they could organize a circle-jerk, let alone fly a plane. It's like they're some extras out of a bad military movie."

"I heard they were activating the reserves for operations here in the Gulf," Chief Monday said. "All kinds of reserves."

In spite of the odd impression the two men had left with the SEALs, they did work quickly and efficiently. A pair of forklifts ran up from where the two had disappeared in the gloom. Going up to the pallets, they scooped up the bulk of the SEALs' gear and turned away.

The forklifts went over to a boxy, high-winged aircraft that the SEALs knew well. It was a Grumman C-2 Greyhound, a little workhorse of a twin-engined plane. The prop-driven aircraft was used to transport men and material to and from Navy carriers all over the world. Their jobs gave them the names CODs, for carrier on-board delivery. The SMD had ridden on board the noisy planes before, and they were about to travel aboard one again.

CHAPTER 15

1905 ZULU
27° 40' North, 50° 48' East
Persian Gulf

The roughly hundred-mile flight to the USS *Midway* should only have taken about a half hour by the clock. If you had asked any of the SEALs on board the Greyhound flying out to the *Midway,* they would have told you the flight was much longer, much, much longer. For those men, that COD flight out to a U.S. Navy carrier took a few minutes longer than eternity.

It wasn't that the flight was particularly rough. Greyhounds were flying trucks, and they rode about as well as one. And the pilot was skilled at flying the bird. The SEALs never did meet the copilot, though they could see the back of his head from where he rode in the cockpit. They were pretty certain that the copilot was deaf, or wearing hearing protection.

What Lieutenant Coudree liked to do when he

flew was talk, and he talked a lot. The men of the SMD riding in the Greyhound were a captive audience, and they knew it.

From the moment the Greyhound completed its takeoff to the time they were on the deck of the *Midway*, Coudree kept up a nonstop barrage of opinion, historical fact, and observations on the geopolitical situation in the Middle East and elsewhere in the world. Over the PA system in the bird, he offered constant commentary on anything that popped into his head. None of the SEALs had ever met anyone who liked the sound of his own voice as much. The man would not shut up; Rockham wondered if he talked in his sleep.

As far as Chief Boyd was concerned, Rockham decided he must have heard everything before. No wonder the man had the expression of a clinically depressed basset hound. Chief Boyd sat near the cockpit of the Greyhound and leaned back in his seat with his eyes closed. Not even Wayne Alexander, who legend said could sleep through a collision alarm, managed to sleep on that COD flight.

Some of what Coudree related to the men was interesting historical information about the *Midway*. By the time they arrived at the carrier, the SEALs had learned that the carrier was built during World War II but was officially commissioned six days after the Japanese surrendered.

During Operation Sandy in 1947, the *Midway* had been the first ship in the world to launch a missile. A captured German V-2 rocket was test-fired from the flight deck. Later, in 1965, some of the first aircraft to fight MiGs over the skies of Vietnam had been launched from the *Midway*. Her planes had helped mine Haiphong and other North Vietnamese ports in 1972. And in 1975, as part of Operation Frequent Wind, the *Midway* evacuated hundreds of U.S. and Vietnamese personnel while Saigon fell to the Communist north.

More recently, the *Midway* had been part of Operation Imminent Thunder, an eight-day combined amphibious landing exercise in Saudi Arabia. Close to a thousand Marines were supported by sixteen ships and more than 1,100 aircraft during the landings that let Saddam Hussein know just what he was facing.

"Not only do we have one of the greatest fleets assembled since World War Two on hand for operations in the Gulf," Coudree said, "we have veterans of that war here as well. The last two active battleships on the ocean are not more than a few hundred miles from here. The battleships *Wisconsin* and *Missouri* are ready to knock Iraq back into its own desert. They're big, powerful, and the world is not likely to see anything like them again."

"You know, he just may be right about that," Daugherty said to Rockham.

"Right about what?" Rockham asked.

"That this may be the last use of battleships in combat," Daugherty said. "It must be something to call in fire from those nine sixteen-inch guns. Like the finger of God bringing fire down from the heavens."

"Okay guy," Rockham said, "you've been riding in this plane too long."

Ignoring Rockham's comment, Daugherty turned toward Chief Monday. "Hey, Chief," he said, "when you were in Vietnam, did you ever call in gunfire support from a battleship?"

"No," Monday said. "The *New Jersey* was long gone before I showed up in Vietnam. I did talk to some of the old hands from SEAL Team One who had been operating in I-Corps up near the demilitarized zone. They called in fire from White Horse—that was the call sign for the *New Jersey*. Said that when those sixteen-inchers finished rearranging the local geography, it was hard to tell there had ever been a target there in the first place."

Leaning back in his seat, Daugherty thought about what it may have been like for enemy troops undergoing a bombardment from shells that weighed as much as a medium-size car. It sounded like the Iraqis might soon be able to tell him just how that felt.

The rest of the men continued to listen to the pilot's nonstop lecture on the present situation in Kuwait and Iraq. As Coudree waxed on in his expressive way about Saddam Hussein's chances to survive the upcoming war, the pilot's own chances for living through the flight were the main topic of discussion among most of the SEALs.

"I don't care if we do crash," Alexander said, "I'm going to kill him if he doesn't shut up soon."

"You can't do that," Kurkowski said.

"Why?" Alexander asked. "It's not like it'll be a mutiny, more like a mercy killing."

"You can't kill him later," Kurkowski said, "because I'm going to kill him now."

"Knock off that kind of talk," Chief Monday growled. "None of you are going to do a damned thing. That is a commissioned Navy officer and gentleman. You will show him the respect due his rank. Is that completely understood?"

The men settled back in their seats with a grumpy nod or two.

"Besides," Monday said as he leaned back, "I'm going to kill him."

There was nothing below the plane but a whole lot of very dark Persian Gulf water as it flew through the night. A number of the SEALs entertained themselves discussing the finer points of killing a pilot and disposing of the body while in flight. These were very accomplished and highly trained men. If such an action were possible, they were the ones who could do it. It was for the best of all concerned that Coudree went into his final speech at that moment.

"I heard that you SEALs joined the Navy to see some adventure. You like living on the edge, jumping out of planes, swimming in the oceans, blowing crap up and shooting off guns. Well, let me introduce you all to one of the scariest things you can do in the Navy—a night carrier landing under combat conditions. That means not much in the way of lights, gentlemen."

There was only one small porthole in the door in the side of the aircraft, and none of the SEALs particularly wanted to look through it. Looking forward and seeing what they could through the front windscreen was bad enough.

In the dark waters of the Gulf, far ahead of them was the phosphorescent glow of the wake of the *Midway*, as she steamed through the calm sea. The flight deck of the carrier was almost a thousand feet long—979 feet exactly, according to Coudree—and that seemed like a very small target to land a plane on. The fact that there were jets crowding the flight deck and other activities going on made their upcoming landing look positively suicidal.

It was too late to dig out and distribute the parachutes from one of the pallets. The only action available was riding out the landing. It was a good thing Coudree was as good as such a colorful character had to be in order to survive the Navy, Rockham thought. If he hadn't been that good, the white-knuckled SEALs on the Greyhound would have seen to it that he didn't survive the flight.

"You know, Shaun," Rockham said as the engines of the plane wound down. "Someone ought to write this guy down. He'd make a hell of a character in a book."

"Nope," Shaun Daugherty said. "No one would ever believe him."

"Stay in your seats until we get belowdecks," Coudree called over the intercom.

While the SEALs sat impatiently, the activity around them on the deck of the carrier ran like the very practiced machine that it was. The deck of an operating aircraft carrier had been described as the most dangerous workplace on earth. None of the SEALs wanted to test out this description, so they stayed buckled in as the plane was moved by the deck crew.

The wings of the C-2A Greyhound folded up at a joint just outboard of the engines. Folding up the wings changed the maximum width of the aircraft from over eighty feet to less than thirty. Moved to the huge starboard lift just behind the island, the command structure rising up above the flight deck on the right side of the carrier, the Greyhound was lowered down into the ship.

The lift was a massive elevator that brought planes up or back down to the lower hangar decks. Once there, the SEALs heard the last bit of talk from their pilot over the intercom when he told them to unlatch their seat belts and get ready to leave the plane.

"Don't have to jump off this one," Coudree said with a smile.

Out on the busy hangar deck, the SEALs were quickly met by a harried-looking young ensign. Ensigns—insultingly known as "enswines" to some—were the lowest officer there was, and they invariably got handed the worst jobs. It was the fastest way to learn about the actual running and layout of a Navy ship. It was also some of the hardest duty time a person could pull in the Navy.

"Ensign McDermott, sir," the young blond-haired officer said. "You're the SEAL unit we were told to expect?"

"I hope so," Rockham said. "Otherwise we made a long trip to the wrong place."

"Yes, sir," McDermott said. "I'm to escort you and your men to one of the pilots' briefing rooms. There's a crew of deckhands here to help you move your gear to the compartment you've been assigned."

"Chief," Rockham said as he turned to Monday.

"Kurkowski, Bryant," Chief Monday said as he turned to the men, "stay with the gear. Make sure everything is properly secured and stowed away. We'll send someone back to bring you to the briefing."

Traveling through the interior compartments and passageways of an aircraft carrier can be one of the most difficult and confusing trips a sailor can make. Ensign McDermott led the SEALs through the maze of passageways and up and down ladders until they arrived at a well-appointed briefing room.

There were two other officers in the front of the room, discussing something in low voices as the SEALs filed in. McDermott excused himself and left to see what he could do about bringing Bryant and Kurkowski to the proper compartment. The SEALs moved up to the front of the room and stood next to the green-upholstered, padded chairs normally used by pilots and crews prior to flying a sortie from the ship.

"Good evening, Lieutenant," the taller of the two officers said as he shook hands with Rockham and Daugherty in turn. "I'm Lieutenant Commander House. This is one of our intelligence officers, Lieutenant Bickman."

"How do you do, sir," Rockham said as he shook hands with both men.

"Please, have your men sit down," House said. "We have some things to go over. It's not much, and as soon as we get things over with, you and your men can grab some chow before you prep your gear."

Things were moving very fast, even for a SEAL operation, Rockham thought. They were supposed to get a briefing, a minimal one by the sounds of things, and then prep their gear?

"Okay, here's the skinny," House said. "We've got a pair of Marine CH-53 Sea Stallions up forward on the flight deck waiting to take you and your men to a location about seventy-five miles northwest of where we are presently. There you are to meet up with another unit that will be taking you further.

"The pilots of the helicopters were chosen because of their experience taking in Force Recon units. They can set you down right on the water and let you and your men drive your boats out the back of the birds."

"Yes sir," Rockham said, "that's a swamp duck technique. We've used it operationally before. But where are we going and what are we expected to do when we get there?"

"Lieutenant," Lieutenant Bickman said as he stepped forward, "we just don't have an answer for that question. We have been kept in the dark about just what is going on, and quite frankly, we aren't used to all of this cloak-and-dagger business. What we do have is a package of briefing material for you and your men. Neither Commander House or myself know what's in the package, and basically, we don't want to know."

"Things are getting very hot around here," House said, "and I'm not talking about the temperature. Congress is supposed to vote tomorrow on backing President Bush if he decides to use force against Iraq. Well, we're here to project that force. The captain and exec are working round-the-clock with the rest of the Persian Gulf group to make sure operations go through as planned.

"We have been ordered to assist you and your men by whatever means are available to us. We're doing that. But this is a conventional ship with a conventional mission, one it's been following since before any of us even thought about joining the Navy. We are not prepared to conduct unconventional operations to the detriment of our prior commitments.

"Chow has been put on for your men if they wish it. You have the use of this briefing room for as long as you need it. Compartments commensurate with your needs have been assigned to you. Gasoline and other supplies are ready for when you want them. Other than that, gentlemen, I leave you to your own devices."

Bickman came up to Rockham and asked him to sign a receipt for a thick package. These were the briefing materials that Rockham was to take with him on his rendezvous at sea with an unknown asset. A second much thinner envelope held the information he needed to carry out his present orders and what he needed to have with him to carry out his mission.

That was it, a set of orders that didn't list a specific objective, a list of equipment, and a timetable. This was not the way that Rockham was used to operating either. The hostility of the carrier officer to a bunch of SEALs arriving on his ship and disrupting his normal routine was something he'd seen before and would probably see again. Not everyone in the Services, not just the Navy, realized the value of Special Operations personnel and the missions they performed. Right now, Rockham knew it wasn't his responsibility to teach those people the error of their thinking.

"Okay," he said to the men, when House and Bickman had left, "I think he made his opinion clear. Now, we've got a lot to do and not much time to do it in. The only real information we have is where we're going and what we're supposed to bring with us. By the looks of these orders, they want us to be ready to do just about anything except jump from an airplane."

A knock at the compartment hatch interrupted Rockham. Mike Ferber opened the door to see Ensign McDermott standing there along with Bryant and Kurkowski.

"Your men had finished up so I brought them here for you," McDermott said. "And a mess steward is bringing down a fresh pot of coffee and some sandwiches."

"Thank you, Mr. McDermott," Rockham said. "You've been a big help."

"Thank you, sir," McDermott said, and he closed the hatch to the compartment.

"Makes you feel like you've successfully house-broke the puppy, doesn't it?" Monday said.

"Hey, at least he's acting like he really is on our side," Ferber said. "Commander House gave me the impression that we were intruding on the real Navy."

"Takes all kinds," Rockham said. "Did your men get everything squared away?"

"Yes," Kurkowski said. "We've got a pretty good-sized compartment assigned to us right off the hangar deck. It's an easy move to get our gear in and out of the place. Here's the keys to the compartment. The chief who was running the deck gang said they're the only set outside of the captain's safe."

"Our ordnance is stowed a short ways aft of the compartment and down a deck," Bryant said, "in the number four starboard magazine."

"Is there enough room in the compartment to rig up the Zodiacs for a swamp duck?" Rockham asked.

"Sure," Kurkowski said. "But we'll have to do them one at a time."

"That shouldn't be a problem," Rockham said. "We load up one boat at a time and run them up to the flight deck. I'm going to meet with the pilots right now and see just how up on the insertion technique they really are."

"I'll bet Ensign McDermott can find them for you," Bryant said. "He's trying as hard as he can to be helpful."

"Hopefully, he won't be too hard to find," Rockham said.

"How much do you want to bet he's within earshot of the hatch?" Monday said.

"No bet, Chief," Rockham said with a laugh. "I wouldn't be surprised if he's sitting in the passageway right outside this compartment. Think he wants a recommendation for BUD/S?"

CHAPTER 16

★★★★

Unlike the higher ranking Navy officers aboard
the *Midway,* Rockham was pleasantly surprised
when he met the crews of the Marine CH-53D Sea
Stallion helicopters that we're going to insert the
SMD at their rendezvous point. Both pilots were
experienced with the needs of special operations,
having worked for years with the Marine Force
Recon units.

Marine Captains Robert Dayton and Wyatt Angels had logged hundreds of hours flying their respective birds. They knew the capabilities of the
helicopters and the needs of the SEALs. For the
first time since arriving in the Persian Gulf theater
of war, Rockham felt that something was going
right.

A lot of the SMD's gear was going to be left behind on the *Midway.* There wouldn't be enough

room on board the two Zodiac F-470 rubber
boats for the SEALs and all of their equipment.
When asked for storage space, Lieutenant Commander House was slow to respond. Finally, he
gave permission for the SEALs to leave all of their
extra gear in the compartment that had been assigned to them. The keys to the room now lay secured in House's hands.

The last detail to attend to on the carrier was to
fill up the fuel tanks for the Zodiacs. Chief Monday carefully checked each fuel container to ensure that it was filled and then properly mixed
with oil, one pint of lubricant to every six gallons
of gasoline. Two eighteen-gallon fuel bladders
and a six-gallon backup gas can went into each
rubber boat to power the fifty-five horsepower
outboard motors attached to the transoms. Packed
in among all of the other gear was a single spare
thirty-five horsepower outboard in case one of the
bigger motors broke down.

The drop point for the SEALs' Zodiacs was almost in the center of the northern Persian Gulf.
They would be more than seventy miles from the
coast of Saudi Arabia, just to the east of the Mar-
jan oil field. It wasn't a hell of a lot farther to occupied Kuwait; only a hundred miles or so away.
If whoever they were meeting up with showed up
late or not at all, Rockham wanted each boat to
have enough fuel to get them back to friendly
shores.

Riding up on the big starboard lift, Rockham
and his men brought the boats up fully laden with
gear. The ten-man F470 Zodiacs were over fifteen

feet long and more than six feet wide. The twenty-inch diameter of the inflated tubes that made up the sides of the Zodiacs reduced the interior size of the boats to only about eleven by three feet. It would be crowded for the nine-man squad and all of their gear inside of one of the boats.

To increase the available room inside of the Zodiacs, the SEALs would ride the boats straddling the tubes, literally sitting on the sides of the boats. Only the coxswains would sit squarely in the back of the boats to drive them along.

The piles of gear in the center of the boats made them heavy and unwieldy to move across the flight deck of the *Midway*. Moving heavy rubber boats was something every SEAL did almost from the first moment of arriving at BUD/S. Every member of the SMD had his own memories of moving heavy rubber boats across the beaches and up and down the sand dunes at Coronado. Carrying the heavy loads of the Zodiacs plus all of their gear was something they were used to.

The pilots of the two Sea Stallions had no trouble getting the SEALs and their gear properly loaded aboard. Wearing their wet suits, the SEALs filed aboard the birds. This was going to be a low-level insertion of the boat, with the helicopters flying just a few feet above the water. After some discussion of the situation, both Rockham and the helicopter pilots had decided that a soft-duck insertion would be better than the originally planned swamp duck.

In a swamp duck insertion, the helicopters would have set down on the water and allowed the Zodiacs to be floated out the back of the birds, through their open rear decks. The soft duck drop would be much faster and leave the helicopters less exposed, drawing less attention from any nearby observers.

For a soft duck insertion, the inflated Zodiac with its gear secured on board would be pushed from the back of the Sea Stallion while the helicopter was just a few feet off the water and moving slowly. Once the boat was in the water, the SEALs would jump off the helicopter and recover it.

Flying along the dark waters of the Persian Gulf, Rockham was thinking about all the things that could go wrong on an operation, and how his men had trained for hours to be certain they did things right. Mr. Murphy was always riding along no matter what they did, and he would take advantage of the slightest mistake to help screw things up royally.

"Coming up on the drop coordinates," Captain Angels said over the intercom. "Target in sight."

Looking out the forward viewscreen, Rockham could see a glowing red light, a burning flare, on the waters ahead. There were no major ships in sight, just the burning red signal. Over his radio, Captain Angels received confirmation that this was indeed the signal they were expecting. The SEALs had arrived at the party, and they would soon finally meet whoever the hell their hosts were.

"Thank you for flying with the Angels," Captain Angels said. "See you on the flip-flop." The truckers' CB reference caused Rockham to grin as his men lined up at the open tail gate. The boat was pushed out and went down into the dark. Only the glow of the activated chem lights attached to the hull showed where the boat had landed. When the boat exited the helicopter, the SEALs quickly followed it off the ramp. Holding onto their swim fins and face masks, they jumped into the darkness and the water only a few feet below.

As the waters of the Gulf closed over their heads, the pilots of the heavy Sea Stallion helicopters twisted open the throttles to their turboshaft engines. With a loud roar, the Sea Stallions climbed and turned for the trip back to their ship.

Bubbles streamed off the SEALs as they sank down several feet after jumping from the helicopters. Bending over, the men pulled on their swim fins and then headed for the surface. The Zodiacs were close at hand for each squad, the two groups of men having hit the water less than fifty yards from each other.

Swimming to their boats, both squads scrambled aboard, slipping their legs over the inflated tubes. Ed Lopez moved to the back of the first squad's Zodiac and primed the outboard for starting. A few pulls on the cord and the well-maintained engine burped and purred to life.

Over in the second squad's boat, Henry Lutz was having a little more trouble starting up the engine. He squeezed the priming bulb on the fuel line and pulled the primer on the engine. After a couple of hard pulls on the starter, the outboard burst into life.

Thankful, they wouldn't have a long session of paddling ahead of them. Second squad headed out after first squad's Zodiac. Both boats were zeroed in on the single black boat that could be seen a few hundred feet away, one person in the boat still holding up a burning red flare.

The eerie red glow of the flare cast a flickering light over the water, illuminating the floating rubber boat enough to show that there were two people in it. As Rockham and his men drew closer, they could see the two figures were also dressed in black, just as the SEALs were.

"So, I wondered when you guys would manage to get here," came a voice over the water.

"Cleveland," Rockham called out. The man sounded familiar to Rockham but he just couldn't place the voice. Playing it safe with the challenge he had been told to use was the best policy.

"Indians," came the proper countersign. "Like you expected to meet someone else out here?"

Lopez moved the Zodiac closer to the other boat, as Rockham motioned him to. In the light of the flare, Rockham could make out the man's face. He wore the same kind of wet suit as Rockham and his men did and held the burning flare up in his right hand. The face looked familiar as a smile spread across it.

"Sam?" Rockham said, recognizing the man holding the flare. "Sam Paulson?"

"The one and only," Paulson said. "At least the only one I know playing the Statue of Liberty holding up her torch in the middle of the Persian Gulf."

"Is that you, Mr. Paulson?" Ed Lopez said from his coxswain's position at the back of the Zodiac.

"Lopez?" Paulson said with an even bigger smile on his face. "Hey, *que pasa,* amigo? Still driving those lazy Team guys around, I see. When are you finally going to just make them get out and swim?"

As Paulson tossed his burning Mark 13 day/night flare overboard, Rockham stared at the other SEAL for a moment. Sam Paulson had been one of the officers crewing a SEAL Delivery Vehicle carried on board the *Archerfish,* the nuclear submarine Rockham and Fourth Platoon of SEAL Team Two had used nearly two years before on their mission into Russia. He had been the navigator for a Mark 8 SDV. The driver of that same SDV was Ed Lopez.

Both men had been badly injured in an incident where the submarine had struck a sandbar. Ed Lopez had broken his arm, the jagged end of the bone slicing through the skin and artery. Only the fast action of a Teammate who was not as badly hurt had saved Lopez from bleeding to death. The Latino SEAL would carry the scar on his lower left arm for the rest of his life.

Having been inside the SDV running an equipment check during the collision, Sam Paulson had smashed his face against the control panel. Shattering his cheekbone and breaking his jaw, the SEAL ensign had been forced out of any active part in the mission. For Paulson, only a bump on his face remained from what had been a very spectacular and colorful bruise.

Though the cost to the SEAL detachment in terms of injuries had been bad, the results of Operation Endurance were well worth it. The mission resulted in the recovery of a defecting Soviet bioweapons scientist and the penetration of a secret weapons testing site on a Soviet island near the Arctic Circle. It was because of the series of inoculations that the SEALs and every man aboard the *Archerfish* had received that the men of Fourth Platoon were chosen to make up the new Special Materials Detachment.

When Rockham was going through the files of the men involved in that deep penetration mission, he couldn't find any information on the whereabouts of Ensign Sam Paulson. Coming up to that same man in a rubber boat a hundred miles from anywhere was not where Rockham expected to run into the other SEAL.

"This is my coxswain, George Weaver," Paulson said. "We call him Kahuna."

The other man in Paulson's boat bent a plastic chem light and shook the tube to activate it. In the bright white glow of the chem light, Rockham could make out the face of a very big Polynesian-looking individual also wearing a wet suit.

"Big Kahuna on occasion," said the six-foot-tall dark-skinned Hawaiian.

"Glad to meet you both," Rockham said. "Now just what in the hell are we doing out here in the middle of nowhere?"

"Why, getting our ride of course," Paulson said.

Reaching into a pouch on his belt, Paulson pulled out a pair of pyrotechnic devices. They consisted of little more than an M60 fuse igniter, an inch or so of time fuse, and a large firecracker, the whole thing held together with waterproof tape. Also held by the tape was what looked like a large metal bolt.

First pulling the safety pins from the igniters, then yanking on the pull rings that had been secured by the safety pins, Paulson ignited the fuse train of the devices. Then he tossed them overboard, where they immediately sank. Seconds later all of the SEALs felt and heard a hard pair of thumps transmitted through the bottoms of their boats as the firecrackers went off.

What Paulson had tossed overboard were two underwater signals, the same kind used during dives by the SEALs all over the world. The thumping bangs of the firecrackers could be heard a long way underwater, even through a ship's steel hull if it was close enough.

There was a ship close enough, even though the men of the SMD didn't know it. Breaking the surface, the water hissed as it flowed around the top section of a periscope rising up almost a hundred feet from the three Zodiacs. This finally made sense to the men of the SMD. A submarine was the only thing they could rendezvous with at sea and not have anything visible above the surface. But why the heavy secrecy? They had been on subs before, and always knew beforehand which one they would be working with—if not the name, at least the type. But the submarine rising up from the water was not one they could have ever possibly expected.

As the periscope rose higher into the air, the mast for an SS-2 radar system broke the surface and came up. Then a thick pipe shaft appeared as the rest of the fittings on a submarine sail came into view above the surface. As the sub moved forward slowly, she continued to surface. Only about ten feet of the twenty-foot-tall sail had come above the water before the massive bow broke through the waves.

"Holy shit!" Daugherty exclaimed. "I do not believe it."

"Neither do I," Chief Monday said. "I've never seen a ghost ship before."

"A ghost ship?" Mainhart said. "What the hell are you talking about?"

None of the men said another word as the big submarine completed surfacing and came to a complete stop a few dozen yards away. Over three hundred feet long, it had a huge, bulbous nose section that made up almost a third of the ship's length.

"What is that thing?" Mainhart said. "I've never seen a submarine like that. Is that a U.S. ship?"

There was a big smile on Sam Paulson's face as he looked at the two boats full of dumbfounded SEALs.

"You haven't seen another ship like her because she's the only one of her kind," Chief Monday said.

"Not quite," Paulson said. "There's a sister ship,

the *Growler*, that's been tied up to a dock in New York as a museum and tourist attraction for the last couple of years. But the *Grayback* came first."

"But what is that thing?" Mainhart said in exasperation.

"That's the *Grayback*," Chief Monday said. "LPSS 574. I worked off of her back in the 1970s when I was with UDT 12 in the Philippines."

"Okay, so it's an old sub type," Mainhart said. "What's the big deal? It looks like a diesel-electric boat to me, and an obsolete experimental one at that."

"Oh, she's a diesel-electric boat," Daugherty said. "But I don't know if obsolete is the right word. You see, the *Grayback* was decommissioned and sunk as a target in the South China Sea on thirteen April 1986. That ship has been listed as destroyed for almost five years now. She was an obsolete specialized design by the 1980s."

"I wonder if April thirteenth was a Friday," Kurkowski said.

"No, it was on a weekend," said John Grant, "a Sunday, I think."

"She looks pretty damned good for a sunken hulk if you ask me," Kurkowski said.

With Paulson in the lead, the rubber boats headed to the ghost ship now at a full stop on the surface. Not quite fully surfaced, the deck of the submarine was just awash and barely above the waves. A deck crew was coming up from the sub's hatches, and the huge clamshell door on the left side of the bow began to rise and open.

The crewmen all worked silently, only saying

the minimum they had to in order to direct the
SEALs. All of the men were wearing normal blue
submariner's coveralls, but none of them wore
name tags, rank insignia, or even the much cov-
eted gold dolphins worn by qualified submariners.
You couldn't even tell if these men were in the
same Navy as Rockham and his SEALs.

There were two round hatches, domed
clamshell doors, on either side of the huge bow of
the submarine. The *Grayback* had been a Regulus
missile-carrying ship built in the mid-1950s.
Commissioned in 1958, it was intended to carry
the nuclear-tipped Regulus II missile as part of the
nuclear deterrent forces of the United States Navy.

The Regulus II was a large-winged guided missile that would now be referred to as a cruise missile. A complement of the missiles would be
carried underwater, sealed in the two bow hangars
of the *Grayback*. In case of war, the submarine
would surface, and a missile backed out of a bow
hangar on a wheeled trolley following a set of
tracks in the sub's deck. With the wings attached,
the missile could be launched against a target
more than, 1,100 statute miles away.

When the Polaris missile replaced the Regulus
as the premier submarine nuclear weapon in the
early 1960s, the *Grayback* was decommissioned.
After an extensive refit in 1967–68 that also extended her overall length by twelve feet, the *Grayback* had a new mission: to transport up to
sixty-seven SEALs or amphibious troops in her
new troop spaces. The huge bow hangars that
could be reached from inside the submarine while

she was underwater had been converted to transport SDVs or rubber boats. The starboard hangar had a divers' decompression chamber installed as part of the new sub's mission equipment.

With the development of the dry deck shelters—removable chambers that could be attached to a nuclear submarine's hatches and transport an SDV underwater—the *Grayback*'s useful life seemed to have come to an end. She had been decommissioned in 1984 and sent on her final dive in 1986. Whatever might be sitting on the floor of the South China Sea, however, certainly wasn't the ship floating in front of the SEALs in the middle of the Persian Gulf in early 1991.

With the help of the deck crew, the three Zodiacs were pulled up on the deck of the *Grayback* and moved into the port bow hangar. Fuel bladders and tanks from the two Zodiacs of the SMD were taken out and secured in a compartment on the deck of the sub. The men all moved quickly and efficiently. The laden rubber boats were stacked inside the bow hangar, and the SEALs entered alongside their boats. The twelve-foot-diameter clamshell hatch slowly closed under hydraulic power, shutting the SEALs inside the hangar.

Red lights were on inside, to illuminate the eleven-foot-tall, seventy-foot-long cylinder. The red lights gave enough light to see and operate by, while still protecting the night vision of the operators inside the compartment. As the SEALs moved themselves and the gear from the rubber boats forward in the hangar, they felt the deck tilt and vibrate beneath them.

"The captain didn't want to stay on the surface any longer than he had to," Paulson said. "The world thinks this ship is dead, and we don't intend correcting that fact."

Who's we? thought Rockham as he went through the hatch in the front deck of the hangar compartment. This was an unknown ghost ship with a nonexistent crew. Who was in charge of this party, and why were he and his men invited?

CHAPTER 17

★★★★

Once on board the *Grayback*, Rockham was looking forward to finally getting a mission-specific briefing on the upcoming operation. There was no question that they were going against the Iraqis, either in occupied Kuwait or inside Iraq itself. Operating against Iran was a possibility, but a remote one since they seemed to be heading away from Iran, which bordered the eastern shores of the Persian Gulf. No, they were probably going to operate against Iraqi interests. But what was the target?

Inside the *Grayback*, the SEALs found themselves in the forward torpedo room. The area was crowded with heavy Mark 48 torpedoes in racks lined up to be loaded into the six forward twenty-one-inch tubes. Among the blunt-nosed shapes of the Mark 48 fish were the deadly encased shapes of A/R/UGM-84D Harpoon missiles. The *Gray-back* may have been an older submarine, but she packed a modern punch. The Harpoon missiles were turbojet-driven cruise missiles that could be launched from a normal torpedo tube.

The first part of a Harpoon flight would be propelled by the rocket that drove it to the surface and up into the open air. Then the turbojet engine would take over to push the missile to speeds over six hundred miles an hour. At Mach 0.85, the Harpoon would take less than six minutes to reach its maximum range of fifty-seven miles. In that short time, it could strike a target with a 450-pound high explosive warhead.

The *Grayback* was well-equipped to be a force projector over a long distance on the water or into the land. Placards hanging from the polished bronze breeches of the torpedo tubes said in bright red letters WARSHOT LOADED, indicating just how ready the *Grayback* was to send that force out and against the enemy.

"The men can handle bringing down your gear and stowing it," Paulson said to Rockham and Daugherty. "Any problems they have, the crew will be glad to help them with things. The captain wanted me to bring you to him as soon as you were on board, so please follow me."

The passage back toward the stern of the submarine went through the crowded torpedo room and then into the forward living spaces compartment. The old missile control and checkout area had come next, but after the conversion of the *Grayback* to a transport submarine, that area was now for use of troops and their officers who brought on board. Besides the living arrangements for the eighty-four enlisted men and officers of the *Grayback*'s compliment, she had berthing and messing facilities for an additional sixty enlisted men and seven officers.

The big ship was crowded with equipment, pipes, conduits, and machinery—all operated or maintained by the quiet men in blue coveralls. In the next compartment aft, Rockham and Daugherty found themselves in the control room. Though not wearing any insignia of rank, the captain of the *Grayback* was an easy man to identify.

"Come to course two-nine-eight degrees, full ahead," Captain Archie Schneller called out. "Run her on the snorkel and charge the batteries. We still have some hours of darkness ahead of us, let's make the best use of them we can."

"Helm, make your course two-nine-eight degrees," Jack Brown, the executive officer repeated, "full ahead."

"Two-nine-eight degrees, aye sir," answered the helmsman at his post behind a large control yoke.

"Engine room answers full ahead, sir," Brown repeated back to Schneller. "Making turns for seventeen knots, batteries are charging."

"Mr. Paulson," Schneller said, "I assume these are some of our passengers, Lieutenants Rockham and Daugherty?"

"Yes, sir," Paulson said. "Their men are getting situated up forward."

"Outstanding," Schneller said. "Gentlemen,

would you please accompany me to our wardroom. Cookie will have some of his excellent coffee available for us. I'm certain you have a lot of
questions to ask, and we don't have a hell of a lot
of time to answer them in."

Following the captain back through the control
room, the four men went down along the passageway until Schneller turned and opened a hatch
into the wardroom. The hatchway was closed
with a simple wooden door, which Paulson shut
behind him. The wood-paneled room was small,
with most of the space taken up by a long table
down the center of the compartment. The table
was bolted to the deck, as were the eight chairs
lining the sides and both ends of the table.

"Please, take a seat," Captain Schneller said,
sitting down at the head of the table, the end near-
est the hatchway. "Feel free to help yourselves to
coffee."

There was a large coffee service at the far, aft
end of the wardroom. Daugherty got up and
poured two cups, one for himself and the other
for Rockham, as Paulson and Schneller shook
their heads at his offer of a cup.

"As you have probably guessed," Schneller
said, "this submarine is not exactly part of the
regular Navy."

"The secrecy surrounding our rendezvous with
this boat pretty well demonstrated that," Rockham said. "Not even our briefing officers knew
what we were going to be meeting up with, let
alone what kind of ship she might be."

"That was because only a handful of people in

the Navy even know that the *Grayback* exists anymore," Schneller said. "And we intend on keeping things that way for a long as possible."

"Who intends?" Rockham said directly.

"The same people who eventually give you your directions," Schneller said. "The Central Intelligence Agency. This boat had very unique capabilities, and there wasn't much chance of her like ever being built again. The Agency saved her from destruction, and the way they did it convinced the world that the *Grayback* no longer existed.

"She did make that dive into the South China Sea. But it was another submarine, lying in wait in the same area, that was finally put on the bottom. That boat was wrecked so there would be the proper magnetic signatures, oil slicks, and debris floating up to show that the *Grayback* was truly destroyed. Then she was moved to a secret facility in the Philippines and given a refit . . . or enough of a refit to move her to safe quarters at another location.

"Now, she's in a position to conduct very secret and clandestine operations for the CIA. Her maintenance comes from what you might call private funds, CIA cover businesses that actually do turn a profit. The money has to be used somewhere. Crews are volunteers recruited from the Navy after a very careful screening process. And damned few outsiders are ever told about her existence. She's officially off the books, which makes her clandestine operations even harder for the wrong people to find out about."

"The Agency is still smarting over the losses

due to spies inside of our own Navy ranks and elsewhere," Paulson said. "When Ron Pelton at the NSA sold secrets to the Soviets, he did an incredible amount of damage to the U.S. intelligence efforts. Some of those efforts uncovered operations being conducted by clandestine Navy subs operating inside of Soviet waters. Ships were almost lost, along with their crews, because of the treason of just one man. The secrecy of this ship's existence helps prevent that situation from happening again.

"Plus, she has a few capabilities of her own that make her very valuable," Paulson went on. "Those forward hangars give the *Grayback* the ability to lock men and equipment in or out at depth. With the hyperbaric chamber in the starboard hangar compartment, we can support extensive diving operations while still having a second chamber to conduct lockouts and recoveries. You'll remember that when we recovered the bioweapon from Morzhovets Island, we lost the use of the DDS when Captain North had us seal the weapon inside her hyperbaric chamber."

"Then there's just the characteristics of a diesel-electric submarine," Captain Schneller said. "This is a very quiet type of submarine. While running submerged on our electric motors, we make less noise then a nuke boat. Even the newest attack submarines have to work to be as quiet as a boat like ours. And the *Grayback* was designed to be able to bottom the hull and still run her machinery. Her seawater inlets and exhausts are all above the keel. We could sit on the bottom and make like a hole in the water until our batteries gave out—and that would take a while."

"Hey, you don't have to sell me on the boat," Rockham said. "My platoon chief operated from her in the Philippines in the 1970s. He had nothing but good stories about his times on the *Grayback*. My only real question is, why are we on this boat, right here and right now?"

"We have a priority mission for you and your men," Schneller said. "One that particularly fits your skills and especially your experience.

"There are no other submarines operating in the Persian Gulf right now. Neither Iran or Iraq have submarine assets in their respective navies. Iran had a midget submarine program, but that went belly up sometime last year when they couldn't get their North Korean boat to work. So we pretty much have this whole gulf to ourselves, aside from a big chunk of the U.S. fleet also sharing these waters.

"General Schwarzkopf is gearing up for what looks to be the biggest land battle since World War Two. All coalition, naval, Air Force, Army, and Marine assets are preparing for a major air campaign to start sometime next week. Schwarzkopf doesn't have the assets or the inclination to spend what he does have looking for weapons of mass destruction—nuclear, chemical, or biological—in spite of the fact that he takes their threat very seriously.

"On the other hand, searching out those kinds

of weapons are exactly why we're here in the Gulf. And we have a very credible report of just where some of those weapons are.

"You know about Saddam's program of extending the range of his Soviet-supplied Scud missiles. Those missiles are probably the most serious political threat in the Gulf region. If he launches against Israel, the coalition of countries President Bush has put together could crumble. If chemical or biological weapons fall on Israeli soil, it will be next to impossible to keep them out of the war. Israel joins in the fighting, and the Arab contingents of the coalition forces will be gone that same day. And if he gasses the Israelis, memories of the Holocaust will make it impossible for their people to stay out of the war.

"This operation was put together to help prevent this war from escalating to the use of weapons of mass destruction. A number of pieces of information came together to point the finger at a high-value maritime target for you and your men. I've been authorized by the Deputy Director of Operations of the CIA in Langley to give you a full briefing on the background for this mission.

"Last week, there was an eyewitness report about a shipment from a suspected Iraqi bioweapons production facility. The material came from a location known as Project 600 and given the cover identity of being a baby milk factory. As part of the cover story, some milk-processing equipment was installed in the factory, but there has been no evidence of so much as a pint of baby formula coming out of the place. The facility is surrounded by a high dirt berm and a concrete wall. There are manned anti-aircraft emplacements inside the factory compound as well as round-the-clock armed sentry patrols. This is the most secure and well-protected baby food plant in the world. Gerber doesn't do this well, and they actually crank out baby food.

"The thinking at Langley is that the Iraqis don't place all that high a value on baby formula. So they gave this plant a priority for penetration and study. Attempts have been made to get inside the site, but that's all I have here. The eyewitness was a local intelligence asset who had been put in place to observe the Project 600 target.

"When a convoy of trucks left the Project 600 compound last week, they were carrying covered cargoes and were under heavy military escort. The bulk of the vehicles left the area heading west. We've confirmed that they later arrived at the Muhammadiyat weapons depot in central Iraq. That location is a confirmed Iraqi chemical weapons storage facility.

"One truck from that convoy didn't head west. Along with its own military escort, it headed east on Highway 10, in toward Baghdad itself. The asset in place decided to follow that truck. It never arrived in the city. Instead, it stopped at a railhead near a place called Daura, just southwest of Baghdad. There, the truck was loaded on board a military train heading south on the Baghdad-Basra branch of the Iraqi State Railway. The military escort went along with the truck, but the asset managed to catch a glimpse of the truck's cargo while they were securing it to the flatcar.

"According to the report, the wind flipped up a tarp covering the bed of the truck while it was being tied down. The contents were described as being two round coffinlike metal containers. They were bolted together at flanges running around a central seam and were about six feet long and more than two feet thick.

"The analysts say that description would fit a warhead shipping container for the al-Hussein missile. They've been keeping an eye out for just such a container since your mission last year. It wasn't until your men took down that ship off the coast of Sudan and did a hands-on examination of an al-Hussein missile that it was confirmed to have a removable warhead. That makes loading and storing a chemical or biological warhead a much more practical proposition."

"But the missiles we found didn't have any kind of warhead at all," Rockham said. "We never found any containers of the type you say this asset described."

"Other sources have been able to confirm the containers and supply us with a description," Schneller explained. "It was a lot easier for them once they knew what to look for. And there were other aspects of this shipment that raised everyone's red flags.

"First of all, it wasn't just any military unit escorting that truck. You don't have a lot of troops even in an oil-rich country like Baghdad driving around in late model Mercedes-Benz cars. But those were what the escorts were driving. Tags on the bumpers of the cars noted by the asset were able to help us identify the unit. They were from the 1st Division of the 1st Brigade of the Special Republican Guards. That's Saddam Hussein's personal Palace Guard. Consider them kind of an insane secret service.

"That unit only guards the highest value sites, usually those used by Saddam himself. They also escort his personal motorcade, and sometimes those of other very high-ranking Iraqi officials. These are not the kind of troops put on a punishment detail to follow around a civilian truck. The only way they would be on the job is if Saddam himself ordered them to, and he would only do that if the truck was transporting something very valuable to him.

"The train the truck was loaded onto was kept under surveillance as long as a satellite was overhead. It turned out there was a hell of a lot more on that train than just general military supplies and vehicles. Some of the flatcars were carrying covered cargoes; one was transporting a very large covered cargo.

"Photo intel analyzed the pictures of the train and have identified what was hidden on one of those flatcars. The only thing in the Iraqi military that fits the size and shape is a MAZ-543 transporter/erector/launcher—TEL for short. The launching platform for a Scud missile."

"We're familiar with that item," Rockham said. "It was part of our intelligence briefing on the op last year. I've never seen one up close, but I know how big the damn thing is."

"It's even bigger with an extended-range al-

Hussein missile mounted in place," Schneller said. "And the fact that the Iraqis are moving even one of them south is a very bad thing for the coalition troops. Iraq hasn't put one into the air yet, but they won't wait long to launch after the fighting starts. So it's a priority for us to find it.

"We lost track of the train carrying the TEL and our mysterious truck after it passed the Imam Anas junction west of Basra. The train switched to a southern track, but then our satellite passed out of range. We lost sight of the train, but we know where it was headed. The rail line south of Basra terminates at one place—the port of Umm Qasr, right above the Kuwait border. There are no other spurs or lines heading in any other direction except for a small loop going past the harbor.

"There are no bridges or other obstacles between Umm Qasr and the Persian Gulf. And a deep dredged channel allows seagoing ships to have access to both the northern and southern routes around Bubiyan Island. The area had been choked with debris and wrecks left over from the Iran-Iraq war, but some of the harbor facilities had been cleared for free passage."

Pulling up a closed and sealed folder, Captain Schneller untied the knot holding the thick envelope closed, breaking the seal in the process, and opened it. Removing a sheaf of photographs, he shuffled through them quickly before laying them out on the wardroom table in order.

The pictures were mostly aerial shots of a harbor facility and some of a roadway across desert sand. Rockham and Daugherty picked up the pictures and were looking at them while the captain went on with the briefing.

"What you see in that first picture is a shot of the harbor facilities in Umm Qasr," Schneller said. "Tied up to the dock there is one of the *Polnocny*-class medium landing ships that Iraq purchased from the Soviet Union back in the 1980s. That type of craft is very close to our LST class," he explained, using the acronym for landing ship, tank.

Pushing one of the other pictures across the table, Schneller pointed to an obviously empty dock. "This picture was taken the next morning on the first pass available of a Keyhole." He pushed out another picture. "And this was taken on the next satellite's pass."

The picture showed the *Polnocny*-class ship again tied up to the dock. Only very subtle differences, such as the placing of a line or the arrangement of gear on the dock, indicated that any time had passed between the picture taken the day before and the one Rockham and Daugherty were looking at now.

"Here's the frosting on this particular cake," Schneller said as he pushed the last picture forward. The shot showed nothing more than a military column of tanks and trucks traveling along a desert road.

"That's the road between Umm Qasr and the customs post just north of the Kuwait border," Schneller said. "The makeup of that convoy has been analyzed by experts. There was no place else for that number of T-72 tanks to have come from except that military train. All that is missing are two tanks, a few other support vehicles, that civilian truck, and the MAZ.

"Estimates of time that the *Polnocny* could have been away from that dock run from seven to nine hours. That estimate includes an hour to load and unload the missing vehicles from that train. Given the speed of that class of ship, she could have traveled from between roughly eighty to one hundred nautical miles. That puts her in range for Kuwait City, Faylaka Island offshore from Kuwait City, and ports in Iran. We don't think that ship went to Iran to deliver weapons.

"Satellite photos show another train loading up. She looks likely to also head down to Umm Qasr. Since active hostilities have not yet officially started, an air strike cannot be called in. And the waters in that area are too shallow and restricted by mines for us to move in with any warships. If the *Polnocny* loads up and leaves port, every effort is going to be made to follow her and see where she docks. The *Grayback* is going to do her best to have you and your men within operational range of that ship wherever she goes.

"Your basic orders are to seize that ship and examine her for information and to determine the makeup of her cargo. A cargo of weapons of mass destruction is to be denied to the Iraqis by all means available. You have a green light to destroy the ship and her cargo if you deem it necessary. And we're here to back you up in that mission."

CHAPTER 18

0056 ZULU
29° 02' North, 49° 21' East
Forward living spaces
LPSS 574 *Grayback*
Persian Gulf

"So that's it," Rockham said. "Our target is an Iraqi landing ship. Our mission is to take it down, search it, and seize or destroy any weapons of mass destruction on board."

"And we don't know where this *Polnocny* is right now?" Mike Ferber asked.

"Sure we do," Sam Paulson said, "we just don't know where she's going or where she'll be when you have to take her down."

"Hell, I'm not even sure where we are right now," Sid Mainhart said. He had been a member of a submarine crew less than two years earlier. "The captain has changed headings at least twice during the past three hours."

"More like three times," Paulson said. "Right

now he's weaving us around four oil fields to avoid detection by any civilian craft. Then the really tricky bit of navigation comes into play."

"Tricky bit?" asked Kurkowski.

"Yes," Paulson said. "There's ten different belts of minefields between the Durra oil field and the Kuwaiti shore. That was one of the missions that Kahuna and I had before you guys showed up, to plot out the minefields in our Mark 9 SDV."

"And your mission was a success?" Pete Wilkes said.

"Well, we didn't find any mines yet," Paulson said. "But we did plot a clear course all the way to Kuwait Harbor."

"You're sure?" Kurkowski said.

"Heck, if this job was that easy," Wayne Alexander said from the back of the group, "everyone would want to do it. Where's the fun in that?"

"Fun, he says," Kurkowski said. "We may be facing four-hundred-pound mines and he thinks it's fun."

"Man, Kurkowski," Alexander said while making a face, "you are really turning into an old lady, you know that?"

The joking around was a little more than Rockham normally allowed the men to have during a briefing, but this was an unusual situation. They were being asked to take down an enemy-held ship in enemy waters. And they had almost no information to go on other than the general layout of the ship.

In the briefing package that Rockham had

brought from the *Midway* were maps, diagrams, deck plans, and layouts of the Soviet *Polnocny*-class medium landing ship. Passing out the materials to the men, he used their input to decide on the best general plan of action. Once they had the specific location of the ship, or the decision had been made to board her while she was under way, the plan could be modified to fit the situation.

"The ship is 267 feet long and 30.5 feet wide," Rockham said. "Her main feature is the big tank deck that makes up the bulk of the third deck. The tank deck is 175 feet long, a little over twenty-two feet wide, and twelve and a half feet tall. She can carry about 250 tons of cargo. That's six tanks or sixty to 180 troops.

"One thing in our favor is that this ship doesn't have berthing facilities for the troops if that's her main cargo. The troops would have to sleep out on the tank deck. From what we know of the Iraqi military, that isn't going to be something they like very well. On board, there's only cargo berthing for thirty men. Those would normally be the five-man crews of the six tanks. So if she had troops on board, they would probably be off-loaded at the first opportunity. If they land just about anywhere in Kuwait, any troops on board would commandeer food and housing from the locals. That still leaves us with a normal crew of five officers and about thirty-two enlisted men to deal with.

"The numbers are against us without knowing just who or what is on board. The ship's complement would be a big enough handful to deal with.

If she has a full load of troops on board, we could see the situation get out of hand fast. There's no way we could deal with that many men. If troops are on board, we abort the mission and pull out.

"We have to plan for the worst, but the word in the intelligence reports on the Iraqi Navy say their ships are running shorthanded and maintenance is not very good. That pretty well matches up with the reports about what their military is like. The regular troops and crew are conscripts for the most part, so if we do a tight sneak-and-peek, we can pull this off before anyone knows we were there.

"That also means we don't have time for anyone to get lost. There are three decks below the main deck and the navigating bridge above. The second deck is pretty much empty. She should be fast to clear. The only major compartment is the berthing area in the fantail.

"The third deck is another matter. That's where the machine, electrical, carpentry, and shipfitter's shops are in forecastle compartments. The rest of the small compartments that line the sides of the deck are for stores. The stern area is the steering gear compartment. The rest of the area is the tank deck where the main cargo would be. That means a team has to move the length of the deck to clear the forward compartments. If there's vehicle or cargo aboard, that would give cover to move. But if she's unloaded her cargo, that's a big open area to move along.

"The hold has the main and auxiliary engine rooms ahead of the twin shaft alleys. Other than that, the rest of that deck is made up of ballast and diesel tanks. The freshwater tanks are on both sides of the shaft alley."

"What are these two compartments near the bow?" Mainhart asked.

"Those are voids to increase the buoyancy of the ship up forward," Rockham said. "This class of ship is intended to beach itself and then unload cargo through the bow doors and ramp. It's called a Ro-ro, for roll-on, roll-off. That's how they can get the cargo unloaded so fast. In good conditions, all six tanks on board can be unloaded inside of five minutes with a decent crew. And she doesn't need any kind of port facilities to operate.

"The main deck has a single superstructure at the stern. This is where the habitable spaces are for the ship's officers and crew. The captain's cabin is at the bow, and there's officers compartments along the port side. On the starboard side are the crew's compartments. Between the port and starboard passages are storage spaces with ladders to the lower compartments forward and aft. At the stern of the superstructure is the mess area.

"The navigating bridge on the upper deck is the most critical target on this op. This is where we have the best chance of finding any intel on the ship's movements. The folks sending us on this little trip want to know where this ship had been and when. They need to know where her last cargo went."

"Why the last cargo, Skipper?" Ferber said.

"Because they know that there was a MAZ-543 TEL aboard then," Rockham said. "They need to know where that Scud launcher went. Knowing where the ship unloaded would at least give them a big boost in just what direction to look in."

"So the ship's log is a major target," Chief Monday said. "What about prisoners?"

"If we can," Rockham said, "we bring one back with us. Otherwise, we aren't equipped to handle prisoners.

"This is a big ship. It's going to take all of us to conduct the takedown and search. First squad will take the critical spaces—the bridge, communications, and engine room. Second squad will handle the mid-decks and security. We have to do this one by the numbers, fast and quiet.

"We go up fore and aft of the superstructure. First squad aft, second squad forward. Ladders to the lower deck are port and starboard at both ends of the main deck superstructure. Fire team one of first squad will go up and take the bridge from the stern ladder. Fire team two of first squad will take down the cabins.

"Shaun, that leaves the lower three decks to you and second squad."

"Like you said," Daugherty said, "it's a big area. But there aren't that many compartments. We can handle it."

"Great," Rockham said. "Without knowing the exact location of the ship or the situation she's going to be in, we can finalize a plan. Once aboard, that's when we learn what her cargo is. If it's what command thinks, we could find a hold full of Scuds. If that's what we find, we destroy the ship."

"Okay," John Sukov said, "so how do we destroy this thing without being taken out ourselves? Limpet mines? That's one thing we didn't bring with us in our loadouts. We do have Mark 135 demolition charges. With a Mark 48 firing device for a clock and a Mark 38 safety and arming device completing the firing assembly, four of those should break the back of even a nine-hundred-ton ship like this *Polnocny*."

"You won't have to take along any charges at all," Paulson said, "at least not any to sink the ship. Kahuna and I can take care of that."

"What?" Chief Monday said, "with the *Grayback*? Not if the target is inshore. The water will be too shallow for a torpedo run. If the target is at sea, that's a different matter. Or are the two of you just going to swim in some demo?"

"Sort of," Paulson said with a grin. "If the *Grayback* can't go in, we'll just use another boat."

"What other boat?" Daugherty said. "You have another sub available?"

"Close enough," Paulson said with a smile. "Up in the starboard hangar is the Mark 9 SDV that Kahuna and I have been using to cover the search grids we're checking for mines. Right now, that nine-boat has been fitted with a Mark 38 standoff weapons system. We've got two Mark 46 torpedoes with ninety-eight pounds of PBXN-103 high explosive each ready to put that Iraqi landing ship on the bottom whenever you give the word."

"You've got a standoff?" Ed Lopez said with a big smile. "Amigo, that would put a dent in anyone's day."

"A standoff?" Sid Mainhart asked.

"The Mark 38 SWS, standoff weapons system," Paulson said. "It's one of the reasons the Mark 9 SDV was designed. With it, a nine-boat can mount two Mark 46 torpedoes in zero-length launching rails. That gives a little two-man wet submersible the firepower to sink a warship from thousands of yards away. And we've got one."

"Sounds great," Rockham said. "So how do you plan to employ it?"

"Probably the best way," Kahuna said, "would be for us to just shadow you in to the target. By the looks of things, this will probably be an over-the-horizon mission in surface craft, especially if the target ends up in a Kuwaiti or Iranian port. And the good money says Kuwait. Iran isn't co-operating with Saddam at all. The Iran-Iraq war has only been over for about two years now.

"One thing's for sure, we know the damned thing can't go up the Euphrates or Tigris Rivers. The water's too shallow in a number of places. Dredging was halted by that same war Iran is still pissing about. Where the water is deep enough up-river, there's too many bridges and other blockages between Umm Qasr and anyplace worthwhile. If the *Polnocny* goes into Kuwait waters, there's not going to be anyplace we can bring the *Grayback* in closer than ten miles or so, at least not to the main harbor at Kuwait City."

"That is way too far for a swim," Rockham said. "And we don't have a Mark 8 SDV available. Your SDV is just a two-man job. So if the insertion is over ten miles or more, detection by Iraqi surface craft may be a problem.

"Over-the-horizon in a small boat may not be as dangerous as you think," Paulson said. "We know that a detachment from Naval Special Warfare Task Group One has been running small boats up and down the Kuwaiti coast for months now. They've been patrolling and conducting strategic recons while trying out the Iraqi Navy. If any Iraqi boats are patrolling Kuwait waters, they haven't been a problem yet."

"Back in Team Two," Rockham said, "we did do practice runs well over the horizon. We took Zodiacs out for over thirty-five miles before bringing them back in. It can be done, but it's a long, wet ride."

"Yeah," Kurkowski said, "but it sounds better than a long swim. Especially if these guys in the nine-boat can cover our asses."

"We can do more than that," Paulson said. "You take the ship down at a shore facility and we can back you up from any counteraction from the ocean side. If we have to pump a couple of fish into the *Polnocny*, it'll look as if she hit a stray Iraqi floating mine. Those have been a problem around here since the mid-1980s. We can also stay on target until you guys are well clear of the area, then launch and pull away ourselves."

"As long as you don't miss," Kurkowski said.

"Hey, like shooting fish in a bucket," Paulson said. "Besides, we can draw in very close before launching. The nine-boat doesn't draw very much water at all, so we can crawl in along the shallows where no one would expect us."

"That takes care of your part in the mission," Rockham said. "Now, it's still up to us to decide whether this op is a go or not."

"I'm in," Mike Bryant said.

"I've done riskier ops," Chief Monday said, "but not by much. Still, this sounds like a good one."

"Hey, came all this way," Ryan Marks said, "I'd hate to disappoint anyone."

One by one the SEALs all agreed that the op was a go. In spite of his reservations about the risks of the operation, Rockham knew that his men would go along with it. The Teams weren't a democracy. The SEALs were a military unit, and a very disciplined one at that. As the unit commander, Rockham could have ordered everyone to go, and they all knew it. But letting everyone have a say in how something went down kept morale high and made the men work that much harder to help support each other in the field. This was the teamwork Rockham wanted to see in his men.

For hours, the men discussed the details of the ship takedown. Practicing it was impossible, since there wasn't time and they were already on-site. They would have to depend on the training they had been conducting for years. It would be enough.

What they could do was pore over the maps and plans Rockham pulled out of the briefing envelope. It was a Soviet-built ship, and that limited some of the information available. There was also the problem of accounting for whatever modifications the Iraqis might have made to the interior of the compartments, machinery, or deck spaces. But the overall and internal layout of the ship could not be changed, which was what the SEALs were memorizing.

Each man discussed what his job would be, where they were expected to be, when, and what they would be doing next. Silence and speed were the two most important assets for the completion of this mission. Creativity on the part of the men helped with a number of the details.

"You know," Larry Stadt said as he looked at a ship photo, "there's not a single port or opening at the stern of the hull."

"So, we weren't going in through a port anyway," Kurkowski said. "And it isn't like you're going to be climbing in through some lady's boudoir window. This is an ex-Soviet military ship, remember?"

"Blow it out your ass, Kurkowski," Stadt said. "What I was thinking is that there's no way out of the aft berthing compartment except by the passageway hatch. The deck ventilators are too small for anyone to be able to get through."

"What are you pushing at, Stadt?" Rockham asked.

"What if we clear the compartment and leave the prisoners there?" Stadt said. "The hatch could be secured and that would leave them inside."

"A steel hull and bulkhead isn't exactly the sort of thing you can just push through, not even with Kurkowski's hard head," Rockham said. "We'll keep it in mind. Once we have the ship secure, that could prove useful as a place to keep the prisoners secure belowdecks."

By that afternoon, all of the men had gone over the general plan and the deck drawings until they could see them with their eyes closed. Sleep came hard to some of them, though Mainhart was right at home even aboard a diesel-electric sub, and Alexander could sleep in a sewer pipe, so neither of them were bothered. It was the unknowns about the upcoming mission, the where and when, that kept Rockham and Daugherty and the others awake.

Throughout the history of the military, quality commanders—men who think about what they could be doing better for their men before sending them into harm's way—have pondered on battles and missions before they took place. Rockham was no different than a leader of a Roman cohort in that respect. And like that leader of long ago, he also had to get the sleep his body demanded, no matter what his mind was doing.

The general routine of the *Grayback* remained constant. She was patrolling along the Kuwaiti coast, heading slowly north toward Iraq. There was no set destination in mind, just a desire to remain in the estimated radius of action the *Polnocny*-class ship could have covered during the missing hours she was away from Umm Qasr.

The *Grayback*'s diesel engine ran as long as Captain Schneller kept the boat near the surface. The radio room ran up the boat's antennas to maintain communications. Both radio and TV signals could be brought in by the updated electronics on board the submarine. The communications package had been upgraded during her clandestine refit by the CIA. Even CNN was downloaded from an orbiting satellite, and tapes made available to the crew for their off-time.

"Captain," Lieutenant Haster, the *Grayback*'s communications officer called out, "I think you should listen to this."

Moving to the radio shack aft of the control room, Schneller held a headset to his ear for several minutes. Pulling up a microphone clipped to the wall, he switched on the 1-MC to make an announcement to the crew.

"Men," Schneller said, "I have just heard over the radio that the U.S. Congress and Senate completed deliberations this afternoon. President Bush has been given the full authority of the U.S. government to use force to expel the Iraqi invaders from occupied Kuwait. This is not the signal for the beginning of active combat—but that may come soon. Next Tuesday is the UN deadline for Iraq to withdraw from Kuwait. Our mission will continue until we are ordered otherwise. That is all.

"We didn't come all this way just to miss the party," Schneller said quietly to himself as he hung up the microphone.

CHAPTER 19

1914 ZULU
29° 04' North, 48° 46' East
Control Room
LPSS 574 *Grayback*
Persian Gulf

"Captain to the radio room," Lieutenant Haster said over the 1-MC.

Leaving his stateroom, where he had been resting, Captain Schneller went forward to the radio room.

"What have you got, Haster?" Schneller asked when he got there.

"Coded message came through for you, sir," Haster said as he handed the captain an aluminum clipboard with a cover closed over the pages inside. "There's more intel downloading from the satellite link now, sir."

"Very well," Schneller said as he looked at the message on the clipboard. "COB!"

Master Chief Runyon, the chief of the boat—or

COB, as he was called—was the highest ranking enlisted man on the *Grayback*. He was standing at his watch station in the control room when Schneller called out.

"Yes, Captain," Runyon said as he came to the compartment hatch.

"Please extend my compliments to Mr. Rockham, and ask him and his exec to meet me in the wardroom as soon as possible."

"Aye, sir," Runyon said. For the captain to ask the COB to run a message indicated the importance of the situation. Runyon quickly went forward to deliver it.

"We are in just about the right place at the right time," Schneller said as Rockham and Daugherty came into the wardroom and closed the hatch behind them. "The target is on the move. A train came in before dusk and unloaded material and vehicles onto the target. Shortly before 2100 hours local time she left the pier at Umm Qasr, and is now moving south. Reconnaissance flights have the ship under constant surveillance."

A chart of the northwest Persian Gulf was unrolled on the wardroom table. Picking up a set of dividers, Schneller leaned over the chart.

"For the last several hours, we've been moving slowly along an oval course in roughly twenty-five fathoms of water," Schneller said. "One hundred fifty feet of water is not a very comfortable depth for a submariner. We prefer a lot deeper water to hide in, but the Persian Gulf doesn't give us that.

"We are here," Schneller said, pointing with the dividers, "at twenty-nine degrees four minutes north, forty-eight degrees forty-six minutes east. The target is just starting to pass here, on the south side of Jazerat Bubiyan—Bubiyan Island. The ship is traveling along the Khawr as Sabiya. That's a fairly narrow and shallow waterway, so it can't be making for anyplace but that mouth of that waterway here, about eight miles north-northwest of Jazerat Faylaka. From there it's a thirty minute run at flank speed to Faylaka for them. Or about a sixty minute run at the harbor at Kuwait City."

Opening up the dividers and setting them to a scale at the bottom of the chart, Schneller spaced out a distance from the *Grayback*'s present location to a spot on the central coast of Kuwait.

"Moving at flank speed underwater," he said, "we can be off the Kuwaiti coast at the northernmost curve of the twenty-fathom line in two hours. That will put us here, at twenty-nine degrees fifteen minutes north, forty-eight degrees eighteen minutes east. That point is twelve nautical miles south of the harbor at Az Zawr on the northwest end of Faylaka or twenty-three miles from the inner harbor at Kuwait City.

"According to surveillance aircraft, the *Polnocny* is making about eight knots along the Khawr as Sabiya. If her speed stays constant, that will get her to Persian Gulf waters in about three hours. That's when we'll learn her final course, to Faylaka, Kuwait City, or elsewhere.

"The winds are blowing from the northwest at one to two knots, giving a Beaufort force of one. That gives you a calm sea state with a wave height of less than a foot. Can you catch the *Polnocny* in open water or do you have to wait for her to dock?"

"With our outboards," Rockham said, "the best speed we can expect to make in those conditions is about eighteen to twenty knots. We barely catch up to a *Polnocny* moving at flank speed. Holding position while trying to put up a boarding ladder would be a bear in the rough water tossed up by her own passage. Even if we got ahead of her and stretched out a line between the boats to catch on her bow, the ride would pound us to pieces before we could ever climb aboard.

"Moving a Zodiac at eighteen knots puts up a bow wave that increases our visibility a lot in very calm waters. So I would say the best we could expect to do to maintain a low profile in closer to shore is ten to twelve knots tops. We have to wait for the target to dock. I don't see any other way for us to do it."

"I agree with your assessment, Lieutenant," Captain Schneller said, "but I needed to hear you say it. A calculated risk is part of the job; a glory hunter just gets people killed. You get your people ready and I'll move us to a launch point. We'll stay in contact with Washington and get the final intelligence dump on the target's location as well as the final go-ahead for your operation."

Though the men of the SMD had been preparing, checking, and double-checking their gear since they came aboard the *Grayback*, with the mission coming up they gave everything a final once-over. In the starboard hangar, Sam Paulson and Kahuna checked their nine-boat. While torpe-domen examined the deadly Mark 46 fish, one on the starboard side and one slung underneath the SDV, Paulson and Kahuna went over the systems that would get the torpedoes into firing range and launch them to their target.

The Mark 9 SDV was a strange boat, even among the strange class of undersea craft. Shaped like a flat, rectangular book with rounded edges, the nine-boat was slightly over nineteen feet long, a little over six feet wide, and only slightly more than two and a half feet thick. In the cramped confines of the wet-type submersible, both the navigator and driver had to lay flat along the bottom of the SDV to operate it.

Since a wet-type submersible was completely flooded when in the water, both crewmen had to wear breathing equipment and wet suits in order to stay alive. Twin screws powered by electric motors and rechargeable batteries pushed the flat SDV through the water at a respectable speed. It couldn't keep up with the faster Zodiacs, but the Mark 9 was able to put out a very heavy punch with its Mark 38 standoff weapons system.

On either side of the nine-boat, small rails were mounted on the end of short fins. Hanging from the rail was a Mark 46 Mod 5 torpedo, a fraction over eight-and-a-half feet long and 12.75 inches in diameter. The little torpedo had originally been designed for launching from aircraft racks or sur-face craft tubes. The Mark 38 SWS used the air-craft attachment point to interface with the torpedo.

A volatile monopropellant, Otto II fuel, which

was close to rocket fuel in performance, drove the Mark 46 to 12,000 yards at a speed of forty-five knots. The active/passive acoustic guidance system of the Mark 46 would zero it in on its target. On impact, the ninety-eight-pound high explosive warhead was greater than any limpet mine and could blast a large hole in the hull of most warships. A single Mark 46, properly placed, would have no trouble sending the *Polnocny*-class ship to the bottom.

The electronics package for activating and firing the torpedoes was complex, and Paulson was going over the circuits and batteries carefully. He had been an active SEAL until he was injured on the mission into Russia that led to the creation of the SMD. He wasn't forced to leave the Teams—his injuries hadn't been that bad—but during his recovery Paulson was approached by the CIA to take time off from his Navy career in order to work with them on a secret maritime project, and as a marine engineer he had looked at the opportunity as a challenge, one where he could make a significant contribution. Paulson knew he was going to miss operating with his Teammates at SEAL Delivery Vehicle Team Two. It was with a great deal of surprise that he found himself in charge of the hangars and assigned SDV to a submarine he thought was long ago destroyed.

George "Kahuna" Weaver had also been a SEAL SDV operator, only he had served in Hawaii with SDV Team One. The big, dark-skinned Hawaiian had grown up surfing on the islands, and found serving in the Navy a natural progression. The challenge of the SEALs was one he welcomed. Later, he had no regrets about accepting an offer from the CIA. The only thing that Kahuna Weaver did miss about the Teams was being able to serve while still staying on his beloved Hawaiian Islands.

The islands were a long way from the coast of Kuwait. Kahuna didn't dwell on home as he concentrated on checking every electrical and mechanical system in the nine-boat—not just because his life depended on it, but so did the life of his navigator, Sam Paulson. Though Paulson was a commissioned officer and Kahuna an enlisted man, they had become fast friends from having worked so closely. Now, they would be going out together on a hot operation with live torpedoes.

In the forward living spaces, torpedo room, and portside hangar, the SEALs of the SMD were working hard to stage their own gear for the operation. Both Zodiacs would be launched inflated. Captain Schneller had balanced the risk of being painted with Iraqi radar against the time it would take to launch the Zodiacs from underwater. Though an underwater launch was barely detectable at any distance, even with radar, raising the boats, inflating, and loading them took time. And time was the one commodity the mission had little to spare.

To launch the Zodiacs, the *Grayback* would surface with her decks awash, and the SEALs would paddle their boats out of the hangars and into open water. So, in spite of all of the modern

advances available to them, the SEALs would begin their mission by paddling a rubber boat—the
same skill they had learned during Basic Underwater Demolition/SEAL training would be put to use
in the field once again.

While Ed Lopez and Henry Lutz, the coxswains
for first and second squads respectively, made sure
of the Zodiacs up in the hangar, down in the torpedo room their Teammates were also working
hard. Weapons and ammunition were broken out
and checked. Most of the men would carry a 9mm
Heckler & Koch MP5-N submachine gun as their
primary weapon. To hold the noise of firing down
to a minimum, the guns would be fitted with a
stainless steel suppressor screwed onto the muzzle.

In their positions of point men and lead climbers
for their respective fire teams, Mike Bryant, Pete
Wilkes, Ryan Marks, and Larry Stadt all would
carry the compact MP5K-PDW, a shorter version
of the MP5-N, with a vertical foregrip that made it
easy to handle with both hands. The personal defense weapon variation added a side-folding stock
to the otherwise almost pistol-size submachine gun.
The MP5K-PDWs were also fitted with suppressors
screwed onto their threaded muzzles.

The suppressors on the guns did not eliminate
the sound of firing, but did lessen it significantly.
For quiet shots, both Mike Bryant and Ryan
Marks carried .22 caliber Ruger Mark II semiautomatic pistols, which were fitted with suppressors that surrounded the barrels and added only a
few inches to the overall length of the weapon.

The suppressors cut back on the muzzle blast of the shot so much that the Rugers sounded little louder than air pistols when fired. Unless a person knew what he was hearing, the sound of a suppressed .22 didn't even sound like a gunshot. The target would never hear itself die.

A 9mm SIG P226 pistol was the standard sidearm for all of the SEALs in the SMD. The SIGs were in low, tactical holsters strapped to each man's hips. To feed their weapons, each SEAL would carry seven magazines for his MP5 and three for the SIGs. That gave them 210 rounds for the submachine guns and forty-five rounds for their pistols. Bryant and Marks would also have two magazines for their Rugers. If the men needed more than the twenty rounds the two magazines gave them, they would by then need to use their submachine guns.

Along with the firearms, each SEAL carried four flash-crash grenades, which were modified M116A1 hand grenade simulators. Fitted with a 1.5-second-delay fuze assembly, the flash-crashes would blast out with a stunning roar and brilliant blaze of light when detonated. The flash-crash would stun and disorient anyone in a normal-size room. In a steel-walled ship's compartment, the effect would be even more powerful.

Along with the flash-crashes, every man's loadout also had a Mark IIIA2 concussion grenade—essentially a half-pound cylinder of TNT covered with plastic—and an M7A2 CS gas grenade. The canister type CS grenade would fill a large area with potent CS super tear gas and drive any unprotected people out of the area where it was used.

To protect themselves from their own gas grenades, the SEALs carried M17A1 gas masks, along with protective helmets, body armor, a sheath knife, a complete first aid kit, an MX-300R radio, boots, web gear, assault vests, and pouches for all of their ammunition and equipment.

Chem lights, Mark 13 day/night flares, flashlights, gloves, Danner CT boots, an SDU-5/E strobe light with an infrared filter, a signal mirror, PRC-112 emergency radio, was also carried. Even a foot-long length of one-inch steel pipe was included with each load, to help open doors that might be dogged down tight by the Iraqi crew.

To secure prisoners, each man would have twelve tie-ties—plastic loops that could be quickly placed over a man's hands and the ends pulled tight. The only way to get a snugged tie-tie off was to cut through it. Three triangular bandages rounded out the prisoner-handling equipment.

Besides carrying their corpsmen medical equipment, Jack Tinsley and Henry Limbaugh were designated prisoner handlers. They had even more tie-ties and triangular bandages on their web gear.

The heaviest loads were carried by the breachers—the men who would open closed doors and hatches. The two breachers in each squad, one per fire team, were the strongest men in the unit: Dan Able, Wayne Alexander, Roger Kurkowski, and John Grant. In addition to the standard gear the other SEALs would carry on the mission, the breachers also had a Remington 870 pump-action twelve-gauge shotgun.

The Remingtons had the stocks removed and pistol grips installed to cut down on the overall length of the weapon. The shorter shotguns were easier to use in crowded passageways. The forty rounds of twelve-gauge 00 buckshot each breacher had for his shotgun would do just as well against personnel as against door locks or hinges.

Along with the shotguns, the breachers wore special backpack frames for their heavy tools; six-pound sledgehammers with cut-down handles; Hooligan tools that were a combination wrecking bar, crowbar, and tearing claw; explosive charges, detonators, fifteen- and thirty-second firing assemblies. Even tubes of adhesive were part of a breacher's load.

Both John Grant and Wayne Alexander would carry an additional piece of breacher's equipment. They had compact DuPont exothermic cutting torches that could slice through steel with a searing hot flame and rush of pure oxygen. The oxygen was in small steel gas bottles with regulators and hoses. The cutting rods ignited electrically at the touch of a button. The rigs could cut open steel dogs and locks, or if necessary quickly weld a hatchway shut.

The two Zodiacs would be handled by the coxswains, Lopez and Lutz, who carried a standard loadout in case they had to go in with their Teammates. For this operation, Rockham would have them stay with their Zodiacs, ready to come in and pull their Teammates out of trouble if things went bad. To give the boats some support firepower, Rockham told the coxswains to pack an M60E3 machine gun and ammunition in the Zodiacs.

The 7.62mm M60E3 light machine gun could be handled by one man like a big rifle. The twenty-pound machine guns could fire a hundred-round belt of linked ammunition in nine to twelve seconds as one long burst. Each machine gun had six hundred rounds of ammunition. That gave the Zodiacs a full minute or more of hammering firepower.

And the SEALs of the SMD might very well need every second of that firepower—though if it came down to a shootout, the SMD would eventually be badly outnumbered and outgunned. They were going into enemy territory, after all. This would be a penetration operation to help gather information, not to try to kill the enemy. If they could go in and get out without firing a shot and still accomplish all of their objectives, that would be, in SEAL language, a "perfect op."

To pull off the operation, the SEALs had to get on board the *Polnocny* from their Zodiacs. As the hook men for their squads, John Sukov and Sid Mainhart were responsible for handling the boarding hooks, which were bent and forged into shape with two prongs turned down and padded with cloth and rubber. The back of each hook had a longer piece, to slip down inside an extendible painter's pole. A D-ring welded to the hook allowed it to have a line or, more commonly, a caving ladder attached.

The painter's pole was a fiberglass rod that came in separate sections that would be screwed together, making a long, ridged assembly. The boarding hooks would be mounted on the painter's pole by shipping the long back rod down inside the top of the tube. A piece of rubber tubing secured the hook to the top of the pole. When the hook was pulled hard, it would slip from the top of the pole, allowing whatever was attached to it to hang free.

The caving ladder that could be attached to the boarding hook was thirty-two feet of twin 3mm steel cables. Solidly attached between the two cables and spaced out at intervals were aluminum rod steps. SEALs climbed a caving ladder by going up the side rather than the face. With the cable of the ladder between a man's legs, a SEAL had a much more secure climb. It took a great deal of upper body strength even to climb a ladder instead of a knotted line. For the breachers, with their heavy loads, the climb would be a strain.

CHAPTER 20

★ ★ ★ ★

2108 ZULU
29° 15' North, 48° 18' East
Forward living spaces
LPSS 574 *Grayback*
Bottom of the Persian Gulf

The physical strain of a climb onto a ship's deck was nothing compared to the mental strain of waiting for an operation to begin. All the SEALs knew that something could prevent an operation from going ahead at the very last moment. You weren't going out on a hot op until you were in the transport and heading in. Even then, operations had been canceled at the very last moment.

Eventually, the last round would be seated in a magazine, the last spot of suspected rust cleaned and oiled, and there was nothing to do but wait for the elements of a situation to align themselves. Some SEALs, like Wayne Alexander, dealt with pre-op stress by going to sleep. His philosophy

was that you never knew when the next chance for
sleep would present itself.

The eternal Team poker game had been started
up again by Bryant, Sukov, Able, and Marks.
Rockham was glad that the men had gotten over
the strain of being with each other so long without
anything to do. Could that have been less than a
month ago? Now, the calm that centered around
the card game was a little island of peace, while the
living spaces around them, and the submarine itself, bustled with quiet activity. That was good, as
far as Rockham was concerned. With the SEALs
geared up for an operation, it wasn't the best time
for heavily armed men to get into an argument.

Once they had arrived on location, Captain
Schneller demonstrated his skill as a sub skipper
by bottoming the *Grayback*, bringing the big submarine down to the floor of the Gulf so easily that
if it had landed on a crab, it wouldn't have
cracked the shell. The soft bottom let the submarine settle in, and she sat down without a list to either side. Putting up an antenna buoy, the
Grayback would wait while in full communications with both the local coalition electronic resources and with the CIA back in Langley.

The *Grayback* had been pushed hard by her
captain and crew to give the SEALs as much time
as they could in the target area. It was dangerous
for the submarine to be in shallow waters during
the day, since any passing aircraft could spot her
on the bottom. Two things were working in the
submarine's favor to help avoid detection. The
Persian Gulf in the area they were moving through

had a dark mud bottom from thousands of years of land runoff down the Tigris and Euphrates Rivers, so the hull wouldn't stand out. Second, there weren't any known submarines in the area because none of the countries surrounding the Persian Gulf had navies with active submarines. So the coalition forces weren't looking as hard for subs as they would have in another theater of war. Any subs spotted by coalition ships or aircraft would be treated as suspect, but probably not simply fired upon.

As Rockham stood watching his men, a seaman entered the compartment and told him that the captain wanted to see him in the control room. It had been almost two hours since Schneller had told Rockham that they would be moving at flank speed to get on station. He knew they should be at that location now. Following the sailor, Rockham went up to the control room, where Captain Schneller was standing over the chart table.

"Mr. Rockham," Schneller said, "a decision has to be made now regarding your mission."

Though he let nothing show on his face, Rockham's heart sank at the thought of their mission being scrubbed at the last moment. Even though he didn't like the way the mission had evolved—the lack of solid information about the target ship's location and no time to practice—Rockham knew how disappointed his men would be to gear up for an op—mentally and physically—only to have it be a no-go at the last moment.

"Satellite imagery and air reconnaissance show that the *Polnocny* was able to make better time through the Khawr as Sabiya channel than we originally estimated," Schneller said. "She has reached the mouth of the channel and headed southeast toward Faylaka Island.

"We have final authorization to launch the operation. That message came over our secure, encrypted radio link only a few minutes ago. The final go command is to be given by the ground commander on site. That's you, Mr. Rockham.

"Exactly where the *Polnocny* is going to land is still a question. By your own estimations, it would take your boats an hour to reach Faylaka Island and nearly twice that to get to the harbor at Kuwait City. The target can be at Faylaka in less than half an hour, Kuwait Harbor in an hour. What are your intentions?"

"In spite of our having two boats," Rockham said, "I can't split my unit to cover both targets. I don't see any other way to do the mission—we wait until the target has docked."

"I concur," Captain Schneller said. "That's the only way to complete this mission with the best possible chance of success. With our on-board electronics package, we can receive real-time information from all the surveillance systems concentrated on this area. That will give us the most immediate and critical intelligence on the target. So right now we wait and see what the Iraqis do. Not the most comfortable situation to be in."

"No sir," Rockham said, "it isn't. But it is the way for me to lessen the risks my men have to take. This is a difficult enough operation for us without stacking the deck against ourselves."

Returning to the forward compartment, Rockham told the men the good news as well as the bad. The operation was a go, but they were still in a holding pattern for the launch time. None of the men said a word. They knew that their skipper was doing the best possible job he could for them, and they appreciated it. The poker game went on, and Alexander continued to snore.

Inside of thirty minutes Rockham was again called up to the control room to speak with the captain. Sitting with a porcelain mug of coffee in his hand, Schneller was looking at a sheaf of pictures fresh from the printer. Lieutenant Haster stood at the captain's shoulder as he looked at the prints.

"It seems the Iraqis have pulled one on us," Schneller said, looking up. "The *Polnocny* has steamed to within a few hundred yards of Faylaka Island and continued on past."

"So she is heading for the harbor at Kuwait City," Rockham said.

"No, not according to her present heading," Schneller replied. "The target has passed through the channel north of Faylaka and is presently following a heading of 237 degrees. To get to the harbor at Kuwait City by the most direct route, they would have to be on a heading of 259 degrees. Unless they are maneuvering to avoid obstacles we know nothing about, that ship is heading for another destination."

Moving over to the table, Rockham looked down at the chart of the local area. "Is there anything on that course that she could be heading for?" he wondered out loud.

"Yes," Schneller said, joining him at the table. "The protected harbor at Ra's al Ard. That's right here, on this point of land below Kuwait City. It's about eight miles from the harbor at Kuwait City and juts out directly into the water of the Gulf."

"That's it," Rockham said with certainty. "That's where they're heading. But why? What's around there? Hiding a missile site within Kuwait City would be next to impossible, considering the size of a Scud's TEL vehicle. We would have had reports from the Kuwait resistance by now."

"We may have one lead as to what's in that area," Schneller said as he pulled up a clipboard. "There's an intelligence report of a suspected missile facility at the Girls Sciences School near the town of Al Badawiyah. That's about thirty kilometers south of the harbor at Ra's al Ard. The report indicates that the site probably holds HY-2 Silkworm missiles. But many of the support people would also be valuable at a Scud site. Then there's the heavy military guard presence at the school.

"But you're right. Something the size of a Scud TEL would have been reported by the resistance."

"I really hate to say this," Rockham said, "but we have to wait for further intelligence. If the *Polnocny* ties up at Ra's al Ard, we can go in and take her down."

Taking up a set of dividers, Rockham set them to a scale on the chart and calculated the distance from the *Grayback*'s location to the harbor at Ra's al Ard.

"It measures out to just less than sixteen nautical miles," Rockham said. "That's about an hour and a half travel time for our Zodiacs. The target will take less than an hour to get to Ra's al Ard, if that's where she's going."

"More like forty-five minutes," Schneller said. "But she will take some time to dock. So she should be tied up and ready to unload at the pier in an hour, less if she noses into a boat ramp or the beach."

"No ramps show on the chart," Rockham noted. "And this whole section of Kuwaiti beach is heavily fortified with obstacles and mines, especially so close to Kuwait City. They want to keep our Marines off that beach. I don't think they can put one of their own landing ships in there. No, the pier is it, I think."

Schneller and Haster watched Rockham head forward to tell his men of the new developments in their mission.

"I don't think he's very interested in waiting," Haster said.

"No, he isn't," Schneller concurred as he took a sip of his coffee. "But he's doing all the right things to ensure the best chance for his men and the success of the operation." Looking over at Haster, Schneller added with a smile, "He is a bit intense, though, wouldn't you say?"

Rockham and his men had another long hour before they had solid information to go on. Returning to the control room, Rockham waited near the compartment where both the radios and the intelligence receivers and printers were located. A television screen flickered blue in the subdued light of the submarine. All lighting had been switched over to red to give the SEALs and the crew the opportunity to develop their night vision before the submarine had to surface.

"We have a live feed coming in from the Keyhole," Haster said as the TV screen lit up with a picture. "The operation has some priority. They've assigned satellite assets just for this operation tonight."

Hearing but not really listening to Haster's comments, Rockham watched the TV screen intently. Sam Paulson had come up to his side and was also looking at the screen.

"They've switched to thermal imaging," Haster said.

In the eerie picture, men and running machinery glowed brightly with radiant energy while colder items looked dark and dead.

"There's almost no one on the pier or anywhere on the main deck of the ship," Paulson said. "If she's unloading, they're taking their time to do it."

"I don't think they're unloading or loading," Rockham said. "There's nothing at the bow of the ship or by any of the deck hatches. If they had unloaded, the cranes would still be hot at least. Look at them—they're dark and cold. And the stack is barely putting out any heat. The engines must be idling, if they're running at all. I think she's either tied up for the night or waiting for something.

"Right there," Rockham said as he pointed to the screen. "There's the heat signature of a body on the port side forward of the superstructure. And there's another closer to the stern on the starboard side. I only see one other guard up near the port side of the bow. Look at that glow. I think he's smoking a cigarette.

"Three guards for a ship in an occupied country. They must be pretty sure of themselves and their security."

Looking around at Paulson and the others who had come up, Rockham said with a grin, "Let's show them the error of their ways. We launch as soon as we are ready."

"We'll be on the surface in fifteen minutes," Captain Schneller said.

Paulson didn't say a word; he wasn't there anymore. Looking up, Rockham could see him heading up forward, where he last saw Kahuna.

Once the men received the green light, they moved quickly and easily into action. Though only one of their number having been on the *Grayback* before, all of the SEALs moved with smooth precision through the submarine's spaces. They had paid attention their last few days on the boat and knew the forward section well.

"Last package!" Alexander called out as he climbed up the ladder into the port hangar. He was bringing up the last of the materials the men would take with them on the operation. Everything else was loaded aboard the Zodiacs. The only thing that had to be done was to open the deck locker and pull out the fuel containers once the submarine had surfaced. Chief Monday would take less than two minutes to complete the recovery of the fuel while the men were preparing to launch the Zodiacs. He would have no trouble opening the locker even with the decks awash.

The *Grayback* was still submerged for the time being. In the starboard hangar, Paulson and Kahuna were in position inside their nine-boat. Several members of the submarine's crew were operating in the now flooded hangar. Since it was at night in open waters, the working crew hadn't bothered with closed-circuit breathing systems. They were working with standard twin 71.2 cubic-foot air tanks on their backs.

Inside the nine-boat, both Paulson and Kahuna were breathing from Mark 15 underwater breathing apparatus. The Mark 15 UBAs were electronically controlled closed-circuit constant oxygen, partial pressure systems. The UBAs would adjust their gas mixtures automatically, so Paulson and Kahuna could work easily and safely at any depth to which they took the SDV. In addition, the two men could breathe off boat air—the compressed air carried in tanks inside the nine-boat. The Mark 15 UBAs didn't exhaust any bubbles into the water, which made them the preferred breathing system for SDV crews.

As far as Rockham and the men of the SMD were concerned, they didn't need breathing equipment. Snugged up behind each man's back was a pair of jet fins. The webbing of the UDT lifejackets the SEALs wore was looped through the heel straps of the swim fins. The bottom blades of the fins were underneath the web belts around each SEAL's waist. Each man also carried a diving mask. In case the SEALs had to abandon the target or swim for any reason, a pair of swim buddies would help each other get their fins out and donned.

With a soft, wet whooshing sound, the hatch of the starboard hangar started to cycle open. The SEAL in the port hangar could only hear some noises—occasional clanks and grinding sound—as the sub's crew moved the SDV out of its hangar on a wheeled cradle. There was no sound as Kahuna turned the speed control open and the nine-boat launched from the *Grayback*. Soon enough it would be the SEALs' turn to launch.

The *Grayback* surfaced slowly and the water poured into the hangar as Chief Monday operated the flooding control. The water swirling around the men's feet was only about a foot deep when it stopped rising. With the experience he had developed years ago in UDT 12, Chief Monday worked the controls and the huge domed hatch slowly lifted up, exposing a cloudy night with no moon showing across the dark expanse of the Persian Gulf.

As the rest of the SEALs pushed the Zodiacs forward and out of the hangar, Monday stepped forward to the fuel locker on the outside deck of the boat. Gasoline was just too dangerous to carry on board a submarine if it wasn't absolutely necessary. Monday also knew this from long experience, and he was quick and efficient at opening the locker and unlashing the fuel containers inside.

The lightweight bladders and fuel cans would float away if they weren't secured, so several of the men stepped forward to help. With an eighteen-gallon gasoline bladder in each hand, Kurkowski went back to second squad's Zodiac while Chief Monday secured the locker. Ryan Marks had the smaller six-gallon can with him as he got to the Zodiac. In each boat, the coxswains quickly secured the fuel containers up in the bow, where the tilt of the boat would help the gasoline and oil mixtures flow back to the engine.

Within minutes of opening the hatch, the outboards of both Zodiacs were quietly purring and pulling away from the *Grayback*. Several members of the submarine's crew who had come up to help the SEALs launch cycled the hangar hatch shut. The operation was under way.

CHAPTER 21

★ ★ ★ ★

2317 ZULU
29° 16' North, 48° 16' East
Zodiacs Papa One Bravo and Papa Two Echo
Persian Gulf

The *Grayback* was two miles behind them as the Zodiacs carrying the SEALs of the SMD sped quietly across the water. The sea was almost completely calm, and the rubber boats skipped across the placid surface, driven by their fifty-five horsepower outboard motors. Under the water nearly thirty feet below them and falling behind was the nine-boat with her deadly armament of torpedoes.

Crouching low across the inflated side tubes of the Zodiacs, the SEALs grimaced against the slight salt spray and held on for the ride. To the left of their boats, even in the darkness, they could see the dim shoreline of occupied Kuwait. There were few lights showing. It was hard to tell if that was because of blackout conditions or because the Iraqi occupiers had cut back on the electricity. Either way, the darkness would be an aid to the SEALs. They did their best work in the dark; it was like a second home to them. The saltwater they were skimming across would always be the first home of the Teams.

It was 0218 hours local time, almost two-thirty in the morning. This was the time the SEALs liked to be on the move. While most people slept, they slipped through the darkness to accomplish their objective.

The Zodiacs would take about an hour and twenty minutes to cover the twelve nautical miles from their launch point to the harbor at Ra's al Ard. The nine-boat behind them would take two hours to cross the same distance. That left a forty minute window where the SEALs would be at the target without the means to sink the boat if necessary. As far as the *Polnocny* landing ship getting away from them, the discrepancy in time wasn't too great a risk.

From what they had learned from the thermal images of the satellite downloads, it would take fifteen to twenty minutes to get the *Polnocny* to raise steam and be under way in her present condition. By the time the target was out of the harbor, the nine-boat would be well inside the range to put a fish into her.

What might matter more to the SEALs were the changes that could take place at the target while they were at sea. Three guards on watch had been seen on the main deck. There could be more or there could be less on duty as the SEALs spent their time at sea. But these concerns couldn't worry the men on the rubber boats. They would deal with whatever came up at the target—it's what they trained for.

The moonless, overcast night sky cast faint light on the dark waters of the Persian Gulf. Below the surface of the inky blackness, the black fiberglass hull of the nine-boat cut through the depths. The electric motors driving the twin screws at the back of the nine-boat made no sound as the SDV passed through the deep. Silent as a hunting shark, it moved forward on the same 300 degree compass heading as their Teammates in the Zodiacs on the surface.

Though the Mark 15 UBAs did allow the crew of the nine-boat to talk to each other, neither man had anything to say. While Paulson kept an eye on the compass and navigation systems, Kahuna drove the boat. When it came time to launch their torpedoes, Kahuna would be aiming the craft while Paulson pulled the trigger.

The two SEALs had been working in the Gulf waters for weeks, looking for explosive mines planted by the Iraqis. So far, about sixteen mines had been located, so the dangers of the minefields had been established; they were not the result of Iraqi propaganda. Now, instead of using their Doppler navigation and sonar systems to try to locate mines, the men in the nine-boat were carrying their own explosives through the water in the warheads of their torpedoes.

There was a glow from chem lights activated and set in holders inside the nine-boat, so the occupants were not working in the dark. The illuminated dials and indicators of the controls and other systems of the boat added to the dim light of the interior. With their breathing masks covering almost their entire faces, Paulson and Kahuna resembled space creatures come to visit Earth's oceans. In fact, the flat, rectangular shape of the nine-boat looked like it could have been some kind of Martian creature, so the otherworldly appearance of its occupants fit the overall picture.

In all three craft, the men were occupied with their own thoughts. They were out on a hot operation in enemy-held territory. This was something all SEALs worked and trained for years in order to accomplish. None of the men liked conflict, but their mission right now was to ensure that the conflict soon to start around them did not spread out to a possibly global conflagration.

By 0317 hours local time, the dark lighthouse at the point of Ra's al Ard was in sight. The SEALs could not have expected the Iraqis to leave them a working lighthouse as an aiming point, but even a dark lighthouse was a landmark, and a solid indication of the locations of the two Zodiacs. Around the point where the lighthouse stood, less than 150 meters to the west, was the entrance to the inner harbor.

The harbor itself was a nearly hundred-meter-wide square behind a fifty-meter-wide entrance. It was at the end of the concrete pier. Secured to the western end of the biggest pier was their target, the *Polnocny*-class ex-Soviet medium landing craft.

Crouching near the bow of the lead boat, Rockham could see that they were fast approaching the target. While the Zodiacs were still almost half a klick away, Rockham raised a clenched fist. At the rear of the boat, Lopez took the outboard motor immediately out of gear.

With the motor shut down, the Zodiac immediately slowed and soon stopped. Seeing the actions on the other boat. Daugherty signaled Lutz to cut the engine on their boat. The two Zodiacs drifted close to each other as second squad coasted to a stop.

Near the stern of second squad's Zodiac, Henry Limbaugh reached out and grabbed hold of the 14mm black nylon line that ran around the top of the buoyancy tube of first squad's boat. Near the bow of first squad's Zodiac, Mike Bryant did the same thing. With both SEALs hanging onto the lines, the two rubber boats bumped quietly together and rocked in the slight swell.

Looking through their 7×50 power binoculars, both Rockham and Daugherty carefully studied the *Polnocny* where she rested secure against the concrete pier. There were no lights showing on the main deck, and only a few lights on the pier were on to illuminate the roadbed that ran along it. Nothing moved; nothing looked unusual.

This was the time for patience. Careful observation of a target could tell a man a lot—like just what kind of trouble he was about to walk into. For more than fifteen minutes there was no movement along the main deck of the landing ship. No

lights shone through the portholes in the superstructure or the half-dozen ports in the main hull.

Then there was movement. A single man
stepped out from the stern of the ship and moved
along the deck on the port side. He was flapping
his arms in the cold night air. Cold was a relative
thing. The SEALs could ignore temperatures that
were painful to experience. But the present situation didn't offer any danger from the cold. It was
midwinter in the Persian Gulf, and to the SEALs
air temperatures in the high fifties were not really
cold.

Observing for ten minutes more, Rockham
watched the man walk along the deck until he
huddled down behind one of the large eighteen-
barreled 140mm barrage rocket launchers amidships on the forward deck. The big rectangular
launchers were covered with tarps and gave good
cover against the slight wind coming in off the
water.

Finally, Rockham reached down and pulled up a
black paddle from the bottom of the Zodiac. Except for the coxswain, each man in both boats did
the same thing. Moving their paddles outboard,
they maintained a low profile while moving the
boats through the water. There was only a faint
splash and gurgle of the paddles as the rubber
boats slipped in. The rally point was behind the
SEALs, in case they were broken up and had to
swim out to sea. Rocking quietly in the current, an
inactivated buoy indicated the mouth of the harbor.
A secondary rally point was planned down along
the coast. To get to the offshore wreck that was the

secondary rally point, each SEAL would have to negotiate any Iraqi patrols, as well as the known mines and obstacles along the beach. The rally points were an important backup to the SEALs extraction plans, but none of the men wanted to use them.

Instead of coming in directly to the target, Rockham directed the Zodiacs toward the concrete pier. The heavy rocks and rip-rap—concrete forms resembling a giant child's toy jacks, breaking up the waves before they could damage the pier—made fair cover for the SEALs' approach. Salt spray and the cold breeze was more of what Rockham was looking for along the breakwater, those uncomfortable features should help keep any local guards from looking out to sea and the darkness that hid the Zodiacs.

Moving parallel to the shore, the Zodiacs came up to the end of the pier and slipped into the entrance to the harbor. A short distance past the end of the pier rose the bow of the target. There wasn't enough room for the Zodiacs to pass the ship, running between it and the pier wall, so they slowly moved along the port side of the craft.

While the coxswains of both boats held up their suppressed MP5-Ns, the rest of their Teammates slipped the rubber boats past the hull. On the port side of the Zodiacs, the SEALs held the rubber boats away from the steel hull, not allowing the boats to bump the hull and make a sound. Silently, they slipped along to the planned boarding points.

First squad moved to the stern of the big landing ship, where the fantail was located. Under the
cover of some tackle and machinery hanging from
the stern of the *Polnocny*, first squad brought their
Zodiac to a halt. With Dan Able and Mike Ferber
holding him steady, John Sukov stood up in the
bow, the painter's pole in his hand. Mike Bryant
held the caving ladder hanging down from the
hook at the top of the pole. He would be the first
man up the ladder once Sukov had secured it to
the deck only a few feet over their heads.

With the men ready, Rockham keyed the microphone to his MX-300R twice. Two clicks
sounded in each SEAL's earpiece. Less than half a
minute later two answering clicks were heard.
Now both squads were coordinated for the climb
up to the deck.

Reaching up with the hook, Sukov easily placed
it over the deck coaming. With Pete Wilkes holding the bottom of the caving ladder, Bryant set
himself to go up to the edge of the fantail deck.
Keying his mike three times, Rockham waited
only a few seconds until he heard an answering
three clicks. At a nod from Rockham, Bryant
quickly went up the ladder until he was just below
the edge of the main deck.

Reaching into his shoulder holster, Bryant
pulled out his suppressed Ruger Mark II pistol.
Clicking off the safety with his thumb, he let the
muzzle of the pistol lead the way over the coaming
of the deck. As the eyes in the black balaclava-
covered head of the SEAL cleared the edge of the
deck, he froze in place. Squatting down in the

shelter of a small boat resting in a cradle at the port side of the ship was an Iraqi sentry.

In his position at the boat, the Iraqi on the deck only had to move his hands away from his face and open his eyes to see Bryant not six feet away. Without moving, Bryant held his position. His dark eyes centered on the Iraqi while staying focused on the front sight of the Ruger. Bryant watched the man he was about to kill.

The Iraqi on guard pulled his hands away from his face as he leaned his head back. Rubbing his eyes, the man finally opened them and looked around the deck. He hadn't been caught sleeping at his post, but the uncomfortable position he had been squatting in would make his knees hurt badly. And just what—

When he could see the man's eyes, Bryant squeezed the trigger of the Ruger. With a sound like a wet cough, the pistol fired. The reduced velocity rimfire round launched a 40-grain lead projectile that was almost half an inch long. The bullet sped from the muzzle of the pistol at less than a thousand feet per second, well below the speed of sound. Without even a sonic crack to mark its passage, the bullet entered the right eye of the sentry. The sound of the ejected brass case hitting the hull was lost in the sounds of waves lapping against the steel hull.

With his brain struck, the sentry crumpled without a sound. Bryant tracked across the deck, leading his eyes with the muzzle of his pistol. No other targets offered themselves to his deadly marksmanship. While crossing the deck, he made sure to also look up onto the bridge deck. Except for the open twin muzzles of a Soviet AK-230 30mm antiaircraft gun centered on the bridge deck, nothing looked back at him.

Pulling himself quickly up onto the fantail, Bryant moved past deck machinery to the rear bulkhead of the superstructure. With his MP5K-PDW in his left hand, he slipped the Ruger back into his shoulder holster. Switching hands on his MP5K, Bryant swept the deck with the muzzle after ensuring that the selector switch was thumbed into the last detent, or full automatic position.

Some paint was peeling and there were spots of rust on almost every surface of the ship as Bryant looked around. There were hatchways into the superstructure on either side of him. Both hatches were shut against the night air. The lack of any way to walk past the superstructure helped Bryant ensure the security of the fantail as he went back to where he had climbed aboard.

Without looking down, he stuck his left hand out and waved a signal down to his Teammates in the Zodiac below. Meanwhile, the muzzle of the suppressor attached to his MP5K swept back and forth across the deck, duplicating the movement of Bryant's eyes.

As Rockham started up the caving ladder, Bryant stepped back into the shadow of the largest piece of machinery on the deck. He recognized it now as a partially covered winch. At the cover of the winch, he maintained a 360-degree security while his Teammates came aboard.

On the port side of the ship, just behind the amidships line, the same drama was unfolding for Ryan Marks, the lead climber of second squad. There was no sign of another sentry as Marks led the way to bring his squad up and on board. If there had been another Iraqi guard, Marks would have dealt with him as efficiently and mercilessly as Bryant had dealt with his.

The men of the SMD had taken down an enemy ship less than six months earlier. Not only had they trained extensively for the kind of operation they were conducting at that moment, they had direct combat experience in just such a situation. The details were different, but not the reactions of the men involved. That experience helped the SEALs as they moved quickly and silently to take control of the *Polnocny*.

To secure the superstructure, first squad would move in on the starboard side of the stern bulkhead. They would enter through the starboard hatch and move into the passageway before splitting up into fire teams. Rockham, with fire team one, would go up and secure the bridge and radio room. Mike Ferber, leading fire team two, would go belowdecks and take down the engineering spaces. With those critical areas secured, the ship couldn't move or communicate.

Second squad had the bigger job, or at least the most area to cover. While Daugherty and fire team one secured the main deck, Chief Monday would take fire team two down into the deck spaces. The most important part of Daugherty's part of the mission was to maintain a watch on the deck and the harbor surrounding the ship. They would be in a position to warn their Teammates if anyone came into the area by water or land.

The intent of the mission was to conduct a soft assault for as long as possible. Using stealth and movement, the SEALs aim was to secure the ship long enough to examine the tank deck and secure any and all documents, charts, and other sources of information.

While the rest of the unit was taking down the ship, Ed Lopez and Henry Lutz stayed with the Zodiacs, hidden up close to the pier and almost underneath the ship. Both men held their MP5-N submachine guns at the ready. On the folding aluminum deck plates in front of them was a loaded M60E3 machine gun. If silence was called for, the suppressor on their MP5-Ns would hold down the noise of firing. If things hit the fan and noise didn't matter anymore, the M60E3 belt-fed machine guns were set to add their power to a fight.

At the fantail, first squad was preparing to enter the ship. There were no accommodation ladders leading up to the bridge deck. The penetration had to be made from inside the superstructure. Lining up at the hatchway, first squad set up behind Dan Able, the breacher who would open the hatch. Jack Tinsley maintained watch as rear security, and the other members of the squad were between Tinsley and Able. Once Able opened the hatch, Mike Bryant as point man would be the first through the door.

As each man prepared for the entry, he snugged up behind the man in front of him. The tight formation allowed every man in the squad to know where his Teammates were. The squad would not move until a signal—a squeeze to the shoulder—had been passed from the rear man to the front. Not until a man was ready for the entry would he pass the squeeze signal forward. When the breacher felt the signal at his shoulder, he knew the line of men behind him, the train, was prepared.

With his men in position, Rockham keyed his microphone and spoke softly into it. "First squad ready."

Fire team two of second squad was lined up and ready to enter the port side of the superstructure. At the port side forward ladder inside the superstructure, they would move to the interior decks. Daugherty and his men would stay under cover at the forward part of the superstructure and keep watch across the main deck until the orders to move out came from Rockham.

While the rest of the unit was setting up, Able prepped his hatchway. Reaching into an upper pocket of his vest, he pulled out a plastic bottle of oil, twisted the cap open and squirted oil on each of the hinges in front of him. The hinges were on the far side of the hatch, and he had to lean in front of it to lubricate them. But the simple act of putting some oil on the hinges could very well prevent them from squealing when the hatch was opened. The devil was in the details.

"Second squad ready," Daugherty whispered into his mike.

"Execute . . . execute . . . execute," said Rockham.

Set at the side of the hatch, Able felt Bryant pass him the signal by squeezing his shoulder. Only a single dog held the hatch shut, and Able turned it with his hand. Pulling the hatch open, he backed to let Bryant and the train go past him and into the passageway.

The train stacked up in the passageway. Now Dan Able was acting as rear security while Tinsley joined the train in the passageway. There were plain wooden doors lining the passageway, hatches for the crew's compartments. To the right of the hatch they had just entered, a ladder led up to the bridge deck and down into the engineering spaces.

Moving at a fast shuffle, Rockham and the three other members of fire team one—Bryant, Able, and Sukov—went up the ladder in a tight tactical formation. Mike Ferber, as the leading petty officer of the first squad, led his fire team belowdecks.

Just as Chief Monday entered the superstructure, the other Iraqi on guard got up from the bow of the boat and walked back to the superstructure. He was cold and hungry, and a hot cup of tea from the galley sounded like a good idea. He never felt the .22 caliber bullet enter his left eye and pass through his brain. His last conscious thought was of hot tea.

Holding his Ruger muzzle up into the air, Ryan Marks watched the Iraqi sentry fall bonelessly to the deck. The thud of the body was dull, but almost louder than the shot that killed the man. Daugherty looked on with a grim expression on his face as he continued to watch the main deck.

CHAPTER 22

★ ★ ★ ★

0131 ZULU
Mark 9 SEAL Delivery Vehicle
Ra's al Ard Harbor
Kuwait City
Persian Gulf

Less than a kilometer offshore from the entrance to the harbor at Ra's al Ard, the nine-boat lay floating with her upper deck barely awash. Having slid the hatch covers back in their runners, both Paulson and Kahuna were watching the mouth of the harbor. They had pulled their masks off and were sitting up to look out over the water.

Even through their waterproof binoculars, neither man could see any action on the deck of the *Polnocny*. They had heard and understood the messages coming over their own radios. The takedown of the Iraqi ship was happening even as they watched—and there was nothing they could do to assist their Teammates. All they could do was watch, and wait to see if they would take a more active part in the mission

With Bryant in the lead, Rockham followed his shooting partner as they set up to take down the bridge. The bridge would have the bulk of the information they were trying to gather on the op. Analysts who specialized in such things would take the raw information and produce worthwhile intelligence from it. But none of that could be accompanied if Rockham and his men failed in their mission—and the takedown portion of the op was just beginning.

Setting up at the hatchway to the bridge, Dan Able reached up quietly and tried to push on the handle to the hatch. Though it was made of steel, the hatch looked like a standard door that would be found on a typical house. The door was locked.

Silence and surprise were working for the SEALs so far, and now Able had to decide to use speed or possibly stealth to open the hatch in front of him. The bridge would probably have a watch, and might have locked the hatch behind them. Speed was what it would take to keep an alarm from being sent out.

Reaching behind him over his right shoulder, Able grasped the duct-tape-covered short handle of his six-pound sledgehammer. The tape made for a secure grip. Standing behind the breacher, Mike Bryant could see what his Teammate was about to do. He reached down and pulled away the Velcro strap securing the handle of the hammer to the pack frame Able had on his back. Then

Able, pulling up on the handle to the sledgehammer, unshipped the head of the tool from the canvas pouch on his pack frame. He measured off his distance and waited for the go signal.

At the rear of the formation, John Sukov had already passed the squeeze signal up to Rockham. In turn, Rockham squeezed Bryant's shoulder. Finally, Bryant reached out and squeezed Able's shoulder.

The train was set. With one hard swing of his strong arms, Able struck the hatch just above the handle. With a loud smash, the hatch flew open, the lock having sheared completely through.

Darting around Able, Bryant went through the hatch and onto the bridge. As he cut to the right, Rockham, coming through the hatchway behind him, cut hard to the left. Neither man saw anyone standing watch at the wheel or anywhere on the bridge. What both SEALs did see was a black-haired man sitting up on a bunk at the rear bulkhead of the bridge. He was shaking his head, as if trying to wake himself. He clearly had no idea what had gotten him up.

Before the man could recover and react, Rockham was at the side of his bunk and tossing him out on the floor.

"*Haedi*," Rockham snarled at the man to keep silent. "*Inta sajeen*," he said, telling the man that he was a prisoner.

Whether the man understood the very bad Arabic or just felt the muzzle of the suppressor grinding into his spine didn't matter. He stopped struggling. While Bryant kept watch on the rest of the bridge, Sukov stepped forward and began to secure the prisoner.

A set of tie-ties were slipped around the man's hands and pulled tight against his wrists. As Sukov was snapping out a triangular bandage to use as a gag, Rockham put up a hand. Sukov stopped and waited.

"Tatakallam Inglizi?" Rockham said as he asked the prostrate man if he spoke English.

"A little," the man said in strongly accented English.

Just then, Daugherty's voice came over the MX-300R radio. "Bravo leader, Bravo leader."

"Bravo leader," Rockham replied as he keyed his microphone.

"We have company coming in from the west," Daugherty said. "A whole bunch of company in a convoy."

Moving over to the starboard windscreen, Rockham looked out over the harbor to the feeder road that led into it. Trucks and other vehicles were coming into the harbor area—and they were heading toward the pier. There was only one ship there, and Rockham was standing on its bridge.

Somebody was coming, and they were coming in what looked like real numbers.

Moving back to his prisoner, Rockham pulled the man's head up by the hair.

"Who is that?" Rockham demanded. "Who are you expecting?"

"Troops," the frightened man said. "Republican Guard troops. We are to transport them. They're early."

"Damn," Rockham said with venom in his voice. Keying his radio, he put out the order that he didn't want to give but knew he must.

"Abort. I say again, abort," Rockham said in a clear, loud voice. "Papa One and Two, meet us at the side. Everyone, abort."

As Rockham gave the order, Bryant stepped to the rear compartment behind the bridge. His MP5-K was up and he would have immediately opened fire on anyone he saw. The time for stealth was over—they had to salvage what they could of the mission objectives.

The rear compartment was the radio room, exactly what Bryant had expected from their studies of the deck plans. Stepping over to the radio desk, he grabbed every notebook and piece of paper he could find. Stuffing the documents underneath his body armor, he pulled up his weapon and fired a long burst into the ship's radio.

"Commo's out," Bryant said as he stepped back onto the bridge.

Sukov was securing the bandage gag over the prisoner's mouth. Looking up over the bunk the man had been lying on, he saw a photograph of the man they were holding, and in it he was wearing a uniform with a lot of gold braid on the shoulders.

"Rock," Sukov said, "look at this. I think we've got the captain here."

Stepping back from the desk he had been ransacking, Rockham stuffed the black leather-bound book and papers he had found into a waterproof bag. Bryant handed over the materials he'd grabbed from the radio room and Rockham stuffed them into the bag.

"I'll be damned," Rockham said.

Pulling up the prisoner, Rockham shoved the muzzle of his suppressor under the terrified man's chin. "Captain?" he said. "Are you the captain?"

Too frightened to lie, and kept from speaking by the gag, the man could only nod his head against the pressure of the weapon threatening him.

Making an instant decision, Rockham turned to Sukov.

"Bring him along," he ordered. "He's the best source of information we'll get out of this mess."

Turning, Rockham pumped his fist up and down in the air and headed toward the rear hatch.

"Move out," he said as he headed down the passageway.

The ship's executive officer, confused and wondering what all the running about was, stepped out from his cabin on the main deck. As he moved into the passageway, he saw the amazing sight of his captain draped over someone's shoulder, being carried off like a sack of onions!

That was the last thought the man had. Bryant, moving as rear security, cut him down with a quick pair of two-round bursts. They had to abort and leave the ship immediately. There was no time for courtesies.

As they left the ship, the SEALs swept through the passageways of the *Polnocny* like a scouring hurricane. Only a few more men stuck their heads out from behind compartment doors. The SEALs dropped the sailors with quick, accurate head shots. Not a man suffered, or even moved much, as he suddenly fell dead.

At the port side of the ship, Rockham looked down and could see both Zodiacs waiting.

"Over the side," he ordered, and the men quickly followed his command.

Before jumping in the water himself, Sukov bent down and pushed his bound prisoner over the side. The SEALs were climbing into the Zodiacs as the bound man hit the water with a clumsy splash. Fast action on the part of John Grant and Henry Limbaugh pulled the prisoner up and into the Zodiac before he drowned.

From his spot on the deck, Rockham conducted a quick head count of the men below him. There were seventeen. All his men were off the ship. As the Iraqi troops started up the road leading to the pier, Rockham was the last SEAL to jump off the ship. The powerful hands of his men pulled him into the Zodiac even as the coxswain twisted open the throttle.

Both boats moved away from the *Polnocny* with the troops only a minute away. As the black Zodiacs disappeared into the gloom of the night, Rockham looked back and cursed. They had gotten away without any losses. But it looked like only the second field operation of the SMD was coming up a crapper. They had a prisoner and a handful of documents.

"Shit," Rockham said, "we never even got to the tank deck."

"Yes we did," Chief Monday said.

Looking around, Rockham realized that the

two squads were badly mixed up. He was on the same boat as Daugherty and Chief Monday. The prisoner and Sukov were on the other Zodiac.

"What do you mean, Chief?" Rockham asked.

"My fire team was already on the tank deck when you called for an abort," Monday said. "As the men pulled out, I snapped pictures of everything on the deck. It was filled with vehicles, no tanks or TELs, but there were several tracked antiaircraft artillery vehicles as well as radar sets and tracked SAM launchers. Taking out just the surface-to-air missile launchers would be worthwhile.

"You'll be able to see all of this for yourself once these films are developed." Monday held up a waterproof bag that had the outlines of a camera held safely within it. "I didn't think it mattered anymore so I went ahead and used a flash. Popped that shutter as fast as I could forward the film and focus. Think I can be a fashion photographer?"

Rockham laughed as he looked at his platoon chief. The big man had ears like jug handles and a thatch of unruly black hair. His lopsided grin showed big teeth. And right then, Rockham thought he was the best guy he had ever known.

As the Zodiacs sped away from the harbor, Rockham pulled up his MX-300R's microphone.

"Bruiser, this is Bravo leader . . . Bruiser, this is Bravo leader."

The radios were encrypted so that even if the Iraqis could hear the transmission, they wouldn't be able to understand it. Still, the operational security habits of a career in the Teams did not go away easily. Rockham maintained the use of code names as he called to the nine-boat.

"Bravo leader, this is Bruiser one, over," came Paulson's tinny and converted voice over the radio.

"Bruiser, you are clear for the fight," Rockham said. "You are clear for the fight. Confirm, over."

"Bravo leader, I confirm clear for the fight, clear for the fight. Bruiser one out."

With the order he had just given, Rockham had told the men on the nine-boat that they had permission to fire as soon as they had the shot. It would be better if the landing ship was out in deeper water. But even putting her down at pierside would damage the Iraqi war effort.

As the Zodiacs moved away from the harbor, Paulson and Kahuna prepared to move closer. They saw a flurry of activity on the deck of the *Polnocny*.

"Looks like they found a casualty or two," Kahuna said.

"Yes," Paulson agreed. "But someone has fired up the diesels in the engine room. Look at that exhaust smoke pour from the stern. You can see it from here. Let's wait and see how fast she gets under way. Maybe we can put a fish into her away from the pier."

As the two SEALs watched from their SDV, the landing ship cast off from the pier and began to move out into the channel. Whoever was piloting the big ship wasn't very good at it. The ship actually brushed against the old tire fenders of the pier, tearing one off as it passed.

"Man, someone is new at their job," Kahuna said.

"Well," Paulson said, "let's button up and help them retire before they get any worse."

Both men pulled their breathing masks back on and slid their hatches shut. The lethal black SDV silently passed back under the surface of the water with barely a ripple to show it was ever there.

Less than two kilometers from the mouth of the harbor, the water was over a hundred feet deep. As the two SEALs had watched the big ship stagger away from the pier like a drunken sailor, neither of them thought they would have much trouble staying ahead of the ship for at least a couple of miles. Once it had steadied down to a course, they would put a torpedo into it, holding the second as a reserve.

Kahuna kept the nine-boat on a steady course just ten feet below the surface. Over his headset, Paulson could hear the noise of the *Polnocny* as it lumbered through the water. His computerized Doppler navigation system also helped him track the big ship.

"Bring her up to the surface," Paulson said into his mouthpiece microphone. "This is too important a shot to miss, and I want to take a visual bearing."

"Roger that," Kahuna said, and pulled back on the plane's control.

Sliding back his hatch cover before they broke the surface, Paulson prepared to lift his head and take a sighting. Less than a thousand meters away was the *Polnocny,* and it was moving in a northerly direction.

Ducking back down, Paulson spoke to Kahuna over the communication system.

"Bring her around to course two-two-five," Paulson said. "She's less than a kilometer away and we have to set up the shot fast. The water's deep enough here to make salvage at least a little harder."

The black SDV swung around and settled into its new course. Over his headphones, Paulson could hear the passive homing system of the starboard Mark 46 torpedo activate and start tracking their target. When he had a good, solid lock, Paulson prepared to fire.

"Torpedo away," he said as he fired the first ever torpedo attack from a miniature U.S. Navy submersible. For that matter, as far as Paulson knew, it was the first war shot from a U.S. submarine since World War II.

The motor of the Mark 46 fired off with a bang and a roar. Immediately, the sleek torpedo disengaged from its rail and sped on its way. The homing system on the nose of the torpedo kept it centered on the *Polnocny* only eight hundred meters distant. At least the ship was far enough away for the fuze in the torpedo to fully arm, Paulson thought as he listened to the high-pitched burr in the water.

The two SEALs didn't have long to wait to hear the results of their shot. In thirty-five seconds the Mark 46 had crossed the distance separating the

294 SEALS SUB STRIKE

SDV from the landing ship. With a thunderous explosion, the warhead detonated as the torpedo struck just forward of amidships on the starboard side of the *Polnocny*.

The explosion of the torpedo's warhead was impressive, and the SEALs felt the shock of the hit through the water and into their SDV. But that explosion was nothing compared to the blast as hundreds of pounds of fuel on board the SA-6 Gainful missiles ignited uncontrollably. The torpedo had impacted not six feet from one of the missiles on its launch vehicle, and the blast of the torpedo set off the rocket motor. Then the eighty-eight pounds of high explosive in the warhead detonated, setting off the other two missiles on the launch vehicle.

The resultant blast and fireball flashed through the tank deck, ripping the *Polnocny* open like an aluminum soft drink can that someone put a blasting cap into. The shock wave was physically painful for the SEALs as it passed through the water and through their SDV. Coming up to the surface to check on the results of their shot, and to let the blood drain from their masks where their noses bled, Paulson and Kahuna looked at the stunning result of their torpedo.

"Man," Kahuna said, "just what in the hell was in that torpedo?"

"I don't know," Paulson said, "but I'm going to be really careful with the other one. I think we better get out of here before anyone notices."

"It may be a little late for that," Kahuna said as he pointed to the northwest.

Roaring out of the Kuwait City harbor were two Iraqi-built Swari-class patrol boats. The eleven-meter-long boats displaced only seven tons, but pushed by powerful engines, they could move across the water at up to twenty-seven knots. The two 14.5mm KPV heavy machine guns mounted on the patrol boats didn't particularly bother the SEALs. Water stopped bullets, even big ones. The thirty-two 57mm high explosive warhead rockets in the pod on the back of the boats, however, were another thing entirely.

Pulling their breathing masks back into place, Paulson and Kahuna got back down inside their nine-boat and pulled the hatches shut. Both men knew that the chances that they'd been spotted by the two patrol boats, looking past the burning oil and wreckage of the *Polnocny*, were just about zero. But nearly zero wasn't the same thing as no chance at all. The nine-boat headed out to sea on a course that would take it back to the *Grayback*.

CHAPTER 23

★ ★ ★ ★

0402 ZULU
29° 14' North, 48° 16' East
Control Room
LPSS 574 *Grayback*
Persian Gulf

The *Grayback* was barely making headway forward, only moving enough to maintain stability.
On her deck, the crew of divers from the sub were
winching in the cradle they had just landed the
nine-boat on. Paulson and Kahuna, inside the boat,
were now waiting out the final part of the recovery procedures. With the nine-boat secured inside
the hangar, the water would be pumped out and
the two men could step out of their SDV and walk
into the submarine.

The fact that there was still a live Mark 46 torpedo mounted to the nine-boat made the dive
crew particular about following procedures. But
the catch—bringing the boat in and securing her

to the cradle—had gone smoothly. As the waters around the *Grayback* brightened from the rising sun, the great round hatch over the starboard hangar began to cycle closed.

"Recovery crew says they have the boat, Captain," Master Chief Runyon said as he hung up the handset of the 1-MC.

"Very good, COB," Captain Schneller said. "Exec, please come to course one-one-zero and full speed. Head us to deeper water."

"Helm, come to course one-one-zero degrees, all ahead flank," Lieutenant Commander Ferro, the *Grayback*'s executive officer, said.

"Course one-one-zero degrees, aye sir," the helmsman repeated from his place at the controls.

In a smooth, wide turn the *Grayback* began moving away from the shore of occupied Kuwait and a very upset Iraqi Navy group. She headed out to the deeper waters of the Persian Gulf and the relative safety they offered.

Turning to Rockham, Schneller smiled. "That's it Lieutenant," he said. "Everyone is back and accounted for. You cut the time pretty closely when you came in on the radio and requested a surface pickup. Dawn was breaking, and we're kind of allergic to the sunlight this close to shore."

"I know sir," Rockham said, "but it was the only way we could bring our captive aboard without risk of downing him."

"Oh, I agreed with your assessment of the situation," Schneller said. "But I still didn't like exposing this submarine to possible observation. I much preferred being able to pick up Lieutenant Paulson and his craft while submerged."

"His message that they had taken out the *Polnocny* was pretty good news all on its own," Rockham said.

"And just what has been done with your guest?" Schneller asked.

"Right now he's sitting on a bunk in the forward living spaces, bound and blindfolded," Rockham said. "There's two of my biggest men with him at all times, even when he goes to the head. That's the only time his hands are untied and the blindfold comes off. He already knows he's on a submarine—but he has no idea which one or what his location is. Besides, he's not very interested in looking around when he's on the head—not with the muzzle of a suppressed Ruger pointed at him from six feet away.

"There isn't a chance of him getting to that weapon before he has several rounds put into him. I know I couldn't do it. John Grant is the fastest man I've ever seen. And the prisoner has already been told the target for the bullets wouldn't be a lethal spot, just a very painful one. Grant said that it really makes it difficult for the prisoner to do his business when there's a pistol pointed at him. And when he comes out of the head, the blindfold and tie-ties go right back on. He is not a happy camper."

"Well, he's going to be even less pleased when we get him off this boat," Schneller said. "He is to be picked up as soon as it's safe for us to surface.

We'll put him in a rubber boat, then a helicopter will gather him and his escort and fly them to the *Midway*."

"His escort?" Rockham said.

"Yes, the orders also said they wanted you to report back to the carrier with him," Schneller said, "along with all of the information, films, and materials you brought back with you. You are to be flown to coalition command headquarters in Riyadh. There are some very high-ranking people interested in your debriefing."

"But what about my men?" Rockham said.

"Not a problem," Schneller said. "We'll surface later tonight near the *Midway*. That will let your men get their boats into the water with all of your gear aboard."

"I should probably take my platoon chief with me when I go in to report," Rockham said. "He was eyes-on inside the tank deck where he took the pictures. Said the hold was full of vehicles and equipment. His observations would be valuable."

"And your men?" Schneller asked.

"My exec and leading petty officer can take care of the unit while I'm gone," Rockham said.

"Then taking your platoon chief along sounds like a good idea," Schneller said. "There should be more than enough room for the three of you aboard the helicopter from the *Midway*."

"If not," Rockham said, "I'm certain Chief Monday wouldn't have much trouble making our guest ride on the skids."

"Sounds like most Navy chiefs I know," Schneller said with a laugh.

"Captain," Runyon said, "the SDV is secured and the crew's aboard."

"Thank you, COB," Schneller said. "Well, Lieutenant Rockham, shall we go forward and greet your Teammates?"

"An excellent idea, sir," Rockham agreed with a grin.

In the forward living spaces, Sam Paulson was stripping off his wet suit. His driver, Kahuna, was already in the head taking a well-deserved fresh-water shower. As Paulson stripped off his suit, the decidedly unique aroma of undersea and under-wear spread through the compartment. Paulson was looking forward to a shower himself but was still excitedly explaining about the nine-boat's last part in the mission.

"You should have seen it let go," Paulson said. "It must have been a hell of a blast. We felt it pass right through us almost a klick away. Any closer and we could have been casualties ourselves."

"You know," Mainhart said, "that is why there's a minimum range on torpedoes."

"Hey, you do what you have to," Paulson said as he vigorously rubbed his wet hair with a towel. "The choice was to nail the target or take a chance on the ship getting away. We were close enough that the torpedo would have had to malfunction in order to miss—not that a piece of Navy ordnance ever malfunctioned before. Besides, that ship was zigzagging like there was a drunk at the wheel."

"Probably just some crewman they grabbed up," Chief Monday said. "We took the ship's cap-tain as a prisoner and brought him back with us."

"No shit," Paulson said. "Where is he?"

"Aft with a couple of our people," Rockham said.

At Captain Schneller's suggestion, John Grant and Wayne Alexander had taken the still blindfolded captive back to the crew's mess deck to get him something to eat. Maneuvering a blindfolded man through a crowded submarine was something new for the SEALs. In spite of their inexperience, Grant and Alexander managed to get this guest back to the mess deck with a minimum of bangs and bruises. The prisoner was acting dull and uninterested, only making a grunt when he banged his shin or forehead on an unseen hazard.

The only thing they had learned from the man so far was that his name was Hazma and that one of the guards killed on deck had been named Muhammad. Apparently, he had been the sentry Marks had dropped just as the sentry had been about to discover the SEALs on board the *Polnocny*. Seeing Muhammad's body before being forced to abandon his ship had made a strong impression on Hazma and dropped the man into a deep depression. Tinsley said he was in shock over his situation. That was something all of the men listening could understand.

Swapping stories continued for a while as the men unwound from what had been a hectic night. Rockham let them blow off a little steam before beginning a more formal debriefing. Luck had been riding with the SMD this time, and all the men knew it. They had managed to pull success out of a situation that had turned very bad, very fast.

Each man sat and told his observations on how the mission had unfolded. A tape recorder sitting on a rack took down every word for later transcription. The men would be formally debriefed later, once on board the *Midway*. But with Rockham and Chief Monday heading in to Riyadh, Rockham thought taking a debriefing interview tape with them, even an informal one, would help deliver even more timely information to the intelligence analysts.

Four hours later, Rockham, Chief Monday, Hazma, and Jack Moody—a crewman from the *Grayback*—were on the surface in a Zodiac watching a helicopter approach them from the southeast. Hazma was no longer blindfolded, but his hands were still secured in front of him with tie-ties.

The crew of the SH-3H Sea King helicopter had seen a lot over the years serving in the Chargers, Helicopter Squadron 14. With their mission being both antisubmarine warfare as well as combat search and rescue, the crew had experienced their fair share of men in rubber boats in the middle of the ocean. But they'd never seen four men in a boat, two in uniforms holding bags, one in a wet suit, and the third in a badly fitting set of blue coveralls while also wearing a blindfold and with his hands tied.

Instead of using the rescue hoist to winch up the three men below, Lieutenant Robert Harridan decided to set the Sea King down on the water and just bring the men aboard through the side hatch. The Sea King had a boat hull for amphibious operations. Though they rarely set down on the water, the men in the boat had someone bound and wearing a blindfold, and whoever or whatever the man was, he sure as hell wouldn't be able to help get himself aboard the bird.

The big five-bladed rotor of the Sea King slowed and changed its pitch after landing. That way, the blades didn't cause such a terrific downwash and the rubber boat could be paddled right up to the door. "Pappy" Ricks, the oldest crew chief in the HS-14 squadron, helped the men aboard. The two men in uniform were fit and well-tanned. Pappy knew who they were as soon as he felt the grip of the men when he offered them his hand.

"Welcome aboard," Pappy shouted over the noise of the GE turboshaft engines. "What about the fourth man? The guy in the wet suit?"

"He's staying," Rockham shouted.

Pappy just shrugged his shoulders. These men were probably SEALs, and he had heard a lot of stories about them over his nineteen years in the Navy. He'd also seen enough of them in action to believe most of the stories. If one of their number was going to stay back, it was because he probably had a better ride waiting—like a Great White shark.

"Passengers aboard," Pappy said into the boom microphone attached to his helmet. "The boat's clear."

"Roger that," Harridan said. He twisted the throttle as he pulled up the collective pitch lever.

The sixty-two-foot-diameter set of rotors picked up speed and blurred into a gray disk as the helicopter lifted up from the waves, water pouring off the curved hull and tanklike outriggers.

In the Zodiac, Moody watched the helicopter lift and start moving away with the SEALs and their guest. Now he had to get the attention of the *Grayback* to send up divers to help him get the rubber boat back down into the hangar. As he reached into a pouch for the pyrotechnic signals, he chuckled, wondering what the helicopter crew would have thought if they knew how close they'd been to a submarine. Many of the Sky Kings assigned to carrier wings also had the mission of antisubmarine warfare. But they rarely got to play tag with a real sub, especially not an unknown one.

The first pyrotechnic signal hit the water with a splash, sinking deeply before firing.

On board the Sea King, Harridan switched the radio over to the *Midway*'s control frequency. "Mama Bear, Mama Bear," Harridan said, "this is Lightning One-niner, over."

"This is Mama Bear, One-niner," came over the headsets in a crackling voice. "What is your message? Over."

"We have the packages, plus one," Harridan said. "ETA 1225 hours. Over."

"Roger that, One-niner," the radio voice said. "Packages plus one, ETA 1225 hours. We'll hold lunch for you, Mama Bear, out."

"Man," Harridan said as he turned his microphone over to the intercom. Now he could talk to his copilot, Harry Everstone. "Have we gone to war early? I'd swear those guys back there brought a prisoner with them."

"Hey, I just help drive the bird," Everstone said. "I learned a long time ago not to look at anything the SpecOps people do. It is not a good thing to learn too much. Not a good thing at all."

Back in the rear of the helicopter, Pappy had heard the conversation from up front. Leaning over to the man wearing the lieutenant's bars, he shouted, "We've got over an hour of flight time ahead of us, sir. What do you want to do with your prisoner?"

That was a question Rockham didn't have a solid answer to. They were on a highly classified mission and were returning with a prisoner to a Navy carrier. They would probably have to fly on from the carrier as well. Sailors knew the meaning of security, and sailors talked, even if just among themselves. Rockham had to do something, but how do you conceal a person walking on the deck of an aircraft carrier?

"Do you have a stretcher?" Rockham shouted.

"We've got a Stokes basket for CSAR," Pappy shouted back.

"Great," Rockham said. A big smile spread across his face as he remembered the Edgar Allen Poe story, "The Purloined Letter."

When the big, gray-painted Sea King set down on the flight deck of the *Midway*, two men quickly got out by the side hatch. One of the men was an officer in a desert camouflage uniform, the other wore the orange flight suit and gear of a CSAR operator. Between the two of them, they pulled a Stokes basket—a curved, metal man-size mesh basket for carrying injured personnel—out of the helicopter. Whoever was in the basket was completely covered with a blanket and tied down so he couldn't be thrown out by sudden movements of their transport.

Coming out of the helicopter next and bringing up the rear of the Stokes was a big, tall man wearing senior chief's insignia on the collars of his desert uniform. The man in the basket must have been important to have a lieutenant and a senior chief acting as his stretcher bearers.

Later, when the crew of Lightning 19 were asked who had been carried off their bird, all they could say was that they didn't know. When pressed for more answers, they just said they didn't have any more information. As Rockham had suggested on board the helicopter, it might be best if the crew simply forgot they were ever there.

"I don't know whose Navy you think you're in, mister," Lieutenant Commander House shouted, "but you do not bring a foreign national on board a Navy ship without notifying the commanding officer!"

"Consider it a spur of the moment thing, Commander," Rockham said as he held his temper in check. "We didn't have anywhere else to go and kind of wanted him with us."

"I don't know if you realized it," House shouted, "but we are not yet in an active state of war with Iraq."

"Not yet, anyway," Chief Monday said.

"Consider him your responsibility," House said as he looked from Chief Monday to Rockham and back again. "And the three of you will remain in this compartment until your transport to Riyadh is ready to lift. There will be someone in the passageway to attend to anything you will need."

"Outstanding," Rockham said. "I couldn't have asked for anything more. Thank you, sir."

Lieutenant Commander House glared at Rockham for another moment.

"It is only because the ship's doctor has declared your man fit and able to travel that I don't have him in sick bay or the brig," House said. "And if he did end up in sick bay, you can be assured that there would be a formal captain's mast at the very least."

With his last words, House stormed out of the compartment.

"Get the impression he doesn't like the Teams?" Rockham said to Monday.

"Maybe he dropped out of BUD/S," Monday said. "I thought the way he was shaking his head back and forth, he might hurt himself. Look, sir, there are a lot of regular Navy officers who have no idea what the SEALs actually do. Had one captain in Vietnam who kept referring to us as pole-carrying assassins, whoever the hell they are. You just have to ignore them and keep on with the mission."

"Right, Chief," Rockham said with a quiet laugh.

There was a knock at the compartment from the passageway outside. Opening the hatch, Rockham looked at a smiling face that was hard to forget.

"My friend!" said a familiar southern-accented voice, *friend* being pronounced more like *fren*. "So we shall share a flight and conversation again."

Lieutenant Coudree, mirrored sunglasses, Stetson and all, walked into the compartment.

Rockham turned to Chief Monday. "And you thought Hell Week was over when you left training," he said with a lopsided smile.

CHAPTER 24

★ ★ ★ ★

"If I don't have to talk to another intelligence officer for the rest of the week, I'll be a much happier man," Rockham said.

Both Greg Rockham and Chief Monday had finally rejoined the rest of their unit after spending what felt like an eternity at the coalition command headquarters in Riyadh. Since the J-2—the intelligence section of the Joint Military Staff—was at the command headquarters, that's where the SEALs had to be. Both men spent nearly two full days being grilled by a succession of intelligence officers. They were wrung out, irritable, and had just spent a long ride in a helicopter crossing more than four hundred kilometers of mostly sand desert between Riyadh and Al Mish'ab.

The officers on the intelligence staff had taken all of the material Rockham and his men had collected from the *Polnocny* during their very short boarding of the ship. The real prizes among the paperwork were the code books from the radio room and the cloth-covered bound book Rockham had grabbed from a desk on the bridge. It turned out that his hunch had been right, and what he'd brought back was the ship's log.

The photos Chief Monday had taken of the tank deck cargo were developed and caused a stir in the intelligence office. Monday was questioned repeatedly about the missile launchers he had seen along with the trailers, trucks, and mobile antiaircraft guns. The chief's best recollections were frustrating to the intelligence efforts since he had not been able to do much more than snap a rushed series of pictures. Some Air Force officers pointedly asked him why he didn't check the weapons and missiles more closely since they would probably be used against coalition aircraft in the upcoming conflict. They were not quite ready to experience an angry Navy SEAL senior chief's response to that line of questioning.

In no uncertain terms, Chief Monday told the officers that if he had stopped to examine the weapons, they wouldn't have the information he did bring back. And they shouldn't worry about that particular shipment of hardware since the ship had been blown up after it was boarded by Iraqi troops.

The angry reaction set the officers back a little. But nothing else the SEALs had done caused as much of a reaction as arriving with a prisoner. It turned out that Rockham had not brought back just any prisoner—Hazma had been the commanding officer of the *Polnocny* for over five years.

The Iraqi Navy captain was a gold mine of information once he was turned over to the professional interrogators at J-2. Rockham later found out that at first Hazam was reluctant to talk to his interrogators. That changed immediately after he was told he might be given back to the SEALs. Then, he couldn't answer questions fast enough. As for the fact that Hazma was a prisoner of war when hostilities hadn't officially started, that minor detail was ignored by the staff officers.

The rest of Rockham's men had come ashore in their Zodiacs near Al Mish'ab. That was the forward facility where Naval Special Warfare Task Group One had their high speed boats. Once they identified themselves to the offshore patrols, the two Zodiacs were escorted into the small harbor. The officers and men from NSWTG-1 knew enough not to ask just where in the hell two Zodiacs full of SEALs had come from at the crack of dawn on the Persian Gulf. But the men of the SMD received more than a few curious glances from their Teammates in the task group.

Finally sitting down in the quarters assigned to his men, Rockham leaned back and accepted a cold can of beer from Shaun Daugherty.

"Beer, huh?" Rockham said. "You've been in-country in a dry Muslim nation for what, a day and a half? And already you have cold beer. I'm not going to hear about this, am I?"

"I really don't think so," Daugherty said with a

grin. "But if it makes you feel bad, you can always give it back."

"Go away boy, you bother me," Rockham said in a very bad W.C. Fields impression.

"So, just what kind of intel did they develop from our information?" Mike Ferber asked.

"We should be getting the full report by the end of the week," Rockham said. "They are very hush-hush and scurrying around like ants in Riyadh. I would say things are going to be happening very soon."

"Today is the UN deadline for Iraq to leave Kuwait," Daugherty said.

"And that doesn't look likely to happen, from what we've seen," Larry Stadt said from where he was sitting across the room.

"No, it doesn't," Rockham agreed. "Apparently, that cargo we took out was a very significant load. The Riyadh planners were less than pleased that we hadn't been able to closely examine it."

"Yeah, like we had a lot of time before the Iraqi Army showed up on board," Kurkowski said.

"Exactly," Rockham said, "but that doesn't change the fact that we were looking at a ship full of very high-value assets. This fight is going to start as an air war, and the fly boys are going to be pounding everything they can for weeks before the ground campaign starts.

"That ship had a hold full of antiaircraft systems, as well as some other items that were very significant. What the hell they were doing being shipped away from Iraq—and especially away from Baghdad—before the shooting war starts was the question the J-2 people wanted answered.

"There were two SAM-6 Gainful surface-to-air missile systems in that hold, along with two ZSU-23-4 quad self-propelled antiaircraft guns."

"Those were the four-barreled tanks?" Stadt asked.

"Yes," Rockham said. "Each one of those barrels is a liquid-cooled 23mm cannon with a cyclic rate of up to a thousand rounds a minute. Those four barrels can rip a helicopter out of the sky, and that radar dish on the turret behind them can track a bird across the sky.

"The SA-6 is a low to medium altitude missile system that caused a lot of casualties among Israeli pilots back in the 1973 Middle East war. Iraq has nearly two hundred of the launch vehicles and no one knows how many missiles. What they don't have a lot of are the Straight Flush radar systems that work with the launchers. That was the radar set on the track inside the hold. So whatever those systems were supposed to protect, Saddam considered it pretty damned important."

Rockham stopped and took a drink from his beer while his men considered what he had just told them. It sounded like their mission had raised more questions than it answered. It turned out they were wrong.

"What about that MAS-543 TEL and the Scud?" Daugherty said. "Do we have a lead on where that missile or those suspected warheads went?"

"More than a lead," Rockham said, then swallowed his beer. "The ship's log said where they were delivered. The captain didn't know exactly what he was delivering, and it looked like he didn't want to. But he did note where the ship went and when. Those vehicles were unloaded at the Az Zawr port city on Faylaka Island.

"They may not be set up and ready to use just yet. There was a trailer radar set on board the *Polnocny* that was probably earmarked for wherever the Scud is. That was an RMS-1 End Tray meteorological radar on the trailer. That's used to support artillery and missile units. The truck was a Mercury Grass VHF communications system. So it looks like we took out their commo and their weather station. Without eyes or ears, they're going to have a hard time operating. It's not a good idea to use a chemical or biological weapon if you don't know which way the wind is going to blow."

"So when are we heading for Faylaka Island?" Mike Bryant asked.

"Once they locate the launch site, we should get the go ahead," Rockham said. "The planners have given the site the code name 'Snowfall.'"

"Somebody had a sense of humor," Henry Limbaugh said. "Snow's kind of hard to find in the desert."

"Apparently, so's this missile site," Rockham said. "Faylaka Island is about fourteen klicks long and seven klicks wide. That's nearly a hundred square kilometers to cover, and it's not all sand. Rocks, ruins, and buildings are all over the place. The age of some of the ruins goes back thousands of years, and they are considered world-class archaeological sites. They are off-limits to coalition bombing or naval gunfire."

"So, we'll have to go in and take the place out by hand?" Daugherty said.

"Looks that way," Rockham agreed. "It shouldn't take the Keyhole satellites long to cover that island and give us a target. But priorities are shifting since we didn't come up with warheads or a missile on board the *Polnocny*. They have officially put us on alert status as of right now. The code name for the mission is 'Operation Black Snow.'"

"Then here's to Black Snow," Kurkowski said as he raised his beer.

The rest of the SEALs responded, toasting a possible hot operation. At least during this trip to Saudi, they were able to do something and not just sit on their hands and wait.

It was only the next day that Rockham's words about shifting priorities proved prophetic. With a thunder of aircraft engines, Operation Desert Shield had ended. Operation Desert Storm began with an avalanche of bombs and missiles. On their TV sets back home, people in the United States were able to see live pictures broadcast from Baghdad of streams of red tracers climbing into the night sky. President George Bush came on live TV to announce that the liberation of occupied Kuwait had begun.

Within twenty-four hours of the beginning of the war, Saddam launched Scud missiles against Israel. The code words Viper Snake went out over

Israeli radios at 0150 hours local time on January 18. It was the warning for a flight of Scuds being detected coming in to the little country. Eight missiles impacted into population centers around Israel, six in the Tel Aviv area and the other two in Haifa. The 350-pound high explosive warheads smashed buildings and killed civilians. But the terrified population did not experience what they feared most—a wave of poison gas from the Scuds.

Israel failed to bite at Saddam's poisoned apple. Coalition forces changed their focus to attack Scud sites in western Iraq, where they would be within range of Israel. Other Scuds came in to Saudi Arabia, and most were smashed from the sky by U.S. Patriot missile batteries. None of the Scuds had the dreaded chemical or biological weapons Saddam was reported to have. If there were such weapons, it seemed he was saving them for a final punch.

Meanwhile, Rockham could not get a solid answer on the results of the search for Snowfall. Finally, a frustrated intelligence officer flatly told the SEAL that priorities had changed drastically with the beginning of the air war. Assets such as Keyhole satellites and reconnaissance planes had much higher priority targets than finding a single Scud launcher. Besides, didn't Rockham know that the threat of weapons of mass destruction was just an empty one?

On January 19, Saddam unleashed an unexpected environmental weapon such as the world had never known. His sanity was questioned as he opened up the oil pipes and began dumping millions of gallons of crude oil into the Persian Gulf. As the huge oil slick spread out, the Saudis estimated that it contained over 450 million gallons. It was considered by some the greatest intentional environmental catastrophe in human history. Then, on January 25, he ignited the oil wells of Kuwait.

The massive black clouds of burning oil could be seen from space as they were spread to the east by prevailing winds. Satellite observation was effectively blocked in large areas of Kuwait and in the northern Persian Gulf. The frustration of the men of the SMD could be felt by anyone entering their quarters, though no one did. While an active air war raged around them, they could just sit and do nothing.

Running into their quarters, Daugherty was obviously excited about something as he looked for Rockham.

"Rock," he said from the door to Rockham's room, "they found Snowfall!"

Rockham was moving almost before his feet hit the floor.

"What is it?" he said. "What did they find?"

"It was from a drone," Daugherty said as they headed out of their quarters, "an RPV launched from the battleship *Wisconsin*. It was flying across Faylaka Island when it took fire from a bunch of ruins. They say the picture shows a suspected Scud TEL hidden among the ruins. Communications said there's transport coming in for you at the pad."

"Get everyone up to speed on a full gear

check," Rockham said. "I'll get in touch with Command and see if we're going to get a green light on Black Snow."

Within an hour Rockham was on a Blackhawk helicopter heading to Riyadh.

Headquarters at Riyadh was even more security conscious now that the air campaign had begun. To get to the meeting, Rockham had to be escorted through a blockade of guard posts by a grim-faced Army sergeant. The sergeant spoke little more than terse sentences, and those only to the guards who stopped and challenged him. The guards looked like they could be even tougher hard cases than the sergeant. They were backed up by men behind loaded M60 machine guns locked on tripods and looking out through shooting slits in sandbag emplacements.

The last stages of the trip were down an elevator shaft running three stories underground. Rockham was taken to a room that looked like any other briefing room he had been to during his career in the Teams, only this room was forty feet underground and constructed of a thick layer of concrete.

There was more brass in that room that Rockham had seen in one place outside of the Pentagon. There were two admirals; Army generals with one, two, and even three stars on their shoulders; and two blue-uniformed Air Force officers, one with one star and the other with two on his shoulder. The colonels and scattered civilians in suits didn't stand out among that crowd. The one man who did stand out was the very big individual sitting at the head of the table.

With his short, gray haircut and round face, his solid gaze and no-nonsense manner, General Norman Schwarzkopf made an immediate impression. The fact that he was also six feet four inches tall and weighed around 250 pounds made the man fit his nickname, "Bear." What Rockham didn't want to see was a demonstration of Schwarzkopf's other nickname—Stormin' Norman.

"Have a seat, Lieutenant," one of the admirals said.

As Rockham sat down, one of the other officers spoke up.

"Did you have a chance to read through the briefing documents on the helicopter?" an Army colonel asked.

An armed escort watching a briefcase full of documents and pictures had been on board the Blackhawk with Rockham.

"Yes sir, I have," Rockham said, having studied the contents during the nearly two hour flight. "And I've put together a tentative plan of action."

"Tell us what you think," an Air Force general said.

"According to the intelligence reports," Rockham said, "the Scud is located in the middle of a group of ruins dating back to Alexander the Great. The single view of the TEL before the RPV moved out of range showed it to be inside an excavation covered with a metal roof of some sort."

"They disguised it as a archeological dig," another officer at the table said. "Covered it with a sheet metal shed that could be moved in minutes. It's like hiding a sneaker in a shoe box. We would never have seen it except for the low-flying RPV."

When the officer noted Schwarzkopf glaring at him for interrupting Rockham, he quickly shut up.

"The ruins are the key factor, as I understand it," Rockham said. "We can't call in fire from any of the Navy ships, not even gunfire directed by an RPV drone. The drone would just get shot down too quickly, and we can't just destroy that kind of historical site.

"I suggest that my men and I go into the site, infiltrate the area, and confirm the missile and its warhead. Then we can destroy the missile and its support structure. If necessary, we can bring in a precision bombing strike and paint the target with a compact laser designator."

"But how are you going to insert?" another admiral asked. "The oil slicks have covered much of the beaches on Faylaka Island. You can't swim through the oil, and we can't bring in a helicopter insertion. Before you could ever get to the target, they could be in a position to fire."

"What if we jumped in, sir?" Rockham said. "Conducted a high altitude, low opening parachute insertion over the island. A HALO drop would give them a very difficult target to see as we came in, and it would put us on the island quietly and quickly."

"Not practical," a general in an Air Force uniform said. "The Iraqis would detect you coming in. We've taken out most of their radar sites, but they still have some mobile ones that are operational. If we put up the air cover to take out their mobile radar as soon as it was activated, they would know something was up. They could reinforce the units on guard or at least put them at a high level of alert."

"They couldn't detect us if we jumped in from an undetectable aircraft," Rockham said.

"What?" the Air Force general said. "An F-117 Stealth? That's a fighter, not a jump platform. There's barely room on board for the pilot, and nothing to spare for a jumper."

Looking up at General Schwarzkopf, Rockham wondered about the level of security clearances in the room."

"Go ahead, Lieutenant," Schwarzkopf said. "Tell us what you have in mind."

"Not a stealth fighter," Rockham said, "a stealth bomber. A B-2 out of the States. My men and I are one of the few operational units that are qualified to jump from a B-2. We've already done it."

"So that was you," the other Air Force general at the table said.

"Yes, sir," Rockham said.

"Impossible," the other Air Force general said. "That aircraft is still undergoing flight tests. There are only two in existence right now. It would be an unacceptable risk to field one right now."

"A greater risk than my men and I trying to swim in through an oil slick?"

"That's not what I meant," the Air Force general said. "I—"

The whole room jumped when Schwarzkopf

slammed his hand down on the table for attention.

"Enough," he growled. "I have been listening to reports on this subject since yesterday. That Scud is considered a very viable threat to my troops along the border. Since it has been identified as an al-Hussein missile, it is even a threat to our headquarters here, let alone what it could do to the civilian population if it does have a biological or chemical warhead. Saddam is an idiot and a thug, but he is crafty. There has to be a reason that missile is so carefully hidden. He knew he couldn't move it after the air war started.

"I am sick of the Air Force limiting what they decide should be available to conduct this campaign. You didn't have the A-10s here when I wanted them. You thought fighters and bombers were the only way to go. Well, you were wrong then, and I think you're wrong now. The American taxpayers paid for those very expensive toys of yours, not you personally.

"Lieutenant Rockham," Schwarzkopf said as he looked straight into Rockham's eyes, "I give my full approval of your operation. You have a green light to conduct Black Snow as quickly as the assets you need can be made available. And they will be available with no foot dragging.

"We have no time to waste gentlemen. This campaign will be moving forward quickly. Make it happen. That is an order."

CHAPTER 25

★ ★ ★ ★

It seemed to Rockham and his men that they had been doing nothing but traveling over the last two days, first from Riyadh back to Al Mish'ab, then down to Dhahran to take a long flight to the Navy base on Diego Garcia in the Chagos archipelago near the middle of the Indian Ocean. That trip had covered nearly 3,000 miles and was long enough. But the trip back was a real killer.

Secured in their ACES II seats in the weapons bays of the B-2, the SEALs couldn't get up and move around, talk, or even pee. There wasn't much question that some of there men were at least getting some sleep, but Rockham wasn't one of them.

The B-2 was big, bad, black, and stealthy. But it

wasn't very fast, and it certainly wasn't comfortable. For more than six long hours the SEALs had ridden in the belly of the aircraft, armed to the teeth and ready to be dropped like a bomb. They would be the most precise of precision weapons. Smart bombs had been the talk of the air war. They were nothing compared to the destructive power of the SEALs.

The Diego Garcia base had been chosen because that was the closest one to the Persian Gulf that held enough security for the B-2. The bomber came in after a flight that took it halfway across the globe. After it dropped the SEALs, the B-2 would continue its flight back to the States. It was a monumental effort on the part of the crew. And one that would probably never be unclassified.

The yellow warning light had been glowing only a few seconds before Chief Monday called over the intercom for an oxygen check.

"First squad, count off," he said.

The tension everyone was feeling didn't ease much, even with the solid presence of their chief going by the book.

"One, okay," Rockham said.

"Two, okay," Bryant said.

"Three, okay," from Able.

"Four, okay," from Sukov.

"Five, okay," Ferber said.

"Six, okay," from Wilkes. Then a long pause.

"Goddamnit, Alexander," Monday bellowed, "wake your fucking ass up!"

"But Chief," came a hurt sounding voice over the intercom. "I am awake. Seven, okay."

Men in the Teams are not easily impressed. There are certain traditions that go with being men of the sea that even the SEALs cannot ignore, no matter how impolitic they may be. The stream of uninterrupted invective that Chief Monday put out over the intercom was truly inspiring to the men. Several of them wished they could take notes on some of the more colorful and inventive references to Alexander's parentage and background. The remarks referring to his personal habits would have made even a hardened SEAL blush.

"Uh, Eight, okay," Tinsley said over the intercom as the laughter and comments faded. The count continued. For the moment, the tension among the SEALs in the weapons bay was gone. Then the lights came on as the drop point came closer, and finally the blue light came on. They were only moments from the drop.

"Twenty-five klicks to Piranha," Colonel Abrams said over the intercom, using the code name for Faylaka. "Good luck, SEALs."

The weapons bay doors opened, the green light flashed on, and it was time to drop. Yellow and black handles were pulled up, and the bottom of the world dropped away.

With his arms bent and his hands up, Mike Bryant felt himself in a good, stable, modified frog position as he took his place as the lead jumper. His balance was good as the wind rushed up and moved his upper cheeks. They were just about the only piece of exposed skin on his entire body.

The rest of the SMD lined up behind him, tracking on the flashing SDU-5/E strobe light secured to the top of Bryant's helmet. An additional green chem light was attached to the back of each man's parachute pack. The dim illumination could only be seen if you were looking for it, and it was a safe backup if the strobe light suddenly failed.

They had exited the B-2 at 32,000 feet in a single stick. The difficulties in tracking across the sky in the dark of the oil clouds had the men all flying as a single V-formation rather than as two sticks. The oily smoke smeared across equipment and goggles as the SEALs continued to fall.

They were all dropping at terminal velocity now, about 125 miles an hour, or 184 feet per second. Mike Bryant had checked, double-checked, then looked at his oxygen system again. This was a combat jump and his Teammates were depending on him. There wouldn't be a repeat of his experience back in Nevada.

They were all in freefall and still had over two and a half minutes to drop. They would be opening at 2,000 feet—so low that there wouldn't be a lot of time to deal with a canopy malfunction. At the same time, any Iraqis on the ground would have damned little time to notice the SEALs coming in before they were on the ground.

They broke out of the smoke and cloud cover at just under 6,000 feet. The dark island below them was only slightly lighter than the Gulf waters they could see surrounding it. The unit was in a good formation as they tracked across the sky. Crossing their hands in front of their faces as the signal, each SEAL in turn pulled his ripcord.

A forest of fast-moving black mushrooms floated down toward the ground. Each SEAL's canopy had opened flawlessly and they all had good control. One of the most dangerous parts of the jump was coming up. Rockham only had the older satellite images and reports from Kuwatis who had lived on Faylaka to tell him just what the ground was like. His drop zone had been chosen at grid coordinates TN 456568.

Luck followed good planning. The SEALs came in to a landing on a gravel and sand plane. All the men came down inside an area less than fifty meters across. They quickly collapsed their chutes and pulled open their rucksacks. Weapons strapped to their sides were pulled off and stripped of rigging tape. Loaded magazines were already in place as bolts were drawn back and released. The scraping click of the bolts slamming home told anyone making the mistake of being within earshot that there were some very dangerous men armed and ready on the island.

As his shooting partner stood watch, the other SEAL in the pair dug a hole in the soft ground with a folding entrenching tool. Parachutes and harnesses were bundled up and stuffed into the ground and the sand pulled back across the dark cloth canopies. As a last detail, the entrenching tools were abandoned and pushed under the sand.

The SEALs were running light, but were still heavily armed. The MP5 submachine guns had been switched for M4 carbines, shorter versions of the M16A2 rifle. Each man had a dozen magazines for his M4 in four pouches on his web belt. One additional magazine was seated in the weapon, but no one thought the number thirteen was unlucky in this case. The more than 360 rounds in the magazines still weren't considered enough by several of the SEALs. Bryant, Marks, and Stadt had also stuffed an extra bandoleer of 160 rounds into their rucksacks.

Able, Alexander, Kurkowski, and Grant were armed with M60E3 machine guns. The big men handled the large weapons as if they were just heavy rifles. Each of the automatic weapons men had six hundred rounds of ammunition with them. Alexander had stuffed an additional four hundred into his rucksack.

The automatic weapons men had a lot of ammunition, but that was just counting rounds. The grenadiers—Lopez, Lutz, Sukov, and Mainhart—had more than thirty rounds of ammunition for the 40mm M203 grenade launchers mounted under the barrels of their M4s. Most of the 40mm grenades were M433 high explosive dual purpose rounds. That round could punch a hole through two inches of steel armor while still spreading hundreds of lethal fragments over a five-meter radius.

Bryant and Marks had their suppressed Mark II Rugers, and all of the SEALs had SIG P226 pistols

strapped to their right hips. One magazine was in
the grip of the SIG, with two spares in pouches on
the straps holding the thigh holsters in place. In
addition to two radios, ten pounds of C4 explosive, four M18A1 claymore mines, and half a
dozen green or red M18 smoke grenades scattered
among the squads, each SEAL had four M67 fragmentation grenades.

All of this was strapped to their bodies or in
their rucksacks as the SEALs prepared to move
out. Not a word was spoken. They were well behind enemy lines and knew it. For several minutes the men just held their positions, with their
weapons up and out in a security perimeter.
Then they just listened. No vehicles were seen or
heard. There were no lights shining in the darkness, and no voices came up from out of the
black. Off in the distance, to the northwest, they
could see glowing lights. The battleship *Missouri*
had started an onshore bombardment of bunkers,
antiaircraft sites, and artillery batteries. The intent was to draw off any troops around the Scud
location, to try to convince the Iraqis that an invasion was imminent.

The diversion seemed to have worked. There
was no traffic on the roads to the north or south
of the SEALs' position. No native Kuwaitis were
known to be on the island; the Iraqis had expelled
them all to the mainland. Now the island only
held Iraqi forces, and a determined group of
SEALs. They were in place on Faylaka Island, un-
detected, prepared, and fully armed.

Over 2,500 meters away, more than two and a half klicks, or 1.6 miles, were the ruins where the MAZ-543 TEL lay under cover. It was shortly before 2400 hours local time, midnight, on February 23. One of the mission parameters that had been set for Rockham was that he and his men were to have the missile site secured or destroyed by 0200 hours local time at the earliest. If the mission had not been completed by 0400 hours, they were to withdraw to the primary extraction site and wait for the helicopters to come in for them.

The reason for the tight time schedule hadn't been explained to Rockham, and he hadn't asked about it. Sometimes, a junior officer had no business asking about things that didn't directly concern him. As long as the timetable didn't put his men or the mission at risk, Rockham was satisfied with it.

The men had a lot of ground to cover and not a lot of time to do it in. Moving in a staggered file formation, the SEALs separated the squads to go forward in bounds, alternating between each other in the classic leapfrog maneuver. The staggered file formations gave the best general files of fire for all of the men. In case of enemy contact, they could quickly move into a V-formation; the wedge shape would give them the most concentrated fire to the front while still covering either flank.

The leapfrog maneuver had one squad covering the other as it moved forward. The forward squad would only bound ahead a hundred meters before stopping and going to ground. While the forward squad covered, the rearmost squad would move forward and pass the first. Then the tactic would be repeated.

Leapfrogging slowed the forward movement of the entire unit, but it was the safest and most effective tactic to use when enemy contact was probable. The SEALs were surrounded by Iraqi forces who didn't know they were there, and Rockham intended to keep the situation that way. If at all possible, enemy contact was not to take place—yet.

Moving at the head of the file as first squad bounded ahead, Bryant was the point man, responsible for detecting anything the SEALs might run into. Back in the squad, Rockham was paying attention to the compass heading the unit was following, but as far as picking the pathway they would move on, that was the point man's job.

The area of the island they were in was mostly flat expanses of sand and gravel. There were shallow dunes to hide behind but that was about all. Even the scrub brush was limited. As far as Bryant was concerned, the only reason to move over the sand was to make it easy to detect mines.

Reports said that Faylaka was heavily mined along the beaches and easier approaches. The landing zone the SEALs had used was well inside the island, off the more obvious patrol routes and not likely to be mined. The sand was constantly moving in the wind, and land mines could be uncovered one moment and buried too deeply to function only hours later.

Mines were a danger that Bryant watched for as he moved ahead. Any disturbance in the ground, an odd line uncovered in the sand or a button sticking up, had to be constantly watched for. In one or two more bounds he would switch off the point position with Pete Wilkes. It wasn't that he was particularly tired. But you had to remain alert and sharp when moving on point.

The patrol had only moved about five hundred meters from the landing zone when Bryant held up his left fist clenched tight at shoulder level. That was the sign to the patrol behind him to stop. Opening his left hand, Bryant held it up to his ear as if listening. Looking back, he watched his signal being passed down through the squad.

As he felt the blood pumping through his head, Bryant listened to the sound of an approaching vehicle. Off to the right, a short stretch of road led to the main road circling the island. Someone was traveling up that road, and the men of first squad were within fifty meters of the road's end.

Hearing the noise of an oncoming vehicle, Rockham put the squad into an immediate action drill. Facing the patrol, he pumped his arm up and down while backing up in a crouching position in the direction of the road. Stopping, he swept his arm in a long arc off to his left. He watched the men repeat it back and then react to his signal for a hasty ambush lined up to his left flank.

It was an Iraqi UAZ-469 coming up the road with its headlights out. Only the dim illumination of the blackout lights gave the driver any clue as to what the road ahead of him looked like. With a squeal of brakes, the UAZ came to a halt near the end of the road, not twenty meters from where the SEALs lay in ambush.

Each SEAL held his fire and watched as someone in uniform got out of the passenger side of the vehicle and walked to the end of the road. Scarcely breathing, Bryant watched the man move as he held him in the sight of his suppressed Ruger. He wasn't more than ten meters away from Bryant, who lay in the dunes aiming his weapon.

After looking about, the man from the vehicle turned and shouted something at the UAZ while shaking his fist. None of the SEALs could understand the stream of Arabic. Another man stepped out of the other side of the UAZ and a rapid conversation took place.

As the two men argued, neither one looked particularly concerned with what was going on about them. After a moment, when the two went through what looked like a Three Stooges act, with both men pointing in different directions, they climbed back into the UAZ. They turned around then and drove off without knowing just how close they had come to a sudden death.

Afterward, the SEALs resumed their patrol route. Crouching and moving, they crept forward from cover to cover, each squad protecting the other, and each SEAL keeping his squadmates always in sight.

Coming to a road, Ryan Marks signaled a halt. As second squad was now in the forward bound, it was up to Daugherty to respond to what was going on ahead of the patrol. Marks signaled Daugherty to move forward. Creeping low to the ground, Daugherty moved up to Marks. According to the map, they were at a point where they should be expecting a road. Now the squads had to cross the open area quickly.

Turning back to his men, Daugherty made a rolling forward motion with his hand in front of his body, then pointed to his left. Each man in turn passed the "skirmish line, left" signal. Daugherty swept his left hand forward, and the men fell out to line up along the road. When he saw that all of his men were ready, Daugherty lifted his arm up over his head and pumped it up and down.

That was the signal to move out rapidly, and the entire squad crossed the road in a rush. Once they were on the other side, the SEALs got into a hasty perimeter and kept watch in all directions. Now it was time for first squad to go through the same procedure. It only took a few minutes, and the move was made in almost total silence. Only the quiet brush of cloth and the soft thud of boots could be heard, and then only if you were listening for it.

The SEALs were now within a hundred meters of their target. Looking over a low dune, Bryant could see the long, low silhouette of the camouflage archeologist's shelter in front of him. Between the shelter and the SEAL patrol stretched a maze of rock walls and foundations. This was what they had been expecting—a warren of openings, passages, pits, and walls. These were the ruins of Alexander the Great. They had stood here for thousands of years. The stones had been laid out more than three hundred years before the birth of Christ. And they hid the weapon the SEALs had come to destroy.

CHAPTER 26

2235 ZULU
Map Sheet NH 39-9, Grid Coordinates TN438586
Snowfall
The ruins of Alexander the Great
Faylaka Island
Persian Gulf

Moving at Bryant's signal, Rockham low-crawled up and looked over the dune. The two men watched for movement and saw none. While their point man and patrol leader were laying down ahead of them, the rest of the squad maintained a careful watch in a full circle around their position. Knowing they were close to the objective, Daugherty brought up second squad and closed the distance between the two elements of the patrol.

Coming back down off the dune, Rockham sliced his hand across his throat. Then he held up his hand in front of his face with the fingers spread and pointed over his shoulder. The message, "Danger, enemy ahead," was passed back on through both squads and returned. Holding out his arms, Rockham brought them together, indicating the men should close the interval between them.

Now was the time to assault the objective. Just because they couldn't see any enemy troops in the ruins certainly didn't mean they weren't there. Assumptions got men killed, and Rockham wasn't going to make any. Pointing to Daugherty, he held the vertical edge of his hand to his face and pointed along the dune. Daugherty understood the signal and brought his men forward to set up security along the slight rise.

Looking to his own men, Rockham held his arms up in a V to tell them to move into a wedge formation. As the men came up, he moved back to where Bryant was lying down, still watching the ruins. Pointing to his eyes and then holding his hand spread in front of his face, Rockham asked his point man if he had seen any of the enemy. After repeating the signal back, a simple shake of his head was all the answer Bryant needed to make.

Waving his point man forward, Rockham began the final movement into the ruins.

The remains of a large rock wall almost completely enclosed the area of the ruins. In several spots the rocks had crumbled or been torn down by locals and time. In a low crouch, the SEALs of first squad moved forward under the covering guns of their Teammates across the top of the dune.

The muzzle of his M4 held out ahead of him,

Bryant moved slowly into the ruins. Rockham was just a few feet behind his shooting partner as they went into action, automatically switching mind-sets to a close-quarter-battle mode of operating.

Off about thirty yards to the left was a raised mound of dirt and rocks, the muzzle of a tripod-mounted DshK 38/46 12.7mm heavy machine gun sticking out of the top. Set up as local aircraft and helicopter defense, the gun was situated so the muzzle could be depressed to cover the surround-ing area. That was a dangerous gun to face, and the squad all noticed it.

With all of his senses at their highest pitch, Bryant moved down into a corridor of rock. There was no other way to reach the metal shed less than fifty meters in front of them, not if they wanted to stay under cover. As he moved forward, he care-fully and deliberately placed each step. If a toe of his boot touched a rock that moved, he lifted his foot to place it on firmer ground. Like a hunting cat, the skilled young SEAL moved forward pace by pace.

As careful as Bryant was, however, there was no accounting for the movements of the enemy forces. As he came up to a low pile of rocks and began to move around them, whatever it was that bothered the Iraqi soldier, no one ever found out or even cared. He just stood up and bumped right into Bryant.

The mouth of the startled man opened to yell as he scrabbled to bring up the AKM-47 hanging from a sling at his right shoulder. There wasn't any time for subtleties. With the man's chest shoved up against the muzzle of his M4, Bryant pulled the trigger.

The blast of fire from the M4 tore through the Iraqi and rang out across the compound.

The time for silence was over. Rockham made an instant decision to assault the compound. If he had called for a withdrawal, many of his men could have been killed trying to get out of the maze of rocks. If they moved fast and struck hard, the shock of the SEALs' assault could overwhelm even a much larger force. That could prove enough for the SEALs to reach the missile. That was their mission, and the lives of thousands could weigh in the balance against the eighteen SEALs.

Surprise was still on their side, and Rockham intended to use it to his best advantage.

"Flank left!" he shouted.

The men behind him were already in motion as Rockham pointed his M4 at a startled Iraqi coming around a corner. As Rockham opened fire, so did Bryant. Their two quick bursts slammed the Iraqi back against the stones. As the body slipped down against the stones, Lopez fired his M203 and they heard a thump.

Seconds later a red-orange flower of flame bloomed at the heavy machine gun position. The Iraqi gun crew never had a chance to man their weapon before they were torn to pieces by the fragmentation of the exploding grenade.

More 40mm grenades began detonating among the ruins as Lutz and Mainhart, positioned up on the dune line, took advantage of their higher position to rain fire down behind the stone walls of the ruins. The deep booming of 7.62mm AKMs were matched by the sharper staccato cracks of M4s firing on full automatic.

A pop sounded out, nearly lost among the roaring weapons. On the far side of the compound a brilliant white light glared, silhouetting the Iraqis. Mainhart had fired a modified M583 white star parachute flare from his M203. Having cut off the parachute from the flare, Mainhart was able to backlight at least part of the ruins, making targeting the Iraqis easier. The SEALs on the ridge knew that their Teammates hadn't reached the far side of the compound yet. They could see them moving into and around the ruins in front of them. So anyone moving on the far side of the compound was quickly cut down.

The loud, heavy knock of the M60E3 machine guns sounded over the rest of the gunfire. The big guns were in four of the SEALs' hands, two in the ruins and two on the dune line. Those hands sent controlled streams of steel-jacketed projectiles into the rocks. Some bullets smashed into stones and screamed off as ricochets. Others spent their energy punching through Iraqi flesh.

The ruins became a roiling cauldron of death. Positions the Iraqis thought they could defend became their final resting places as they fell back and died from the power of the SEALs' onslaught. Over it all, the ghosts of Alexander the Great's troops looked on as men continued the ages-old dance of war.

Hand grenades exploded inside the old foundations as SEALs tossed then around blind corners. When the blast of the grenade rang out, the explosion was quickly followed by a shooting pair of SEALs as they charged into the area, firing their weapons at anything left standing. Short, quick bursts of fire made doubly sure that any downed Iraqis were not going to get up behind the passing SEALs.

But not all of the fire was so one-sided. As Sukov and Able dashed into a square foundation area where they had just tossed an M67 grenade, neither man noticed the pile of boxes next to the old door opening. Sukov went through the room and into the corridor beyond. Out of the far side of the boxes, a stunned Iraqi who had missed being hit by any of the grenade fragments, pulled up his AKM and opened fire.

Soviet-made 7.62mm slugs slammed into Sukov's back, knocking him against the far wall. Spinning around, Dan Able fired a long burst from his M60E3 into the man who had just shot his Teammate. The Iraqi was literally picked up off his feet by the hammering projectiles, his AKM continuing to fire into the air as a dead finger depressed the trigger. The soggy mess that slipped down the wall only resembled a man from the waist down.

Jumping over to where Sukov was struggling to rise, Able bellowed, "Man down! Man down!"

Bent down over his shooting partner, he looked in all directions to see if there was danger or help on its way.

"Don't move," Able shouted. "I'll get a corpsman. Man down, man down!"

"Oh Jesus, it hurts," said Sukov as he put his hand behind his back. The rucksack Sukov had on was torn to shreds. But the hand he pulled back had no blood on it.

"What the fuck?" Sukov said.

"Shit," Able exclaimed as he looked at the rucksack. The remains of one of the unit's HST-4 SATCOM radios and the KY-57 encryption device attached to it were little more than wires and scrap circuit boards. The rest of the damage had been stopped by Sukov's body armor.

"Damn, brother," Able said. "You're not hit. But I don't think you're ever going in the air with this rig again."

"Well, screw me," Sukov said.

Approaching the main objective, Rockham and Bryant were leapfrogging each other as they moved through the rock walls. As soon as anyone who wasn't a SEAL showed their face, one or both of the men put a short burst of bullets into it.

"Magazine," Bryant shouted as the bolt locked back on his M4.

As Bryant kneeled and reloaded, he shoved the empty magazine into his shirt. Standing over his shooting partner, Rockham kept watch.

"Ready," Bryant said as he stood up.

They were only a few yards from one of the entrances to the metal shed. There were two long excavations to either side, sticking out at right angles to it. This was what they had come for.

Stepping up to the sides of the entrance, Rockham reached inside a pouch and pulled out a M67 fragmentation grenade he had brought for this moment. The target inside that shed was a Scud missile and possibly a biological or chemical warhead. Shots fired around this very deadly object had to be very carefully aimed. And the use of high explosives was completely out of the question. Rockham and Bryant knew this and had prepared for it.

Pulling the pin from the grenade, Rockham looked at Bryant and nodded. At the return nod from his shooting partner, Rockham shouted, "Grenade!" and tossed the deadly green ball into the opening.

There was a clank and scrabbling sounds. Without waiting for the explosion, the two SEALs moved into and through the opening.

The grenade didn't detonate. It never was going to. That was the plan. Rockham had removed the blasting cap from the M213 fuze, and the six and a half ounces of Composition B explosive was just so much weight in the fragmentation body. But the Iraqis inside the shed hadn't known that.

Moving to the right and left, Rockham and Bryant moved up to the rock walls but not against them. The shed covered a deep excavation, and the bulk of the area was taken up by the huge MAZ-543 TEL. The weapon was impressive, but neither SEAL spent any time looking at it. As the startled Iraqi who had taken cover from the expected explosion looked up, he was met by a burst of fire from Bryant's M4.

In the opposite direction, Rockham saw a huge Iraqi disappearing around the front of the MAZ.

"I have a runner!" he shouted.

He quickly moved to the front of the vehicle, ducked down, and snatched a quick look around the corner. Behind him, Bryant was keeping watch with his weapon pointed down toward the rear of the shed. They knew there was an exit point on the far side of the vehicle, and their runner was probably long gone. But that was not the thing to expect, and the SEALs were not going to suddenly dash around the corner of the MAZ and walk into fire.

Moving back-to-back, Rockham and Bryant stepped around to the front of the MAZ. A sudden burst of AKM fire roared out, echoing off the metal walls. There was a moment's silence, then a scream, followed by words shouted in Arabic.

"*Laa! Laa!*" the man shouted, then something like, "*Awgfu!*"

Time to bite the bullet, Rockham thought, and he ran around the corner of the MAZ.

The huge Iraqi was standing over a body in coveralls. He was pointing his weapon, not at the SEALs, but at the MAZ. As the big man turned, both SEALs opened fire and cut him down.

Moving fast, Rockham and Bryant went up to the dead Iraqi and made sure he wasn't going to be getting up again. There was a side door into the MAZ. According to their briefing, this was where the missile erector was controlled. Standing at either side of the door, Bryant kept watch while Rockham prepared to yank it open.

When he did, Bryant stepped back as Rockham leaned into the opening with his M4 leading the way. Kneeling on the floor of the cramped control compartment was a sobbing Iraqi wearing another set of coveralls. He was muttering incoherently in Arabic.

"Quiff," Rockham shouted. *"Irfaa idak!"*

As the kneeling man looked up at the commands to halt and put his hands up, he stared in astonishment at the two SEALs.

"Ameriki?" he said. "Americans? You are Americans?"

In spite of the man switching to English, neither SEAL was in the mood to waste any time on him. Reaching into the compartment, Bryant jerked him out and dumped him on the ground. With Rockham keeping watch, Bryant pulled the man's hands behind his back. Yanking a set of tie-ties from a pocket, Bryant quickly fastened the man's hands together at the wrist.

The fire outside the building was dying down. Occasional shots still rang out, but they were from SEAL M4 carbines and not AKM-47s. The SEALs only carried enough ammunition to continue their relentless barrage of fire for about five minutes. The assault had taken only four.

Now the men had to move fast to complete the destruction of the objective and pull out. After checking with Daugherty over the MX-300R, Rockham asked for a sitrep. The SEALs had the entire compound secured. As the two officers were talking, the rest of first squad was ransacking the area to make sure no Iraqis were in hiding, as well as searching to locate anything of informational value.

"Echo One," Rockham said over the radio to

Chief Monday, "regroup, run an ammunition count and redistribute. We are out of here in three mikes. Send in Bravo Four, Papa Two, and Bravo corpsman."

"Roger, Bravo leader," came back over the radio as Monday prepared to carry out Rockham's orders. Sukov and Lutz were the unit's Explosive Ordnance Disposal experts, while Tinsley was one of the bio/chem experts as well as being a corpsman.

"Now just who in the hell are you?" Rockham said as he looked down at the bound man on the ground. "And what in the fuck am I going to do with you?"

The other SEALs Rockham had called for over the radio came into the compound, Sukov looking the worse for wear. They immediately went to work carefully examining the MAZ-543 TEL and the long, green missile across the top of it. There was no nose cone on the missile, and Rockham was concerned that they had come across another dry hole as far as weapons of mass destruction were concerned.

He was wrong.

The man on the ground struggled to talk.

"I am Abu Waheed," he said. "I am—was—a technician for Saddam Hussein's weapons program."

"And just who is this?" Rockham said as he nudged the body in coveralls with his foot.

"That is my friend, Jaleel," the man said with his voice choking. "He was also a technician on the program."

"And this guy tried to kill you?" Rockham said as he pointed to the body of the big man in uniform. "Why?"

"That pig is Colonel Kassar," the bound man spat out. "He was in charge of this installation and the special weapon. He must have had orders to kill us rather than let us be captured."

"Special weapon?" Rockham said.

"I think he means this, Skipper," Sukov said from behind the rear of the TEL.

Rockham walked over to the back of the vehicle where Sukov, Lutz, and now Tinsley were standing. There was a big open container in front of the SEALs. Laying in it was a green painted warhead.

"Just what is that?" Rockham said. "Is that what we've been looking for?"

"I would say so, Skipper," Sukov said as Tinsley nodded. "This is a warhead to that al-Hussein Scud sitting there. There's handling gear here ready to lift it up to the launcher."

"Bryant!" Rockham shouted. "Bring that prisoner over here."

As Bryant dragged the man over, Rockham looked down at the big warhead. Now they had to destroy it or hold it secure until relief came in to carry it out. It was not going to be easy.

"Just what is this thing?" Rockham asked Abu Waheed as Bryant dragged him up.

"That's the special weapon," Abu said. "We only managed to load the one here. The other is just a normal high explosive warhead."

There was another container in the corner,

which Sukov had opened. It also held an al-Hussein warhead, also green but with different markings.

"What's the special one loaded with?" Sukov asked.

"Anthrax," came the chilling answer, "weaponized anthrax. It has been freeze-dried and treated with an anticlumping agent before being milled to three to five microns in particle size."

"This guy sounds like the real thing to me, Skipper," Tinsley said.

"I think so too," Sukov agreed.

"Great, so how do we destroy this thing?" Rockham asked.

"You can't," Abu said simply.

Just then a radio in the MAZ crackled into life. Arabic came out of the speakers in an increasingly loud voice. Then there was nothing.

"And just what was that?" Rockham said.

"It sounded like Colonel Moel," Abu said. "He's in charge of the Republican Guard unit assigned to the security of this site."

"Well, he didn't do a very good job of it," Bryant said.

"That's because he took the bulk of his unit to the north," Abu said. "They were expecting your Marines to come ashore there after the bombardment."

"And he said what?" Rockham asked.

"He asked for Kassar several times," Abu said. "Then he just cut off."

"Great," Rockham said. "So we have an unknown number of Iraqi Republican Guards coming in and no way to destroy a weapon we can't let them have."

"There is a way to destroy the warhead without spreading the agent," Abu said as he looked around. "But it will be very dangerous."

"What, it can blow the warhead?" Rockham said.

"No, my idea will destroy the agent inside as well as the warhead," Abu said. "You can't just blow it up or disarm the fuze. All Moel would have to do is set it off with an explosion. The anthrax would spread to Kuwait City, possibly killing thousands."

"But those would be his own troops!" Bryant said.

"That wouldn't matter to him," Abu said. "He would just be following Saddam's orders to destroy Kuwait rather than let it fall into your hands."

"Okay," Rockham said, "just what is your idea?"

As Abu explained how the warhead could be destroyed, Rockham just stared at the man. Sukov nodded but looked unhappy. Lutz and Tinsley shared Sukov's opinion that the idea would work and that it would be the most dangerous thing any of the men had ever attempted.

CHAPTER 27

★ ★ ★ ★

2249 ZULU
Map Sheet NH 39–9, Grid Coordinates TN438586
Snowfall
The ruins of Alexander the Great
Faylaka Island
Persian Gulf

The SEALs were not in the best possible position, in spite of being in control of their objective site. Rockham had just heard the most insane plan ever to destroy a weapon, and from an enemy national who had helped design it. Only the insistence of his EOD and biological weapons people convinced him to even try the crazy scheme.

There were even more pressing dangers to his men and their mission with the upcoming arrival of an unknown number of enemy troops with who knew what kind of support. About the only thing Rockham wasn't expecting was a preassault artillery barrage. The Iraqis wanted their missile and its warhead back. They didn't want to blow it up themselves.

The news from Chief Monday regarding the ammunition situation also wasn't the best. But that was something Rockham knew he could deal with right now.

"Chief," Rockham said to Monday, "we have to hold this position for as long as we can. There's a live bio warhead in there, a real one. And it has to be destroyed. There's no way we can hold this position indefinitely. So you have to buy us enough time so we can take a shot at destroying this thing.

"Take half of the men and start stripping the dead of weapons and ammunition. Take anything that can be carried easily. We'll use that up before we fall back on our own hardware."

Chief Monday just agreed and started directing the men. There was more than enough ordnance around to give them the ability to make the situation difficult for anyone coming into the ruins.

Leaning up against a wall, Ryan Marks was taking a drink from his canteen while sorting through an open box of hand grenades. He had already opened up the brown-painted metal can full of URZGM delay fuzes and had unwrapped them from their dull paper envelopes. Next, he was going to start screwing the fuzes into the bodies of the RGD-5 fragmentation grenades filling the box.

"Hey, Marks," Kurkowski said, "I've got a surprise for you."

Coming into the small enclosure, Kurkowski

set down the two PKM light machine guns he was carrying in his right hand, holding the weapons by the handles attached to their barrels. In his other hand Kurkowski had four of the rectangular two-hundred-round belt boxes that attached to the PKM. Over his shoulders were additional lengths of ammunition belts.

Sticking up from Kurkowski's shoulder was what looked like the skeletonized butt stock of a third PKM. As one of the unit's automatic weapons men, Kurkowski's scrounging machine guns made complete sense. All of the SEALs not on perimeter watch had been combing the ruins for weapons, searching in the dull light of their red-lensed penlights.

"Oh, gee," Marks said. "How sweet, a machine gun for my very own. And I didn't get anything for you."

"Not that, smart ass," Kurkowski said as he straightened up. "This."

Unslinging the weapon from behind his back, Kurkowski lifted up an SVD Dragunov sniper rifle complete with PSO-1 scope.

"I found it, and it just looked like you had to have it," Kurkowski said. "And here's some magazines to go with it. I have no idea how that scope's zeroed, but that's your problem."

Lifting up a small canvas bag, Kurkowski handed over three of the ten-round magazines that fed the SVD. As a sniper, Marks appreciated the long range weapon. He was satisfied with his M4 carbine and the pile of AKM-47s he had collected. But the SVD was a special weapon that fit his personal skills.

"Okay," Marks said. "This really is cool, man."

"Hey," Kurkowski said as he picked up the PKM machine guns and their ammunition cans, "don't mention it."

The rest of the SEALs were doing much the same thing, gathering weapons and ammunition, checking the guns out and loading up magazines. Wayne Alexander had found a PKM of his own, along with three of the two-hundred-round ammunition cans. He also had located a pair of RPG-7v antitank rocket launchers. He was sitting down, pulling the propellant charges out of the green plastic tubes they were shipped in. Once he had the charges unwrapped, he was going to screw them onto the bases of the pile of PG-7 rockets sitting next to him.

On the other side of the rock wall surrounding the ruins, Pete Wilkes was laying out the firing wires to a pair of M18A1 claymore mines. Inside each mine was a one and a half pound charge of Composition-4 plastic explosive. In front of the explosive, cast into the curved surface of the mine, were seven hundred steel balls. When the mine detonated, the explosive blast would send the balls out at several thousand feet per second. Like a giant shotgun, the claymores would sweep down everything in front of them to a distance of up to 250 meters.

In the metal shed, things were moving along, which didn't necessarily please Rockham. Using muscle power, the SEALs had managed to move a heavy trailer with a large tank on it over to the warhead in its open container. Sukov was carefully wrapping a line of detonating cord around the base of the warhead and up along one side. Overlooking what the SEAL EOD specialist was doing was the Iraqi weapons technician Abu Waheed.

At the trailer, Henry Lutz was preparing a small charge of plastic explosive. Handling the malleable white Composition-4 with the ease of long practice, Lutz pressed the charge around the base of a pipe extending out from the trailer tank.

"You better put a venting charge up on the front top of that tank," Sukov said as he looked up.

"I was planning to," Lutz said. "I'll lay out a main line of detonating cord to hook everything together."

"Do you think this will work?" Rockham asked. "Or is this something that will just get us all killed?"

"Oh, it'll work all right," Sukov said. "Getting us killed will still be a question, though. That big trailer tank is full of red fuming nitric acid. The detonating cord I've wrapped around the warhead will just be enough to crack it open, not set off the explosive burster in the core."

"You're sure of that?" Rockham said. "We're trying to destroy this thing, not set it off ourselves."

"Oh, it will not detonate the warhead," Abu said. "It was designed to withstand the forces of low-altitude reentry. That little bit of explosive cord will not set off the burster."

"Okay," Rockham said. "You bust it open. Then what?"

"The plastic charges will vent this nitric acid tank," Sukov said, "dumping it all over the anthrax. That bug is tough, but this shit will eat anything and kill it dead. The only trouble is, the fumes are like corrosive poison gas. We breathe it or let it touch us and we'll be as dead as the bugs."

"Bugs and gas," Rockham said, shaking his head. "A hell of a place for a simple sailor to be. What's in that other trailer?"

"High-grade kerosene," Lutz said as he looked up from his work. "It works with the nitric acid to fuel the Scud."

"Okay, rig it to blow along with the rest of this mess," Rockham said. "The fire may help cover our withdrawal. Strip every piece of paper from the area and load the Scud and the MAZ as well."

"Already done, Skipper," Sukov said as he stood up. "We have everything in those haversacks over there. The films we shot have been divided up between Lutz and myself. We have to hook up all of the charges and set the clocks is all. There's a thirty-second nonelectric firing assembly already in place—just in case."

"Just in case," Rockham said. "Okay, finish loading everything and let me know. I'll tell you what to set the clocks to when we're ready to—"

"Incoming!" came the call from outside the shed.

Stopping in mid-sentence, Rockham dashed out of the shed to see what the situation was. Monday was looking out to the north and pointing. From their maps of the area, Rockham knew a road lay out there not a few hundred meters away.

"Okay, it's party time," he said. "Sukov, how much time to you need?" Rockham said into his MX-300R radio.

"About five minutes," Sukov said.

"You better make it three, and less would be better," Rockham replied. "Set the clocks for five minutes and let me know when you're ready to pull."

"Okay, Chief," Rockham said. "Now we earn our beer money."

The Iraqi unit approached the ruins rapidly. There didn't appear to be anything in disarray to Colonel Moel. It could have been a simple radio malfunction that caused the communications break with the Scud emplacement. But there had been the sounds of gunfire and explosions in the distance. It was better to be cautious and wrong rather than charge in and find the enemy.

Riding in the T-72 tank leading the small convoy, Colonel Moel was standing up in the turret to see the area ahead more clearly. As they approached within a hundred meters of the ruins, he saw very well. But what he saw were the blast plumes of two RPG-7 launchers being fired.

Alexander and Ferber squeezed the triggers of their RPG-7 launchers almost simultaneously. The thunderous blast of the propelling charge going off almost deafened everyone in the compound. The sustainer motors fired up with a bang about

ten meters in front of the launchers. Speeding on
their way, the two PG-7 warheads detonated
against the armor of the T-72.

Normally, a frontal shot of any kind of portable
weapon does very little to the front of a T-72
tank. That's true when the tank is properly but-
toned up and the hatches are closed for combat.
Both the commander's hatch in the turret, and the
driver's hatch at the front of the hull, were open.
Besides Moel having his head and upper body
sticking up from the armor, the driver had his
head up as well.

Both men were immediately killed in the blast as
the PG-7 rockets detonated against the tank, one
just above the driver's hatch. The flame and shock
wave of the round detonating above the driver
swept through the hull of the tank, killing or inca-
pacitating the occupants. When the ammunition
started to burn, the difference between dead and
just unconscious soon became unimportant.

As the rest of the convoy got off the road to assault the ruins, Chief Monday detonated the claymore mines. The soft-skinned trucks were no
protection at all from the hundreds of steel balls
that came scything out from the explosions. Then
the fire from all along the ruin walls slashed
across the remains of the convoy.

The Republican Guard troops in the convoy
were combat seasoned from the long years of
fighting with Iran. The extensive bombing campaign of the last five weeks had not weakened
their resolve. They wanted to kill the hated
Americans, and this looked like their chance to

do so. No one else could have taken over the ruin site so completely, and without leaving an outward sign.

Then the heavy 12.7mm slugs from the DshK started ripping through the east flank of the Iraqis. Their positions were being destroyed around them. They could only go forward and try to wipe out the interlopers before they were themselves destroyed.

At the Soviet heavy machine gun, Lopez fired a few more bursts and then abandoned the gun. The Iraqis were getting too close for the heavy machine gun to depress enough to reach them. And he couldn't fire to the left without the risk of hitting the shed. Grabbing up his AKM and two bags of magazines, Lopez pulled back to where the rest of his squad was fighting.

The Iraqis were coming on, and the fire the SEALs were putting out wasn't stopping them for long.

"Sukov," Rockham shouted into his radio. "We are out of time here. Pull the fuses and run."

Nodding to Tinsley and Lutz to leave the shed, Sukov watched them go and take their prisoner with them. His back hurt like hell from the hits it had taken that evening, but he wasn't going to pass this job off on anyone. Pulling the pin on the M60 fuse igniters, he waited a moment to see the smoke rise from the two firing assemblies, then also ran from the shed.

As he saw his last man leave the shed, Rockham knew that the area around the ruins was about to get soaked with poison gas, or something much worse. Pulling a whistle from his pocket, he blew two sharp blasts.

"Leapfrog rear," he shouted. "Two's base! One's back!"

The SEALs knew just how fast they had to move. But no one panicked or forgot their training. By the numbers, just as they had trained, the men peeled off to the left, staying out of second squad's field of fire. Each man ran back toward the dunes, making sure that no one was left behind. Rockham was the last man to leave the ruins, and he made the fastest hundred meter dash of his life.

As first squad made it to the dunes, second squad ran through ammunition like water through a hose. The barrels of the enemy weapons they carried had burned hot and then started to glow as the rounds ran through them. If a gun jammed, it was tossed down and another pulled up in its place. The SEALs had so many different AK-47s that they didn't bother reloading some but just tossed them aside and picked up a loaded one.

The PKM light machine guns were another matter. They fired a very powerful 7.62×54mm rimmed round, the same ammunition Ryan Marks was firing from his SVD. The long hammering bursts from the PKMs ripped across the distance between the SEALs and the oncoming Iraqis. Then the explosions rippled through the metal shed.

The blasts were loud, but not that loud. The SEALs had all set off larger charges during their

training. But none of them had seen the horren-
dous results of such an explosion before.

A huge cloud was growing, pink-colored in the
light of the fires starting in the ruins. Some of the
Iraqis knew what they were looking at, and they
screamed and ran. Others tried to run but it was
too late for them.

The cloud was heavy, and it rolled across the
ground as it was pushed by the winds and headed
east. Everything it touched crisped and blackened
instantly, plants, grass, wood, and men. Screams
were cut short as the corrosive horror rolled out.
Now Rockham understood just how this material
could destroy the anthrax they had searched so
hard for.

But the cloud of red fuming nitric acid didn't
kill all of the Republican Guard troops. Many of
them were north of the cloud as it formed. Those
men wanted vengeance now, personal vengeance
against the men who had killed their fellow fighters in such an inhuman manner.

Now the SEALs were running for their lives,
though they still stayed in the formations they had
practiced for years. They were performing the
fastest leapfrog withdrawal they had ever done,
with more than a full kilometer to run to get to
their secondary extraction point. The primary
point was too far in the wrong direction to even
consider now. The Iraqis would catch them before
they ever got there.

So the SEALs headed almost directly south, toward the beaches and the water beyond. There

might be mines and oil on the water, but the sea was always the safest haven for the SEALs.

As the men fell back, Kurkowski pulled up the PKM machine gun he had been carrying. His last full box of ammunition was attached to the bottom of the gun. Across his back was his M60E3 machine gun. There were still two hundred rounds left to that weapon.

The SEALs were all big, strong, powerful men. And they were fighting for their lives. Not just their lives, but the lives of the brothers to either side of them. Each man would make the enemy chasing them pay dearly for each yard they covered, and ten times that price before a SEAL went down.

As second squad stopped to put out covering fire for first squad. Kurkowski pulled up the PKM and shouldered it like a rifle. He held it up by the barrel handle and the pistol grip. The long hammering bursts he put out swept across the oncoming Iraqis, mowing them down like grass. But more came on.

The PKM was never designed to be fired like Kurkowski was shooting his. The brass ejecting from the port of the left side of the weapon punched into his upper arm, bruising and tearing the flesh. But Kurkowski never felt the pain. The damage he was taking was nothing compared to what he was inflicting on the Iraqis. He just continued firing until the bolt slammed shut on an empty chamber.

The powerful rounds fired by the PKM tore into and through the Iraqis. Bullets that went through one man hit another man behind him. Bodies fell and flopped. The path the Iraqis had taken could be followed by the bloody trail of bodies behind them.

These were the Republican Guard, the cream of Saddam's military might. They were fanatic fighters. But they were facing the Navy SEALs—some of the most professional and highly trained soldiers in the world. The Iraqis only had the SEALs outnumbered, not outmatched. The name SEAL was something worth a hell of a lot more than just bragging rights. And the casualties the Iraqis were taking showed that.

The SEALs had casualties of their own. Lopez was hit in the left leg and went down hard. There was no time to bandage the wound. Alexander stopped long enough to pick up the wounded man. With Lopez slung across his back, he slogged on.

Fighting just as hard as his Teammates, Ryan Marks was firing more slowly and methodically. Each round he fired from the long SVD sniper rifle dropped an Iraqi. Kneeling behind a rock formation, he had the Soviet SVD pulled up tight against his shoulder as he looked over the oncoming Iraqis. Each time he saw a man with a pistol or shoulder boards on his uniform, Marks dropped him with a single shot. Those were the signs of an officer or senior sergeant. Drop them and you cut off the leadership of the enemy. But this enemy didn't seem to care.

Rounds steadily boomed out from the SVD. When Marks had gone through a magazine, the reload was so fast that it didn't seem to pause the shooting. Finally, he got up and also ran off with his Teammates.

The hailstorm of bullets from the SEALs, combined with the precise delivery of death from Marks, had caused the pursuing Iraqis to slow. Now, the men of the SMD had a chance to break contact and slip off into the night. But Rockham knew there was something much more important that had to be done. In spite of the risk, they had to try and make contact with Command and tell them the mission had been accomplished, that the warhead and the missile had been destroyed.

As they came up to a sharp ridge line, Rockham raised his fist in the air and called a halt.

"Security out," Rockham said. "Sukov, get on the radio and raise Command."

Sukov stepped over to Lutz, to help him get his HST-4 SATCOM set up. The rest of the men spread out behind the ridge. There wasn't much light from the stars and moon, which were blotted out by the oil smoke, but they could see across the area they had just covered. If the Iraqis were still on their trail, that was the direction they would come from.

As he lay down behind some rocks, Marks pulled up his M4 and checked it. The SVD he had used so well was still slung across his back.

"Break your new toy?" Kurkowski said.

"Nope," Marks said. "Out of ammo and no more shopping days left till Christmas."

Mainhart flopped down next to the two men

and started to pull 40mm grenades from his pouches. Laying them out in front of him, the young SEAL made ready for some fast reloads into his M203.

Having loaded a loose belt of ammunition into his PKM, Kurkowski had a small mound of ammunition belt lying next to his weapon. Pulling up the end of the belt in his PKM, he grabbed it and with a twist of his powerful hands tore the last foot of the belt free.

"Here," he said as he tossed the section of belt to Marks. "Try not to spend it all in one place."

The gleam of a wide smile spread out across Marks's camouflage-painted face. Both the PKM and the SVD fired the same 7.62×54mm rimmed ammunition. He started pulling individual rounds from the metal pockets of the belt. Pulling the empty magazine from the SVD, Marks thumbed the big rounds into place.

"Kurkowski," Marks said as he reloaded, "I owe you one for this and I will repay you. You know, you run your thumb across the top of your cards every time you hold a good hand."

"What?" Kurkowski said as he kept looking into the darkness for the Iraqis.

"In the poker game," Marks said. "You run your thumb across the top of your cards whenever you're holding something decent."

"Damn," Mainhart said, "you told him."

"You knew?" Kurkowski said.

"Everyone knew," Mainhart said. "Well, at least you finding out should make the next game a little more interesting."

* * *

"Boss," Lutz said as he held up the handset.

Rockham took it and pulled it up to his ear. "Home Plate, Home Plate, this is Bravo One, over."

"Home Plate, go ahead, Bravo One."

In spite of the KY-57 encryption device, Rockham still carefully used the proper code words as he reported the situation.

"We found a jewel," he said. "Emerald Green, I repeat, Emerald Green. There is no buyer. Do you copy, over."

"I copy Emerald Green, no buyer. Emerald Green, no buyer."

"Our party was raided," Rockham continued. "We are heading for Lunch."

"I copy that, party raided, heading for Lunch."

Lunch was the code for the secondary extraction point.

"Company," Monday said quietly before Rockham could say another word.

"Bravo One, out," Rockham said, and returned the handset to Lutz.

Twisting suddenly to the left, Monday fired a short burst from his M4. An Iraqi soldier, probably one of the best scouts from the approaching unit, had risen up from the rocks to the SEALs' flank. The short burst fired by Monday ripped into the Iraqi, driving him backward away from the SEALs. As the man fell, his finger convulsed, locking back on the trigger of his AKM-47. A stream of green-colored tracers fired off into the sky.

Though none of the SEALs were hit, the wild firing by the dead Iraqi did a lot of damage. The green stream of tracers pointed out their location to the oncoming enemy. It was as if a big green arrowhead was penciled out across the sky. The Iraqis were quick to open fire on the ridge line.

"Leapfrog rear!" Rockham shouted over the incoming enemy fire. "Two's base, One's back."

As the men from first squad pulled back from the ridge line, the rest of the SEALs opened fire. The spaced-out booming of Marks's SVD was drowned out in the long bursts from Kurkowski's PKM. He wouldn't be able to run with the machine gun while a long belt was dangling from it, so Kurkowski was lavish with his ammunition. The muzzle of the PKM started to glow as the rounds poured through it.

Like a machine, Mainhart was pumping out rounds from his grenade launcher. Starting out firing at long range, he moved his point of aim forward, through the Iraqi position. The blooping noise of the 40mm firing came fast and regularly. Though he would never know it, the young SEAL had three rounds in the air before the first one reached its target. The blossoming orange blasts from the 40mm high explosive grenades sprayed razor-sharp fragments of steel through the Iraqis, and still they came on.

A shrill whistle rang out, and second squad pulled back from the ridge under the covering guns of their brothers behind them.

* * *

"Goddamnit," the Marine general cursed as he stood in the command and control space of his amphibious landing ship. He had just heard the radio communication from the SEALs come over his own encrypted radio. "I will not just sit here and be a decoy while men are dying on the ground."

Turning to his air wing commander, he continued, "You put those helicopters into the air and get them to that island. The ground war has started, and we aren't going to do anyone any good just sitting out here anymore."

None of the Marine forces that had been sitting out in the Persian Gulf were happy with their situation. They had been part of a plan to convince the Iraqis that a part of the invasion would come from the sea. The Iraqi ground commanders in Kuwait couldn't believe that the coalition would waste 28,000 combat-ready Marines and their equipment just floating in the Gulf.

But the Marines had been a good decoy, since the plan had worked. The Iraqis had moved units from several divisions to cover beaches that would never be landed on.

Now, if it wasn't too late, the general decided, maybe those Marine assets could help pull some of their fellow warriors from out of the fire.

At last the SEALs reached the oil-covered beach. They were at Lunch, their secondary extraction site, but there was no one in sight. The Iraqis had slowed and were more studied in their chase of the SEALs, but time was now on their side.

Most of the SEALs had their last reloads in

their weapons. The enemy hardware had long since been expended. As they took cover to make their stand, none of the men had any regrets. They had completed their mission. And if they had to go, their brothers around them were the men they wanted to go with.

There was a roaring, clanking squeal coming from up the beach on their left flank. There was another T-72 approaching, and nothing the SEALs had left would be able to stop it. Tinsley pulled out the remaining demolitions. There wasn't much they could do to a T-72 main battle tank with just a couple of pounds of C-4, but it was the heaviest punch they had left.

Then the beach around the tank erupted in geysers of sand. The T-72 exploded and came apart like a child's plastic toy. Zooming in from overhead was an A-10 Warthog, right then the most beautiful sight any of the SEALs had ever seen. The 30mm GAU-8 seven-barrel cannon under the nose of the plane had ripped up the T-72, and now the pilot was looking for more targets.

As they looked out to sea, the SEALs could see the wingman of the first A-10 come flying in. Behind him was the welcome sight of a trio of Marine CH-53 Sea Stallions coming in to the beach. Their ride was here, and he'd brought friends along.

Relief washed over the SEALs, almost dropping several of the men to their knees in weakness. These were men who had just been facing almost certain death, and now they had a reprieve. They had accomplished their mission, but few would ever hear the tale. What was important was, they were all alive, mostly unhurt, and they were going home.

The SEALs of the SMD had no way of knowing it yet, but the ground war had started that morning at 0400 hours local time. Kuwait would be liberated in one hundred hours.

SEALS
SUB STRIKE

S.M. GUNN

OPERATION BLACK SNOW
0-06-009549-0/$6.99 US/$9.99 Can
In the hours before Operation Desert Storm begins, a bold,
submarine-launched raid by SEALs captures an Iraqi ship
carrying a missile warhead designed to hold
a frightening payload of deadly germs.

OPERATION OCEAN WATCH
0-06-009548-2/$6.99 US/$9.99 Can
The SEALs are dispatched to the Red Sea to intercept
a transport sent by Saddam to the Sudan containing
an enemy stockpile of virulent biological weapons.

OPERATION ENDURANCE
0-380-80829-3/$6.99 US/$9.99 Can
A six-man SEAL team must conduct a search-and-snatch
operation on an ice-covered island in Russian waters
where the secret construction of biological weapons
of mass destruction is taking place.

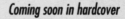